Prologue

by Kristy Dykes

INTRODUCTION

Angel Food by Kristy Dykes
Angel Morgan is intent on her new restaurant, Rue de France, succeeding so she can take care of her widowed mother. Businessman Cyril Jackson III is attracted to Angel but is concerned because she doesn't share his devotion to God. What will it take for Angel to realize the importance of soul food? And will Angel and Cyril ever make a perfect blend (*noun*: two ingredients thoroughly mixed until smooth)?

Just Desserts by Aisha Ford
Once upon a time, Monica Ryan and Gil Butler's families were inseparable, and so were Monica and Gil. But a business disagreement between their fathers put an end to any ideas concerning a happily ever after. Now that Monica and Gil have been thrown into business once again, is there forgiveness in the air, or is one of them plotting to serve the other their *Just Desserts*?

A Recipe for Romance by Vickie McDonough
All her life, Haley has been embarrassed by her parents' old-fashioned restaurant, The Cowpoke Café. When she learns that her parents are retiring and giving her the café, she's stunned. Now she can remodel and recognize her dream of managing an upscale diner. She recruits carpenter Scott Jantzen's help in remodeling. Sparks fly between them, but when she learns his true identity, will her recipe for romance flop?

Tea for Two by Carrie Turansky
Allison Bennett, owner of a financially strapped tea shop, receives an anonymous check that saves her business. Who is her secret benefactor? Peter Hillinger, a wealthy businessman, wants to convince Allison he is the man for her. But Tyler Lawrence, Allison's old boyfriend, returns to town claiming a renewed faith and a changed life. Allison doesn't know whom to trust. Should she follow her head or her heart?

KISS
THE
Bride
~~COOK~~

FOUR CONTEMPORARY ROMANCES ARE
STRENGTHENED BY THE SAME LASTING INGREDIENT

Kristy Dykes ❧ *Aisha Ford*
Vickie McDonough ❧ *Carrie Turansky*

BARBOUR
PUBLISHING

ISBN 1-59789-353-6

Cover Photograph: © Jim Celuch, www.celuch.com

Scripture taken from the HOLY BIBLE, NEW INTERNATIONAL VERSION®. NIV®. Copyright © 1973, 1978, 1984 by International Bible Society. Used by permission of Zondervan. All rights reserved.

Scripture taken from the New King James Version®. Copyright © 1982 by Thomas Nelson, Inc. Used by permission. All rights reserved.

Published by Barbour Publishing, Inc., P.O. Box 719, Uhrichsville, Ohio 44683, www.barbourbooks.com

Our mission is to publish and distribute inspirational products offering exceptional value and biblical encouragement to the masses.

Printed in the United States of America.
5 4 3 2 1

Prologue

HAM and I

I'm sitting in a crowded restaurant, looking at the apron I just bought. *Kiss the Cook* is on the bib and red lips dot the *i*. *Kiss the Cook?* My mind zigzags.

I'm a cook. And I'd sure welcome a kiss. From Mr. Right. Only he's nowhere in the recipe of *my* life. At least not now.

I laugh as I think of The Single Girl's Bedtime Prayer. *Now I lay me down to sleep, Lord give me a man for keeps. If there's a man beneath my bed, I hope he heard each word I said.*

I can't quit smiling. Haley, Allison, and Monica will think the apron's a hoot, too, when they see it. Where are they? I look at the hostess desk and see several people waiting to be seated. But not HAM, an acronym of their names and what I jokingly call them.

HAM and I are in Dallas attending the National Restaurateurs' Convention. We met several days ago when the four of us were riding on the hotel elevator, and it got stuck. You should've seen Monica. She was a basket case at first. I think she must have a touch of claustrophobia.

But after we got to talking like magpies, she never said another word about it. You would've thought we were sitting in a restaurant instead of a steel box suspended between the sixth and seventh floors. It took the maintenance men over an hour to get us unstuck, and by then we were like lifelong friends. As soon as we got out, we headed straight for the coffee shop and chatted for another eon.

We found out we had lots of things in common. Number one, we're attending the same convention. Number two, we're involved in the restaurant business. And number three, we're all single.

Haley's family owns The Cowpoke Café in Tulsa, Oklahoma. But right now she's hostessing at her brother's restaurant, Tannehills. Haley's tall, has honey blond hair and brown eyes, and usually wears jeans and t-shirts. She hopes to own her own restaurant some day—an upscale deli.

Allison and her sister are about to open Sweet Something Tea Shop in Princeton, New Jersey. Allison has light brown hair, dark blue eyes, and she wears those long flowing skirts and ruffled blouses and boots. She's also an artist who paints Victorian still-life paintings.

Monica's family owns The Pie Rack in Missouri. She has caramel skin, light brown eyes, and glossy black hair cut into a cute bob. She's what you'd call girly, with her sophisticated tops, skirts, and matching heels and purses.

And I, Angel Morgan, am about to open a French restaurant called Rue de France in Nine Cloud, Florida, a small town 30 miles from Orlando, where I live.

HAM and I have been together for three days now, laughing and cutting up. After lunch, we're all heading to the airport and our bright futures, as the speaker said in the session called "Owning Your Own Restaurant."

In all our busyness, I'm hoping we'll stay in touch. But our plates are full, overflowing in fact. Like the way they serve food in that Mennonite restaurant down in Sarasota. Yoder's is the name of it.

Haley and Allison breeze into the restaurant. They spot me and wave as they make their way toward me. A flurry of greetings fly across the table as they sit down. Monica hurries in and joins us. After the waiter takes our orders, we talk nonstop for nearly half an hour.

"What's in your lap, Angel?" Haley gestures at me.

I hold up my apron for everyone to see. I'm grinning as wide as a dinner plate.

HAM laughs like a bunch of hyenas, as I expected.

I slip the apron over my head and tie it at my waist. "How do you like it?"

"It's adorable." Allison reaches over and fingers the material. "Looks like it'll wash and wear well."

"Where'd you find it?" Haley asks. "Which vendor? I didn't see any aprons like that at the convention."

"I just bought it. At the gift shop next door." I glance down at it. "You think I should wear it on the opening day of my new restaurant?" I flutter my eyelashes like a ditzy blond, which I'm not. Ditzy, that is. "Like, I really would. I've got all kinds of aprons, but this one. . .well, it takes the cake."

Monica rolls her eyes. "It's definitely food for thought. People'll think you're on the lookout for a man."

"I'm saved, single, and searching, all right." I clasp my hands together and stare at the ceiling. "Lord, *please* send me a man." I burst out laughing. "That's what my great Aunt Myrtle Jean used to say."

"Did it work?" Haley asks.

"Did she get a man?" Monica wants to know.

"Nope. She died an old maid—"

"Is that the one who willed you her building?" Allison asks. "Where you're starting your restaurant?"

I nod, a warm feeling flooding my heart. "Aunt Myrtle Jean was *so* generous. I still can't believe I received an inheritance from a distant relative. She was as sweet as sugar to do that."

"And you're a cute tomato," Haley deadpans.

"And they're as slow as molasses getting our food out here." Monica cranes her neck, looking for the waiter. "I'm so starved, my stomach's gnawing on my backbone."

"My, we're *full* of food clichés," I say. "Those who are one in food are one in life. That's a Malagasy saying. Maybe it'll be that way for us."

"Mackalasky what?" Haley's mocking me.

I playfully look smug and all knowing. "Malagasy is the native language of Madagascar. They produce gourmet chocolates, rare coffees and teas, and exotic honeys."

"You'll have to give me some information on them." Allison looks thoughtful. "Maybe I could sell some Madagascar items at Sweet Something."

"Sure," I say. "I'll e-mail it to you."

"Speaking of e-mailing—" Monica glances around the table "—let's keep in touch, okay?"

"We will," Haley says. "We're like peas in a pod."

"Like scones and jam," Allison pipes up.

"Like pie and coffee," Monica says.

"Like a hand in a glove," I add. "That's what Aunt Myrtle Jean would say. She wore little white gloves all her life. She even had them on in her casket." Suddenly, I think of a joke. I steel myself not to crack a smile. "You want to know what she put in her will?"

HAM nods and leans in close.

"She specified female pallbearers only."

"I've never heard of that," Haley says.

"Me neither," Monica adds.

I wag my head like a bobbly thing on a dashboard. "She said, 'Men never took me out in life, and they're *not* going to take me out now.'"

We laugh till tears come to our eyes.

"I hope that won't come true for us," Allison says when we quiet down.

Haley sighs. "Finding a good man is next to impossible these days." Her voice takes on a serious tone. "Especially when you're in the restaurant business—"

"Those long hours. . ." Monica has a wistful look in her

eyes. "They sort of fend off romance."

Haley tugs on a corner of my apron. "Are there any more like this? I definitely need help finding Mr. Right."

"Me too," Allison says.

"Same here," Monica chimes in.

"Nothing says loving—" I sing the Pillsbury ditty and tap a spoon in rhythm "—like something from the oven—" I pause "—and we—" I motion around the table "—can do it best."

"Let's *all* go buy one of those aprons," Haley exclaims.

"You can't." I untie the apron and slip it over my head. "This was the last one."

"Then you've got to share it with us." Haley gives Allison and Monica a conspiratorial glance. "HAM in agreement?"

"Oink, oink," I say. "Don't get greedy."

Haley's eyes light up. "Be an angel, Angel. If it brings a man into *your* life, you've *got* to share it with us. Remember that movie where the girls passed a pair of jeans around until everyone wore them? Come on. Give us a turn with the apron."

The waiter appears, hoisting a tray laden with towering sandwiches.

"Finally, the staff of life arrives." Monica pats her stomach.

I put my apron back in the bag, smiling as wide as a dinner plate again. I just might surprise HAM and start passing it around.

After I find *my* Mr. Right.

Angel Food

by Kristy Dykes

Dedication and Acknowledgements

To my hero-husband, Milton,
who is my collaborator in the deepest sense of the word—
he's believed in me, supported me, and cheered me on
in my calling to inspirational writing.

If I speak in the tongues of men and of angels, but have not love,
I am only a resounding gong or a clanging cymbal. . . .
If I give all I possess to the poor. . .but have not love,
I gain nothing.
1 CORINTHIANS 13:1, 3

Chapter 1

Angel Morgan still couldn't believe her good fortune. She put the paint roller in the tray and looked around—dreamily—at the building that was now hers, compliments of her late great-aunt Myrtle Jean. It would soon be an elegant, upscale restaurant called Rue de France.

"No fair." Angel's mother, crouched above the baseboard and, smiling, kept up with her steady strokes. "No slacking on the job."

"I, Myrtle Jean Morgan, being of sound mind"—Angel made her voice crack like an old lady's as she held an imaginary will in her hands—"do bequeath to my great-niece Angel Morgan my building in Nine Cloud, Florida, to do with as she sees fit. I also bequeath a sum of money to be used wisely. . . ."

"You could've been an actress." Her mother shook her head, her eyes twinkling.

"I wonder if I'll ever get used to being the owner of my very own restaurant." Angel felt a sense of wonder and awe. She stared out the tall Palladian-style windows she'd worked so hard on yesterday, removing years of grime and neglect. Now they sparkled in the summer sunshine. She would get to the glass door this afternoon, if time allowed. "Pinch me so I'll know this is real, Mom."

Her mother, agile even at sixty-seven, plunked down her paintbrush, dashed over, and playfully pinched Angel on the upper arm.

"Ouch, I was just kidding." Angel laughed as she rubbed the spot, then grabbed her mother in a bear hug. "Oh, Mom, I'm so happy."

"And I'm happy for you." Her mother's voice choked up with emotion. "If anybody deserves this, it's you, hon. It's a blessing from the Lord. You know that, don't you?"

Angel nodded and slowly released her, then walked back to her paint roller. If her restaurant was going to open on time, she'd better keep painting.

Her mother resumed her painting as well. "Of course, you're one of the hardest working people I've ever seen—"

"I'm a chip off the old block."

Her mother waved her hand into the air, as if she was shy of compliments. "How do you say *excellent work* in French?"

"*Travail excellent.*"

Her mother swept her hand around the large, high-ceilinged room. "That's what you've done here."

"Thanks, Mom. I couldn't have done it without your help."

"But the Lord's help, most of all. He's gifted you with determination. . .and fortitude. . .and creativity—"

"Now you're embarrassing *me*."

Admiration shone in her mother's eyes. "You are *so* creative, hon. What a nifty idea, to give the downtown business owners a free lunch right before your opening day. . ."

"In only two weeks, I'll get to meet the important people of Nine Cloud."

"Your father used to call people like that The Brass. He said they dressed to beat the band."

Angel laughed. "Well, I'm going to be dressed to beat the band that day." She glanced down at the paint globs on her clothes.

"Knowing you, you will be."

"That reminds me. I need to design an invitation for the free lunch and get it in tomorrow's mail. I'm lucky I learned desktop publishing in a PR class—"

"You're blessed, you mean. Luck doesn't come into play for a Christian."

"I *am* blessed, Mom. I've got the greatest mom in the world. You've been my cheerleader since I was a kid."

"A champion's worth cheering for."

Angel's eyes misted over. As the white walls turned goldenrod, she thought about her childhood that had been dear and sweet and pleasant—but only because her mother had worked like a Trojan to make it that way. Other women might've given up, but not her mother. Angel's father had died when she was eight, and her mother had found a job as a school-cafeteria cook to support them.

God's the reason we're making it, her mother often said. *He's the most important thing in life.*

Angel sighed contentedly, thinking about her twenty-four years. She'd determined early on to make something of herself, to go somewhere beyond the crackerbox house she'd grown up in on the wrong side of the tracks, and she'd worked hard to see that happen. In high school, she hit the books while her friends enjoyed football games and parties. She did the same in college to maintain a four-year scholarship. For the past two years, she'd worked—slaved actually—in an upscale restaurant to learn about the business firsthand.

The only thing she hadn't attained from the grit and gruel and grind of hard work was her great-aunt's bequest. It had caught her by surprise. Now her dream was about to come true. She was a restaurant owner, and the money would flow in, and she would buy a beautiful home for her and her mother, and nice cars, too. And her mother would never have to work again.

She pushed the paint roller up and down the eleven-foot high walls. Paint one section. Move paint tray with foot. Paint the next section, move paint tray, *ad infinitum* it seemed. But that was okay. Every paint stroke brought her nearer to her goal, and that made her happy.

She paused for a moment and worked her shoulders in circular motions. The only thing that could make life any better for her right now was for Mr. Right to come on the scene. She'd been looking for him for years.

The friends she'd grown up with were all married and either had babies or were pregnant. One had met her husband in church when they were both a mere sixteen. The others met their guys in their early twenties. Not so for Angel. She'd had lots of dates and one relationship that looked like it might lead to marriage. But *her* man—Mr. Right—had never materialized for her.

She scanned the room, pleased with her work. All of the walls were rolled. She put down her roller, poured paint into a small plastic pail, grabbed a paintbrush, and climbed a ladder. As she painted the edges of the wall up near the crown molding, she was careful with her strokes so she wouldn't get golden yellow paint on the wood.

She glanced down from her perch on the ladder, saw her mother, and thought about the love between her parents, something her mother had endearingly talked about Angel's entire life.

Angel wanted that kind of love—if and when it came to her. She breathed in deeply. *I long for the day when True Love knocks at my door.*

"Angel? I called you two times."

"Hmm?" Angel stopped painting and turned, balancing carefully on the tall ladder. "Sorry. I was—"

"Daydreaming." Her mother chuckled, her midsection—the only rounded part on her lean body—jiggling.

"You know me."

Her mother gave a knowing nod. "You're a pie-in-the-sky, Pollyanna girl. But that's okay. I always said you could have as many daydreams as you want, as long as you turn them into reality someday. And that someday has arrived. I'm proud of you, hon. Now. Somebody's knocking at the door. Weren't you expecting some equipment to be delivered? Do you want me to answer it? Or do you want to?"

Cyril Jackson III knocked on the door of old Miss Morgan's building. He had about twenty minutes before an appointment and wanted to welcome the new business owner to Nine Cloud.

A few minutes passed, and he knocked again. He knew people were working inside. He could see them—or at least vague forms—through the dirty glass on the door. One was high up on a ladder. The other was in the far corner, crouched near the floor.

So why wouldn't they answer the door? Or at least call out to let him know they were coming? Surely they'd heard him knock. He wished they'd let him in. This June sun was as hot as an August one, and he swiped his forehead, then knocked again.

As he waited, he glanced down the street and saw the three downtown buildings he and his father, Cyril Jackson II, owned in the long row of buildings lining Main Street.

He felt a sense of place and peace in the quaint, small-town atmosphere of his hometown in central Florida, things big-moneyed developers were seeking to create all over the state. Master-planned communities, they called them.

Just last week, he and his father had ridden over to see a city built out of nothingness near Disney World. It had two-story houses surrounded by white picket fences, a main street with awnings over the sidewalks, and neighborhood schools. These were things Nine Cloud had had all along.

He and his father laughed when Cyril read aloud the snazzy brochures—written by advertisers to lure people to move to the friendly, relationship-laden Southern town—exactly what Nine Cloud was and always had been. Of course Nine Cloud didn't have a hotel like this new town, or street singers at Christmastime, or fancy restaurants and shops, or famous authors visiting the bookstore, or art festivals.

But Nine Cloud had history. . .

. . .and heritage. . .

. . .and pride.

He had to be honest with himself, though, as he glanced at the peeling paint on some of the buildings. Nine Cloud *did* need some refurbishing. But more than a physical transformation, Nine Cloud needed a spiritual transformation. He was praying for several situations. He was interceding for Ted White, owner of White's Hardware, to accept the Lord. And Joe Freeman, the funeral director, needed to get back in church. He dropped out last year when his son died. And some of the teenagers in Nine Cloud were getting into trouble—drinking and things. They desperately needed God.

Lord, he silently prayed, *give the folks of Nine Cloud a new glimpse of You.*

He saw one of the vague forms coming toward the door. "Finally. Somebody's going to answer."

The door opened two inches at the most. "Yes?" A young woman stood in the narrow opening, paint streaks in her blond hair, on her T-shirt, her cut-offs, and her ratty tennis shoes. She brushed her fingers through her hair as if to freshen it up, and more paint joined the paint that was already there.

Good thing your paint's the same color as your hair, ma'am.

"Would you. . .um. . .like to come in?" The young woman opened the door only an inch more.

Haven't you ever heard of Southern hospitality, lady? You're supposed to throw open the door in welcome.

"If you come in, you'll have to be careful where you step. Paint's everywhere."

"I see that." He stepped inside, enjoying the air-conditioning immediately, and closed the door behind him. This was probably Miss Morgan's great-niece. He'd heard via the town grapevine that Miss Morgan had willed her building to her. Yes, it was the great-niece. He remembered seeing the striking blond at the funeral.

She held out her hand, then looked down at it and withdrew it. "I'd shake your hand, but. . .um—"

"Paint."

"Yes. Paint."

"Cyril Jackson, here." He dipped his chin in politeness. "I own Main Street Café, right down the street."

She looked sheepish, didn't speak.

"And you're the owner of the new restaurant Rue de France, right?" he asked.

"You know the name of my restaurant?"

He tipped his head sideways. "You've got a flyer out front. In the window."

"Y–yes. . .of course."

"A French restaurant in Nine Cloud. . ." He stopped himself. He wouldn't be rude enough to voice his thoughts. But he couldn't help thinking them. Hadn't she done any demographics? Marketing studies? Why would she start a French restaurant in Nine Cloud? It sounded like a flop to him.

An older woman with a friendly face walked up and shook his hand. "I heard you two talking. I'm her mother. Nancy Morgan's my name. It's nice to meet you, Mr. Jackson."

He exchanged greetings with her.

"I'm going to go hunt some sweet iced tea, hon," the mother said. "I've worked up a thirst. Would you like some?"

"Sounds good, Mom."

"Try Main Street Café." Cyril pointed to his left. "On down the street. We always have sweet iced tea on hand. And try our fudge-covered brownies. Mama Edwards makes them every morning."

"I will," she called as she bustled out the door. "Thanks for the suggestion."

Cyril looked around. The two women were doing a nice job on the place. The ceiling had been redone. And the brick wall had some type of fancy paint treatment on it that showed traces of its original finish. And the yellow color on the rest of the walls blended nicely with the oak floors, or what he could see of them under the drop cloths.

The young woman stood there, not saying a word.

"Well. . ." He cleared his throat. Was she never going to introduce herself? "I know your mother's name. And I know your restaurant's name. But I don't know *your* name."

Her face reddened. "I'm. . .Angel Morgan." She stuck out her hand, then nervouslike, as if remembering the paint, quickly withdrew it.

"Angel." He rocked on his heels. Appropriate name. Blond hair. Blue eyes. Wonder if she had wings and a halo? "Angel, welcome to Nine Cloud."

Angel berated herself as soon as Mr. Jackson walked out the door. She'd acted like a moron instead of the smooth business-woman she was. She hadn't even displayed proper etiquette.

"I don't know why the cat got my tongue. But I just couldn't think, let alone talk." He seemed so. . .austere. And unfriendly?

She'd wanted to make a good impression on the business owners of Nine Cloud. That was the first step to success. She'd intended to meet them at the free lunch she was going to host, when she'd be dressed in nice clothes.

"And here I am, covered in paint." With a glance at her paint-stained cut-offs and remembering her lack of manners, she knew she'd shot that chance with *this* businessman. And *that* made her frustrated with herself.

She knew who *he* was as soon as he'd said his name. When she'd talked with the attorney who executed Aunt Myrtle Jean's will, he mentioned several business owners, including the one on Main Street who would be her chief competition!

"Mr. Cyril Jackson." She let out a smirk. "The Third." A name for him came to mind. "Mr. Brass," she accused. Then another named surfaced, one she hadn't heard since elementary school days. She couldn't resist saying it now. "Mr. Hooty-Toot."

Chapter 2

C yril sat down in his usual spot in the white-steepled church in the center of town. He'd just finished teaching his middle-school boys' Sunday school class, and he welcomed the quiet time during the organist's prelude.

A couple of the boys had been unusually rowdy this morning, horsing around and making their usual obnoxious remarks. Jason Baxter had tried Cyril's patience in the worst way. But Cyril didn't let him know he'd irked him. Instead, he quietly breathed a word of prayer and asked for wisdom, then continued with the lesson.

When Jason first started attending the class, someone told Cyril his mom had a drug problem, and his heart had gone out to him. He had donated money through the church to be used to purchase groceries and necessities for Jason and his mother. Every Sunday, he brought doughnuts and juice to his class, and he gave the boys freebies—prize items boys of his age enjoyed.

Cyril occasionally took them on outings, showing them a good time while trying to live out the gospel before them, hoping they would make a decision for Christ. A couple of them had done this, but Jason had never responded.

Cyril had done a lot to help Jason, to no avail it seemed. He'd tried to find out what made him tick, tried to get him to open up, but the boy was like a stone wall.

Lord, he silently prayed, *be real to these boys. Give them the strength and will to live for You. Help them to put You first in their lives. And, Lord, help Jason realize his need of a Savior. Let him know You're real and You're there for him. Somehow, speak to his heart. Lord, use someone to get through to him.*

Later, as Pastor Kyle preached, Cyril deemed his sermon a masterpiece. Pastor Kyle and his wife were in their late twenties, unlike the church's former pastor who had been much older. Even though he was young, Pastor Kyle was a gifted speaker.

Lord, let someone respond to Your Word today.

At the close of the service, Pastor Kyle gave a salvation appeal.

A woman walked down the aisle, a stranger. She knelt at the altar, and an altar worker came and knelt beside her.

Jason came barreling down the aisle, tears streaming down his face. He knelt beside the woman.

Cyril's heart lurched when he saw Jason. *This must be his mother.* He remembered his prayer. He'd asked God to use someone to get through to Jason. And God had used his mother! *Thank You, Lord.*

Cyril quickly made his way to the altar and knelt beside Jason. A little while later, he knew the angels in heaven were happy. The Bible said they rejoiced when a sinner found the Lord.

And Cyril was rejoicing, too.

～⤝✦⤞～

After the service, Angel spotted Mr. Hooty-Toot coming down the church aisle. She waved and smiled like a kid opening Christmas presents, and he waved back. She would dazzle him this time—for her restaurant's sake. No cat-getting-your-tongue stuff today.

"Why, hello, Mr. Jackson," she said, as he approached, her voice dripping with friendliness. *Hello to the owner of Main Street Café, domain of down-home cooking.* She'd already heard some locals say his restaurant served soul food, what with its home-style fare and its superb black cook, Mama Edwards. "It's good to see you."

"Call me Cyril." He held out his hand.

She shook it heartily. "Only if you'll call me Angel."

"Sure thing. I almost invited you to church the other day when I stopped by your restaurant and almost asked if you were saved—"

"Of course I'm a Christian, Mr. Hoo—" She caught herself. "Mr. Jackson."

"It's Cyril—"

"I received a pin every year for perfect Sunday school attendance when I was growing up, over in Orlando." She didn't tell him her mother had agreed to be her chef at Rue de France *if* Angel started going to church again.

"Perfect attendance in Sunday school? Learning Bible stories? Memorizing scriptures?"

She nodded. " 'I can do all things through Christ who strengthens me,' " she quoted.

"Now that's what I call *real* soul food."

Angel smiled to be polite. But she didn't want to talk about the Lord right now. She wanted to talk about Rue de France—at every opportunity that came her way. The Lord had His place, of course, but for right now, at this pivotal time in her life, when she'd put all of Aunt Myrtle Jean's money on the line, she needed to push her restaurant.

"You look like you zoned out. . . . I asked if you're ready for your opening day?"

"Opening day?" Angel felt all aglow. "As ready as ready can be. The curtains are hung, the furniture's in place, the menus are beautiful, and the table service is Paris perfect at Rue de France."

"Why'd you decide on a *French* restaurant?" He rocked on his heels, his expression unreadable. But his disdain came through loud and clear.

"I spent a week in April at a Paris cooking school. It was the grand prize for a contest I entered, and I fell in love with France while I was over there. When I decided to open a restaurant, it seemed the way to go. *Vive le difference, monsieur!*"

"Bone jeer, mad a moe sale." He dipped forward in a mock bow.

She didn't think his exaggerated redneck drawl was funny. But she would continue being nice. She couldn't afford to do otherwise. "I'm offering a free lunch to downtown business owners the day before my official opening day. I put the invitations in the mail yesterday. It's on a Monday, two weeks from tomorrow. I hope you'll come by."

His eyebrows went up, then down. "I'll put it on my calendar."

For several moments, she churned out information like she was a publicist, using words and phrases like *upscale* and *elegant* and *patterning after the Paris restaurant where I'd studied.* She didn't care about her shameless self-promotion. Everyone in Nine Cloud would soon see that Rue de France was worth bragging about.

"I plan to serve mostly fine French cuisine," she said, "though I'll have some sandwiches, too. My signature dessert will be *Charlotte au chocolat.*"

"Sounds divine. *Angel's* food is di–vine." He dragged out the last word.

She gripped her purse, viselike. Was he making fun of her restaurant? He'd already made fun of her French. Did he think his restaurant was superior? Probably so. "I hope you'll soon say my food *tastes* divine."

"Sure thing." His affirming words didn't match his tone.

Irritation bubbled inside her like fudge in a pot. Talk about a condescending attitude. Forget he was a mover and a shaker in this town. The word *influencer* lit up like neon lights in her brain, but she turned them off with an imaginary flick of the wrist. Forget he was single—the attorney had told her that tidbit of info about Mr. Cyril Jackson III. Forget he was a Christian—he'd just told her he was. Forget her quest for Mr. Right.

In her mind, he was Mr. Hooty-Toot.

❦

Cyril felt a little guilty as he watched Angel shaking hands with Pastor Kyle in the church foyer. He'd maintained a stiff reserve with her and kidded her condescendingly. But her pushy ways brought it out of him. Whatever happened to genteel Southern charm in women? Where were the angelic ways he'd anticipated when he'd met her and learned her name?

Thinking quickly, he determined to make up for his behavior by asking her to lunch. He would display some Nine Cloud friendliness. He could do that much. It was professional courtesy to extend oneself to a fellow business owner. And besides, she was one good-looking woman.

He made his way down the church steps and into the parking lot. He saw her getting in her car and caught up to her just as she shut the door. "Angel?"

She looked up at him as she put on her seat belt. "Yes?"

"Care to get some lunch with me?"

Her brows drew together contemplatively.

"We could talk about Nine Cloud. . .and your plans for Rue de France."

She brightened. "That sounds great."

"What's your choice? B&B Cafeteria? Or Jim's Steak House? Those are the only two restaurants open on Sundays in Nine Cloud."

"Either one's fine with me. Why don't I follow you?"

"You're on."

Five minutes later, Cyril pulled into the parking lot of Jim's Steak House, knowing Angel was following. He searched for a parking place amidst a sea of trucks and a few cars. With their gargantuan tires, some of the trucks were nearly as tall as hundred-gallon drums.

Half of Nine Cloud must be inside. For some reason, every pothole he hit—he counted seven in all—seemed to jar him like they were jarring his car. Probably because Angel was hitting them, too, he decided. She'd gone to considerable trouble to fix up her aunt's old building, and she was probably thinking Jim of Jim's Steak House needed to repave his parking lot.

He walked up to the restaurant with Angel at his side. He grabbed the handle of the glass door, but it was so heavy he couldn't get it open. Obviously, the swing mechanism was in disrepair. He gave it a hefty pull and finally opened it. She walked inside, and he followed her, the door bumping him on the backside.

She slid in on one side of a booth, and he slid in on the other. "Thanks for suggesting this." She opened the dog-eared menu. "I appreciate your friendliness. I'd be eating alone today if you hadn't asked. I don't know too many people yet."

"I'm sure that'll change—"

"Oh, yes."

"You said you're from Orlando?"

"Yes. When I decided to open a restaurant in Nine Cloud, I decided to live here, too. I fixed up the apartment on the second floor of Aunt Myrtle Jean's building. I'm liking it, though downtown is dead in the evenings. But since I'm on the premises twenty-four-seven, it'll be a big help in running Rue de France."

"The restaurant business can be all-consuming, so be careful."

She shrugged. "I'm game. I'll do anything it takes to see it succeed. I've dreamed of owning a restaurant for a long time. I'm ready to work my heart out, as my mother puts it."

Cyril felt something gooey on his fingers, saw the shininess of pancake syrup on the menu—and now on his hand. He pulled his napkin out from under the fork and wiped the goo from his fingers. *She has vim, vigor, and vitality*—an old saying of his grandfather's—and he admired her already. "You said your mother's going to be your cook?"

"My chef. She'll be driving over to Nine Cloud every day. But it only takes about thirty-five minutes. I tried to get her to move in with me, but so far, I haven't been able to convince her. She says her little bungalow in Orlando is just fine for her. Someday, though, after the business takes off, I'm going to buy a nice home in Nine Cloud and get her to live with me. I want to take care of her in her later years, like she took care of me when I was growing up."

He noted the wistful look about her, enjoyed the soft side he was seeing.

They placed their orders and didn't say much for a few minutes, just listened to the songs on the jukebox.

"She thinks my tractor's sexy," crooned the country singer. "She likes my farmer's tan."

When they made eye contact, they got tickled. He laughed,

and she giggled, and her eyes twinkled, and his shoulders shook in mirth.

"What a song," he said, shaking his head.

"I never listen to country music. But it's a hoot."

The waitress brought their drinks and salads.

"Thanks," they said in unison, still laughing.

Cyril asked the blessing over the food.

Angel took a sip of her sweet iced tea, then picked at her salad and finally took a bite.

He was enjoying looking at Angel across the table. Living in a small town, going to a small church. . .well. . .pretty women—especially those with drive and ambition—didn't come along too often. She'd practically dropped down from. . .heaven? *Her name is Angel,* he thought with a smile. He'd been praying for a good mate. He'd asked the Lord for the last two of his twenty-five years—soon after he and Sheree broke up—to send him the right mate. He'd dated several women during that time, though none seriously. *Angel is. . .fine.*

He tried to distract his thoughts and concentrated on his salad. What wasn't brown was wilted. Two miniscule pieces of tomato were the only other ingredients. He pushed the bowl aside and took a long swallow of his sweet iced tea. At least the tea was good.

Angel pulled a napkin from the stainless steel dispenser and took a swipe at something on the table, then wadded it up and put it aside.

Cyril wondered what she was doing. Then he spotted a dead fly—belly up—on his side of the table, between the ketchup bottle and the filthy window. She must've found a fly, too. He went through the same procedure, the napkin swiping and wadding.

They got tickled again.

"Sorry about that," he finally said, still laughing.

"It's not your fault." She fished in her purse and pulled out a bottle of waterless handwash. "This isn't your restaurant."

"No, but I know who owns it." He drummed his fingers on the table. " 'Course, Jim pays a manager to see that things like this don't happen. But even managers have to be managed."

She didn't say anything, just poured some waterless hand-wash in her palm.

He held out his hand, and she poured some in his. He admired her for not chiming in with criticism of Jim's restaurant, though it would've been well deserved. He believed in sticking up for fellow business owners. Apparently she had this philosophy, too, and he admired her all the more.

The waitress brought their entrees and left like she was going to a fire.

Cyril needed butter for his roll. He looked across the restaurant but couldn't see their waitress. Another waitress approached. "Ma'am. . ."

The waitress whizzed by without stopping.

He looked left and right, searching for their waitress, for any waitress. He saw their waitress approaching. "Ma'am. . ."

She whizzed by.

He broke his roll in half and took a bite. Forget the butter. "You said your mother's a cook—"

"The best."

He smiled. "What line of work is your father in?"

"He passed away—"

"I'm sorry."

"I was only eight years old when it happened. . . ."

"That must've been hard."

She nodded. Like she was lost in time, she held a forkful of rice and gravy in midair. "I still remember the day he died." She put down the fork and blinked hard, as if trying to ward off tears. "I was born when they were in their forties—"

"So that means your mother's in her. . .what? Early sixties?"

"She's sixty-seven."

"No way. She can't be."

Angel smiled. "I guess hard work—and raising a child in your forties and fifties—keeps you looking young."

"I'll say. How old was she when you were born?" He laughed. "I guess I'm asking how old you are."

"I don't mind telling you. I'm twenty-four. Mom was forty-three when I was born. And Dad was forty-five. That doesn't sound out of the norm today—"

"Lots of people have children later in life."

"Right. But when I was born, it was fairly unusual. Mom and Dad got married when they were eighteen. They'd been together a long time when I came along. Mom always said they weren't just husband and wife, they were best friends, too." She smiled. "You know what Southerners say. They were so close, they were like white on rice."

He laughed at the familiar cliché.

Her eyes seemed to glow. "They called me their miracle baby." She had a distant, far-off look. "They were the most wonderful parents. . .loving and caring. . .and fun, too. Every afternoon when Dad got home from work, he'd sit with me on the porch swing. And Mom would be in the kitchen, cooking up a storm. And when she'd call us in for supper"—she breathed in deeply—"why, I can still smell the aromas. Chicken frying in the skillet. Biscuits baking in the oven. . ."

He sat quietly, envisioning the homey scene she was painting with verbal brush strokes. And he could feel the sense of nostalgia she was creating, and it was a good feeling.

She blinked hard again. "Dad was a car mechanic. We made it even though things were tight. But after he died, Mom needed to find a job so we could survive, she said. She was elated when she got the job at my elementary-school cafeteria. She said she would be able to be near me all day long. She retired two years ago." She paused.

"But here I've been babbling like a parrot," she continued, "and I haven't even let you say a word. Sorry."

"No need to apologize. I was enjoying it." He really was. He saw why she was so. . .pushy, he'd called it earlier. No, she was driven, he decided. By necessity.

"It's your turn to talk. Tell me some things about you."

He drained his tea glass then looked around for their waitress. Where was the woman? He spotted her near the cash register, jabbering on her cell phone. He stood up, loped across the aisle to an iced-tea station, whisked up a pitcher, and then loped back to the table. In short order, he refilled both his and

Angel's glasses. He sat down and set the pitcher on the table to keep it handy.

"Did you grow up in Nine Cloud?" she asked.

He nodded. "I'm a native. Born and raised here."

"When I tell people I'm a native of Orlando, they always say, 'I bet you've seen a lot of changes.'" She smiled. "You can't say that about Nine Cloud, can you?"

"No. Nine Cloud's been the same since I was a kid. No malls. No huge housing developments. And no superstores." He chuckled.

Angel studied the tabletop, ran her finger over a chipped-out place in the laminate.

"Let me guess what item you'd like to add to my list about Nine Cloud."

She looked up, questions in her sky blue eyes.

"No progress."

"I didn't say that."

"You were thinking it."

"How could you know that?"

"I just do." He wiped his lips with a napkin—a fresh one pulled from the container—then pushed his plate back. He'd finished eating and wanted to get to know her better. "And you know what? You're half right."

"I am?"

"I've been here all my life, and I'll admit, Nine Cloud needs some spiffing up here and there. In fact, it needs more than that. It needs refurbishing. Especially our downtown. I'm not blind. But renovation costs are sky high. And most business owners are barely making ends meet now. They don't have the money to kick in the tens of thousands it would take."

"But if we all got out and used our elbow grease—"

"That won't cut it—"

"It would help. . .and if we'd put on things like. . .like craft festivals to draw people. . .and if we'd erect historical markers and then promote them so people would come see the land-marks and shop at our businesses—"

"But Nine Cloud doesn't want to draw hordes of people—"

She rolled her eyes. "People equal money."

"I know that. I'm a businessman. But you need to attend a town-council meeting sometime. Nine Cloud doesn't want to attract people. They think developers would start building scores of new neighborhoods and shopping centers, and we'd lose our small-town atmosphere if that happened—"

"That's not necessarily so." She went on and on with other ideas, not missing a beat. "And if everybody would bring their businesses up-to-date. . ." She looked around the restaurant.

Cyril's eyes followed hers. With a sweeping glance, he noticed things he'd never focused on before—dilapidated furnishings, peeling wallcoverings, brown water-stained ceiling tiles.

". . .and up to par."

He squelched the *bah, humbug* rolling up his throat but couldn't prevent the low *tsk-tsk* escaping his lips. Who did she think she was, to move to Nine Cloud and two weeks later tell folks their town was archaic? And *then*, to top it all off, to tell them they needed to change it? Oh, yes. She was Miss Pushy.

And I'm drawn to her like a magnet to metal!

As Angel drove home, she couldn't keep from thinking about Cyril. Correction. His Lordship. She'd looked up the meaning of his name last night. *Lord.* That's what it meant.

At lunch today, when she'd mentioned her innovative ideas for improvement and growth for Nine Cloud, His Lordship resisted every one. And like a cloud blotting out sunshine, a coolness had settled over them.

"You're behind the times, Mr. Cyril Jackson III—just like your town. And just like your old-fashioned name."

Chapter 3

"M y, we served a lot of people today." Angel ate the last bite of her signature side salad—apples, celery, pineapple, and pecans served on Romaine with a tangy dressing drizzled over it. She leaned back in the Bentwood chair, enjoying the delectable flavors. "We must've had forty in here."

"The day will come when we'll have forty paying customers." Across the table, her mother stood up and gathered her dishes. "And more."

"And I don't think that day is too far off." An eternal optimist, Angel knew Rue de France was about to explode with success.

"Me neither."

Work awaited, and Angel raked scraps of food from her dinner plate onto her salad plate.

"With the way you've decorated this place, and the good food you're serving, and the excellent service you give to customers, well, you're going to have a thriving business." Her mother added Angel's dishes to her own stack, then made her way toward the kitchen.

"I can't wait to see that happen." Angel looked around at the French-style décor she'd created. Yellow walls. Blue and white striped tablecloths made from fabric bought at the *Marche St. Piere* in Paris. White lace curtains at the tall Palladian windows. Blue and white plates on wall shelves here and there. A blue and yellow tapestry rug in front of the door.

She sighed. The place had a soul, or *âme*, as the French called it. It was the most important thing to get right in any venture, French people were noted for saying. And she believed she'd gotten it right. Rue de France seemed to reach out and hug a person.

Her thoughts shifted to a year or two down the road, and the home she would buy, and the new car she would give her mother, and the other amenities in life that success would bring—all because of Rue de France. Life was grand. And would get grander.

She stared out the windows that fronted Main Street, watched people ambling by, saw the tattered awning over White's Hardware Store, noted the peeling paint on the book-store. If only Nine Cloud would do some downtown renovation, like what a lot of other small towns were doing. Forget reconfig-ured streets for more convenient parking and lush landscaping for beauty, and park benches for ambience—things that needed doing and would certainly bring in more customers. Just do some cleaning, painting, and fixing.

She picked up her stemmed water goblet, made her way to

the kitchen, and opened the broom closet to get an apron. Way in the back, behind several, was the apron she'd purchased in Dallas at the National Restaurateurs' Convention, the one with the cute words on it.

KISS THE COOK.

She recalled HAM—her three new friends, Haley, Allison, and Monica—a thought as pleasant as a bite of *Charlotte au chocolat*. They were a barrel of laughs. When Haley found out the gift shop didn't have anymore KISS THE COOK aprons, she begged Angel to pass the apron around until they all got a turn to wear it. HAM was in agreement. They said they were all needing help finding romance.

She pulled out the apron and ran her fingers over the words on the front.

I sure haven't been kissed in a long time.

For some reason, Cyril Jackson appeared in her mind's eye. Because he'd been here for lunch today? But it was more than that, she had to admit, despite her earlier feelings about him. *He is handsome, and he is a Christian,* she thought with a little thrill as she envisioned his dark hair and eyes and his tall, regal bearing and his upstanding reputation. Everybody liked him and looked up to him.

Her mother was wiping the stainless-steel island with a wet cloth. "Cyril Jackson went out of his way to talk with me today. Several times, I might add."

"He did?" Angel's heart fluttered. *He talked to me several times, too.*

Her mother nodded. "He's a nice young man."

Angel smiled as she leaned against the doorway and looked into the dining room, her gaze wandering to the front of the restaurant. A warmth seeped into her soul, and she knew it wasn't from the sunshine streaming through the sparkling windows.

What if Cyril turns out to be Mr. Right?

She certainly hoped to get to know him better. And see where things would lead. A childhood song fluttered through her memory.

" '*Qué será, será*, whatever will be, will be,' " she sang. " 'The future's not ours to see. *Qué será, será.*' "

Her mother gave her a knowing look. "Whatever will be, will be?" Her eyes gave off their familiar twinkle. " 'The future's not ours to see,' " she sang softly. " '*Qué será, será.*' " She paused and looked toward the ceiling. "Lord, please bring about Your will for Angel in the romance department, whatever it is."

Angel sighed as she put the KISS THE COOK apron over her head and tied the strings at the small of her waist. In her heart a hope grew, as surely as the magenta-colored phlox were growing in their window boxes outside.

⤜⤛

Late that afternoon, Cyril sat in his office that was housed in the building beside Main Street Café, working on his books. To offset an expected downfall in business at his café due to Angel's free lunch today, he'd come up with a good plan. Early that morning he'd faxed outlying businesses and offices and offered free delivery for lunch.

His manager had just informed him that his idea was a

smashing success. Though they'd had few customers in the café during the noon hour, his profits were excellent. In fact, the profits were better than they'd been for a single day in a long time.

Figuratively, Cyril gave himself a pat on the back. "Maybe I'll do that every day." But delivery help was hard to find in the middle of the day. All the teenagers were in school. On second thought, maybe he'd do it once a week, maybe twice.

He smiled. "I need to go thank you in person, Angel Morgan, for the extra money in my cashbox."

Ten minutes later, he walked down the sidewalk to Rue de France. He couldn't wait to see the sunshiny woman in her sunshiny restaurant—even though he'd eaten lunch there less than three hours ago.

And he stepped up his pace.

Angel looked at her watch as she dried her hands on the colorful kitchen towel. Three thirty. Her mother was probably getting into Orlando now. Good. Mom would be home before the bad traffic started.

She hung the towel on a rod, then made her way into the dining room and straightened the chairs from the lunch crowd.

A knock sounded at the door.

Who could that be? Hadn't she displayed the CLOSED sign? A glance that way showed her it was in the window. A peek at the front door showed Cyril Jackson standing there, smiling at her.

"Cyril. . .I'm coming." She dashed across the dining room,

zigzagging around tables, her heart as light as a cheese soufflé. She swung the door open wide. "What brings you here for the second time today? Come on in."

He stepped inside and closed the door behind him. "I could easily say your food drew me back." He touched his midsection. "That was some kind of eating at lunchtime. What'd you call that dessert you served us?"

"Charlotte au chocolat."

"It was delicious." He looked at her apron and smiled.

She glanced down and realized she still had on her KISS THE COOK apron. Her face grew warm, and her heart turned a flip-flop. Did he think she was on a hunt for a man? Hadn't Haley said people would think that?

"Interesting apron." He chuckled.

She whisked it off and slung it over her arm. "Would you. . . um. . .like a piece of pie? I. . .um. . .just pulled three out of the oven. For tomorrow's lunch crowd."

"I'll have to run some extra laps tonight if I do." He touched his midsection again. "That Charlotte stuff at lunch, and now pie?"

"It'll be worth it. It's my mother's recipe. It's not fancy but it's good. It's called chocolate chip pie."

"You talked me into it."

"Come on back." She waved for him to follow her as she turned and headed for the kitchen. They made small talk as she scurried around. She brewed a fresh pot of coffee, placed two wedges of pie on the Eiffel Tower dessert plates she'd purchased at the Paris Chinatown, and garnished them with dollops of

KISS THE ~~COOK~~ *Bride*

whipped cream and fresh mint leaves.

Cyril helped her carry mugs and silverware to the dining room, and they set the table together.

Shortly, they were seated at a table that overlooked a lace-covered window, Angel's heart singing.

Cyril put two tiny sugar cubes in his coffee. "Does each piece equal one teaspoon of sugar, or what? We don't use these things at Main Street Café." He grinned.

"Umm. . .it's supposed to, but you might need to add an extra cube. I don't think they're quite a teaspoonful."

He added another cube, then heavy cream from the dainty-footed pitcher. He stirred until his coffee reached a light golden color. "You know the proverbial saying. . ." She giggled and nodded as she shook out her cloth napkin. "I've heard it a million times in the restaurant business—"

"Me, too."

"You like your coffee like you like your women—"

"—blond and sweet." He finished the saying for her, his eyes roaming her long hair.

She could feel her face heating up, like it did when he'd caught her wearing her KISS THE COOK apron.

"I came by to say thank you, Angel."

"Thank me? For what?"

He told her about his business plan at lunchtime and how successful it was.

"That's a great idea," she exclaimed, when he finished telling her the details. "I'm always on the lookout for new things to try. The PR classes I took in college help me think along those lines. You know. Promo for the business and all."

"I think it goes way beyond classes. I think it's inborn in you."

She shrugged. "I admit I'm full of ideas. My mother calls them daydreams."

"You want me to pray?" He looked down at his pie. "I don't think I can resist any longer."

She smiled. "Sure." She bowed her head as he led in a blessing for the food.

He put his napkin in his lap, took a bite of pie, and swallowed it slowly, like he was savoring it. Then he became animated. "Angel!" His eyes widened. "*This*"—he tapped the plate with his fork—"should be your signature dessert!"

"It's good, isn't it?" She ate a bite and took a sip of her coffee.

"It's fabulous."

"But I wanted something French sounding."

He ate another bite, then another. "This pie'll make you want to slap your grandmaw." He chuckled.

She laughed at the Southern euphemism. "My father used to say that all the time. Except when my mother fixed chocolate chip pie. Then he'd say, 'This is lip-smacking good.'"

"I'll agree with that. And it makes you want to. . .kiss the cook." He was looking right at her, all traces of amusement gone from his eyes.

She averted her gaze, stared down at the table, noticed his plate was empty. "You want more?" She made a movement to stand, but her legs were Jell-O.

He gestured for her to stay seated. "Much as I'd like to, I'd better not."

She sat back down.

"But I'll sign up for another piece *real soon*, okay?"

Real soon held promise. She nodded and took another bite, fancifully envisioning the *real soon* appointment with Cyril. A picnic by a pond? A private, candlelit dinner for the two of them in Rue de France? Nothing could please her more. Perhaps the *real soon* appointment would grow into *frequent* appointments. *Dates* was the better word.

There I go again. Daydreaming.

As Cyril made his way down the sidewalk after leaving Rue de France, there was a spring in his step. A thought hit him, an old saying he'd heard his grandfather say many times. *In the spring, a young man's thoughts turn to fancy.*

No. That wasn't it. *In the spring, a young man's fancy turns his thoughts to love.*

That wasn't quite it either, but it was close. And so were his sentiments. He smiled.

And it's not even spring.

Chapter 4

A ngel picked up her cell phone on the first ring and smiled. It was Cyril. "Hi."

"Hi, Angel."

For several minutes, they talked—about everything and about nothing. If she were a cat, she would be purring. He asked how her day had gone. She asked the same.

"Are you free on Saturday afternoon?" he asked. "Would you like to get a bite to eat with me?"

She was so excited, she could've reached through the phone and hugged him. *He's asking me for a date. And a date leads to dates. And dates lead to a relationship.* There she went again, daydreaming. But that was the only way to succeed in life, in her opinion. Daydreaming led to goals. And goals led to plans. "A man with a plan" went the business adage for success. Only she was a woman with a plan, both for her business and for finding Mr. Right.

"I thought about driving over to the beach and eating some seafood. Jack's Crab Shack isn't fancy, but it has some goooood"—he drew it out Andy Griffith-style—"food."

"I'd love to go."

"Great."

"What time? And is it casual or dress?" *Slow down, Angel.* She laughed. "I guess *shack* tells it all."

"Oh, it's informal all right, but it's as good as all get out."

"I love seafood."

"We might walk on the beach after dinner. Is that okay with you?"

She took a deep breath to steady her heart. "I'll look forward to it, Cyril." *Will I ever!*

Angel checked her appearance in the full-length mirror one last time. Twisting this way and that, she knew her attire was perfect for their date at the beach. Red cowl-necked shirt. Red and black print cropped pants. Black open-toed heels that could easily be removed when she and Cyril walked in the sand.

She pulled out her lightweight black sweater and put it by her purse so she wouldn't forget it. She might need it. Even though it was July, brisk breezes could stir up quickly on any given evening on the beach and particularly tonight. It had been rainy the last two days, bringing the soaring temperatures down.

Twenty minutes later, she was sitting beside Cyril in his car as he drove toward the coast. In the backseat was a basket holding wedges of chocolate chip pie in plastic containers. She'd brought along his *real soon* request.

"What's in the basket?" he'd asked when he picked her up.

"A *pique-nique a la Provencale,*" she'd said with a French accent.

Now she glanced over at him as they drove along, the soft FM music filling the car. She liked his hearty laughter. And his winsome ways. And. . .and. . .him. Period.

Cyril, are you Mr. Right? She hoped so. It had nothing to do with a quick decision. Though she'd known him only a little over a month, she'd waited her entire adult life for the right man to come along, someone whose goals and morals matched hers. She felt good about Cyril—despite their awkward beginning. In fact, she felt more than good. She felt. . .wonderful.

⊱─━━━━━━─⊰

After Angel and Cyril finished eating at Jack's Crab Shack—both of them ordering fried shrimp and finding out it was their favorite seafood—they did just as he'd said. They walked on the beach, the waves lapping gently at their bare feet, creating a pleasant sound.

As she expected, the weather turned a little cool. She untied her sweater from around her neck and pulled it on to ward off the chill. But her heart was as warm as brownies pulled from the oven.

"Cold?" He rested his hand lightly on her shoulder.

She thought her heart would jump out of her chest. "No, not now." Not after his warm touch. For long minutes, neither said a word. She was glad. She was reveling in what was transpiring between them—a pleasantness, and maybe something more.

"Thanks for dinner," she finally said.

"Glad you could come. I'm enjoying the evening with you."

"Same here." She paused. "I've told you a lot about me, but you hardly told me anything about yourself."

He shrugged. "Not a whole lot to tell."

"Try me."

"I grew up in Nine Cloud. I went to elementary school, middle school, and high school here."

"Did you play any sports?"

"Basketball."

"And after you graduated, you. . . ?"

"I went to University of Florida. I wanted to go to our denominational college, but UF was my father's alma mater, so I went there to please him. When I finished school, I came home to help run our family business—"

"Which is. . .besides Main Street Café?"

"We've run the café into the third generation now. But we dabble in other things. . .we have some land. . .and some citrus groves. . .things like that."

She'd heard they owned a large chunk of land that bordered Nine Cloud to the east and west. People in town called it the Jackson land.

"Dad's had me involved in several of our businesses since I was a kid." He smiled. "I've picked my share of oranges and grapefruits, believe me."

"Someday, when I own a home in Nine Cloud, I want an orange tree in my yard. And a tangerine tree, too."

"I have a trio of citrus trees in my yard—orange, tangerine, and grapefruit. And my grapefruit are pink grapefruit. The best and sweetest."

"The best?" She scrunched up her nose, thinking of the sour fruit that didn't appeal to her, cook though she was. "I guess pink grapefruit is the way to go, if you've got to eat grapefruit."

"You don't like it?"

"Well, let's just say it's not my favorite citrus fruit. It's so sour, and you feel like you're wrestling with an alligator to get the meat out of the membranes."

"If I ever fixed one for you, you'd like it. It's all in the cutting and serving of it."

"Okay. You're on."

"All right. As soon as my grapefruit's ripe, I'll fix one for you."

"Deal."

He stopped on the beach, and she stopped. "We've walked a long way."

She glanced behind her, saw the lights of restaurants and hotels far down the beach. Above them, a full moon shone down. Her heart skipped a beat.

"We need to head back," he said.

"Okay."

They turned and started up the beach. Angel was chilly, but she'd be willing to stay out here for hours to be with him. Thankfully, he'd already led them out of the water, and they were now walking on dry, powdery sand.

"I told you about my school life," he said. "But I didn't tell you about my church life."

"I'd like to hear it."

"My mother accepted Christ when I was a kid. I'll never forget that time. It was like somebody gave her a gold mine. She was that excited. I guess she needed some joy." He shook his head. "My father was an alcoholic."

"Oh my."

"He wasn't a down-and-outer, though. Our family's enjoyed financial success for generations back. But he was a social alcoholic. And that's as bad as the other kind because he always had a drink in his hand. Or at least it seemed that way. Ever seen those old comedy videos of Dean Martin clowning around with Frank Sinatra?"

"I'm not sure. . ."

"You know who Dean Martin is, don't you?"

"Yes."

"I've seen them all my life. My father loved Frank and Dean. Anyway, on these videos, Frank's always cutting Dean down about his drinking, and Dean's always cutting Frank down about his carousing with women." He drew a deep breath and slowly released it. "You could safely say Dad was a combination of the two of them."

Angel didn't know what to say. Her father had treated her mother like a queen. They'd enjoyed the love of a lifetime, a unique and sacrificial love. A *faithful* love. She'd been raised in a safe, secure, and loving environment. "I'm. . .I'm so sorry."

He reached for her hand as if he needed the touch of a human being. He grasped it firmly in his. "It wasn't a good life for Mom. Of course I didn't know about these things when I was growing up. She kept them from me. But I knew things weren't good at our house. A kid's no dummy. He can sense things. There were arguments, though Dad was the main one doing the arguing. And when he wasn't arguing, he was away. And there was the weekend drunkenness, and my mother not being able to count on my father for anything, it seemed. And then. . .and then she left him—"

"They divorced?"

"She should've divorced him, I guess. But when I was ten, she told him she was leaving for a while to think things through. She took me with her, and we went to the coast. She and Dad had a condo on the beach, and that's where we stayed. It was during the summer, so she didn't have to worry about school."

He let go of her hand as they walked. "A neighbor in the next condo struck up a friendship with Mom. Mom and the woman—Kendra—started having coffee together a few mornings a week, and Kendra started talking to Mom about spiritual things—"

"Did your family go to church before that?"

He shook his head. "Mom had a vague knowledge about God, but she'd never experienced a relationship with Him. One day Kendra told her you could *know* you would go to heaven when you died, that you didn't have to just *hope* you did. And then she explained salvation. Mom later told me no one had ever done that to her. It was like a lightbulb went on in her head. All of a sudden, she had an overwhelming desire to know God—"

"Sounds similar to my mother's experience."

"Kendra asked Mom if she'd like to invite Christ into her heart, and she said yes. Mom came over to the sofa where I was sitting and grabbed my hand. Tears were pouring down her face. We knelt down in front of it, and Kendra led us both in prayer, and we asked the Lord to be our Savior. It was like a sunburst of joy hit Mom's soul, and I could tell from that moment she was a different person. And I was, too. I remember the feeling distinctly, even though I was only ten at the time. It was like a ton fell off my shoulders. The weight of sin."

"Wow."

"We moved home the next day, and Mom told Dad what happened. At first, things didn't change—for him, I mean. He still drank, though he didn't leave for trips as often. And he still had a quarrelsome nature. But Mom had this newfound joy—and hope—and so our house was different. Anointed, I'd call it. Mom started going to church and got involved, and I did, too. We attended Sunday school, and I joined the boys' program on Wednesdays."

"What about your dad? Did he mind?"

"No. He said he didn't care. He said since her religion made her so happy, he was all for it. And what I'm about to tell you next may sound dramatic. Or it may *not* sound dramatic. I've heard all kinds of conversion stories. I've heard of people seeing visions of Jesus. . .and I've heard of people visiting revivals and being changed by the power of Christ. . . ."

Angel nodded. She'd heard—and seen—stories like those, too.

"And then there are stories like Mom's—of someone sharing the truth in love. But Dad. . .well, one day Mom and I got in the car to go to church, and she was backing out of the driveway. . .and Dad comes running out of the garage and jumps in the passenger seat. She told him we were going to church, and he said, 'I know.' She didn't say anything, and I didn't either. He went to church with us—to Sunday school, too—get that. And at the close of the pastor's message, Dad walked to the altar and told the pastor he wanted what my mother and I had. Dad prayed for Christ to come into his heart. From that day to this, he's never drunk a drop of liquor. And he's lived a life for the Lord ever since."

"That *is* dramatic."

"It's a miracle."

"For sure." Angel marveled at the story. It was amazing.

"There's no telling what would've happened to our family if Kendra hadn't told Mom about Jesus. I don't know where I'd be right now. I might be just like Dad was." He paused, as if deep in thought. "That's why I tell everyone I meet about the love of God. That's why I'm sold out to Him—hook, line, and sinker."

❦

They reached the place where they started walking on the beach earlier, near Jack's Crab Shack. Looking over a sand dune and toward the parking lot that was lighted by streetlights, Cyril could see his car in the nearly deserted lot. It was late.

He opened the car door for Angel. "Have a seat, and stick out your feet."

She laughed. "You're a poet and don't know it." She proceeded to do as he said.

He chuckled. "I'll be right back." He walked to the trunk, then came back to her door. He poured water from a jug over her feet, handed her a towel, and waited while she dried them.

"Thanks." She handed him the towel. "That felt good."

"What? Walking on the beach with me? Or rinsing your feet?"

She laughed. "There you go again with your poetry."

He chuckled as he made his way to his car door, gently shaking the towel in the breeze, got in, rinsed and dried his feet, then cranked up the car.

"I *did* enjoy walking on the beach with you." Her voice was soft as she reached down and slipped on her shoes. "It was. . . wonderful."

"And so is this. . ." He reached for the basket in the backseat, then put it between them. "Let's eat your pie now, okay?"

"Sure."

"But let's get some coffee to go with it. That all right with you?"

"What goes better than pie and coffee?"

You and me. He wheeled into a small restaurant, dashed inside, and in a jiffy was pulling out of the parking lot and onto the highway, two cups of coffee sitting in the built-in cup holders near the dashboard. "You don't mind if we go to one other place before we head back, do you?"

"No. Not at all."

"The condo I was telling you about earlier? Where Mom

and I found the Lord? We walked past it tonight. We still own it."

"Your old stomping grounds."

"Yes. I guess that's why I love the beach so much. It holds happy memories. I'm going to show you another place we own."

"Another condo?"

"No. A house." He sipped his coffee as he drove for a good ten minutes. He turned onto a narrow, private road. At the end of the road, he pulled up to a house that fronted the ocean, the headlights allowing them to see in the darkness. The house was weathered and beaten looking, and the yard was full of sand-spurs. "Dad bought it the first of the year—for the land really. It's a little run-down—"

"It looks like a wonderful place to retreat to. Sort of like a hideaway."

"We're not sure what we're going to do with it." He cut off the engine, rolled down the electric windows, and turned the radio to a soft level. "We'll either remodel it or demolish it and build something in its place."

"A little TLC, and it'd be beautiful."

He laughed. "There you go again. You and your bright ideas." He looked at her, then slowly reached up and caressed her cheek with the back of his hand, first the right side, then the left. He couldn't resist. Then his hands were on the bottom of the steering wheel again, but he kept looking at her intently. "I'm getting to where I like your ideas, Angel. . ." *And you.*

She looked down at the basket in her lap and traced the print of the napkin.

"I apologize for my forwardness," he said. "I shouldn't have done that—"

"Yes, you should have."

He was surprised at *her* forwardness. But he liked it. He reached over, cupped her chin in his hand, and gently turned her face toward him, forcing her to look at him. Even in the moonlight, her eyes were as blue as the ocean and just as mesmerizing.

"I guess I should apologize," she said.

"For what?"

"For this—" She reached over and gave him a warm hug, snuggled to him for long moments, then settled back in her seat. "I—I guess it's the. . .the beach in front of us. . .and the waves lapping gently. . .and. . .and the moon shining down. . . ."

"Whatever made you do it, I'm glad."

⤌⧉⤍

Late that night, Angel pulled the sash of her terrycloth robe tightly about her waist, then brushed her hair that was damp from the shower spray.

She'd taken a hot shower, but it hadn't been to warm up, as she'd thought about earlier when they were walking on the beach. His nearness in the car had done the job.

And it not only warmed my heart, it ignited it.

She remembered the tender moment when she'd hugged him. Then she'd withdrawn from him. He seemed old-fashioned in many ways, and she didn't want to appear forward—which she wasn't.

Hadn't she hugged him for the reasons she'd told him? Hadn't the romantic setting pulled it out of her? Yes, but it was more. It wasn't entirely the romantic setting. It was. . .him.

Chapter 5

I just don't understand small-town mentality," Angel complained to her mother as they cooked. "Why these people don't flock to a French restaurant is beyond me. Don't they realize the uniqueness? Why, how many small towns do you know of that have French restaurants?"

"Maybe it's too much of an oddity to them, hon." Her mother stood at the stove, stirring a honey-colored sauce. "Maybe you need to adjust the menu."

"I've already stopped serving *rouget*—"

Her mother smiled. "Nine Cloud people couldn't seem to adapt to whole red mullet staring up at them from their plates—"

"Wonder why?" Angel laughed. "You'd think rednecks would like red fish."

"Rednecks?"

Angel sighed. "I was joking. Nine Cloud has lots of sharp people. Only *some* of them are hicks." She was thinking of some of the church members. But they were sweet hicks, she had to admit. "And forget the *gigot d'agneau* with *herbes de Provence*. That went off the menu after the first month."

"Lamb *is* a little wild tasting, if I do say so myself."

Angel giggled. "I've got a secret."

"You don't like it either?" Her mother's eyes danced in merriment.

Angel shook her head no. "But I wanted it on the menu because it sounded sophisticated."

Her mother laughed heartily. "Well, at least the sandwiches sell well."

"Those sandwiches are the only thing keeping this ship afloat. But I don't know for how long."

Angel's eyes misted over, but she willed herself not to let the tears fall. She'd been open since June—for two months. If business didn't pick up soon, she might have to close Rue de France. And she couldn't bear the thought.

❧

Late that afternoon, Angel sat at a table in the dining room, doing office work. She glanced out the window and noted the awning over White's Hardware Store. It had another tear in it, compliments of last night's rainstorm and high winds. Maybe now, Mr. White would see the need to replace it.

"Why can't you people see the need for progress?" she said through gritted teeth.

She spotted the peeling paint above the awning. "Decrepit. Antiquated." She couldn't think of any more adjectives. *In desperate need of repair.*

"Repair?" Into her mind flashed a picture of the pastor at church. Last Sunday, Pastor Kyle had announced he wanted the congregation to take on a different kind of project. He wanted their church to rebuild a destitute family's house. And he was proposing to do it in a short amount of time with the help of lots of workers. He had put out a heart-stirring plea for volunteers to sign up.

She would like to help. But there were only so many hours in the day. Rue de France consumed all her time except for the hours she managed to squeeze out to be with Cyril. She smiled at *that* thought.

"The church rebuilding project? My plate's too full for that."

Chapter 6

Standing between the two back pews, Angel gathered her purse and Bible. She was in her usual hurry to get to Orlando and spend the afternoon with her mother. She spotted Cyril rising from his pew near the front. He'd asked her several times to sit with him. They'd spent a good bit of time together lately, and he said he wanted to be with her in church, as well. But she told him if she sat in back, she could dash out and get on over to Orlando to be with her mother. He understood, he said.

She felt a tap on her shoulder.

"Isn't your name Angel Morgan?"

She turned around and saw a petite, seventyish lady in the aisle.

The elderly lady's clothing cried passé, but her manner made up for it with the sparkle on her countenance. "Sweet thang—that's what I call my grand young'uns, so I hope you don't mind me callin' you that. Anyway, we're as tickled as can be that you're attending our church."

"Thank you. I enjoy the services."

She gave Angel an air kiss on the cheek, then a boisterous hug. "The Apostle Paul says to greet the brethren with a holy kiss, but I'm sure he meant the sistern, too." She let out a jolly laugh.

Angel smiled as she breathed in deeply. The elderly lady's hug smelled like the lavender in the French countryside she'd come to love during her time in France.

The lady stepped into the pew in front of Angel, plopped down, and turned to face her. "Like I said, we're mighty glad to have you in church with us. I seen you every Sunday, but this is the first chance I had to say hello. I never can get back here in time."

Angel told her about spending Sunday afternoons with her mother.

"I know. Somebody told me that. That's right commendable. Well, I won't beat around the bush. I come back here on a mission."

"A mission?"

"Yessiree Bob. Pastor Kyle asked me to start a new Sunday school class, and I'm wondering if you'd be a member?"

Angel made a mental note. Put a bouquet of fresh lavender—or some sort of purple flowers at least—in the center of each table in Rue de France.

"I knew your great-aunt. I visited her regularly after she became a shut-in. I was saddened to hear of her passing."

"Thank you, Mrs. . . ?"

"Sister Wilkins."

"Pleased to meet you, Sister Wilkins." Angel smiled at her.

"Same here, sweet thang. In this new Sunday school class I'm starting, we'll be studying a book called *The Dedicated Life for Christ*. The course'll run for three months. Unless we get to enjoying our self so much that we keep going. You know how Sunday school is. Everybody wants to share. I'm sure a-hoping you'll become a member of my class."

"I. . .I'm not. . .sure. . ."

"Oh, there's Cyril." Sister Wilkins clasped hold of Cyril's hand as he walked by.

He stopped in the aisle.

Sister Wilkins pawed over his hand as she looked up at him, her eyes as twinkly as stars. "How's our resident bachelor today?" She winked at Angel. "Do you know this young lady?"

He smiled at Angel. "I certainly do."

Angel looked away, thinking of the romantic times they'd had recently. Her breathing was so short, she was afraid it was jiggling her cotton top.

"Cyril, I was just telling her"—Sister Wilkins gestured at Angel—"about my new Sunday school class. I was asking her if she'd join it." She turned to Angel. "I checked, and you aren't enrolled in any of our Sunday school classes, so I thought you'd be a prime prospect. Cyril here"—she thrust her hand toward him—"is joining. Pastor Kyle's doing a rotation thingy in Sunday school and asked Cyril to take a break from the middle-school boys and help me get this new class a-going. Will you commit to us?"

Angel hated being put on the spot like this. *If I join this class, the next thing you know, they'll be asking me to do other things...*

"I know you'll find it interesting. And we need to become more dedicated to Christ. All of us. Studying how to do it will help...." Sister Wilkins's voice trailed off, question marks forming in her faded blue eyes.

Angel fiddled with the zipper on her purse. Sister Wilkins was speaking the truth. Angel couldn't deny it. And her mother would readily agree.

"Won't you please come?"

Angel's cell phone rang, and she was glad for the interruption. She whipped it out of a side compartment of her purse and noted it was her mother. She turned to Sister Wilkins. "If you'll excuse me, I'll only be a moment."

"Go right ahead, sweet thang."

Angel took the call and told her mother that yes, she would pick up some butter and that she would be on her way in a few minutes. Then she closed her phone.

Sister Wilkins shifted in the pew, the scent of lavender wafting through the air again. "We all need to make time for the work of the Lord."

Angel squeezed the tiny phone in her hand. The work of the Lord? All she knew right now was the work of Rue de France. Well, the *lack* thereof. With hardly any customers, she was consumed with worry, not work.

" 'Only one life, 'twill soon be past, only what's done for Christ will last.' That's an old poem—"

"I know. My mother quotes it all the time."

Sister Wilkins rose to her feet, wincing in pain. "I got a

hitch in my get along." She laughed as she touched the small of her back. "Just don't get old, folks. Just don't get old."

Cyril made eye contact with Angel, and they both laughed with Sister Wilkins, enjoying her antics.

"Well, I know you got to go. I heard you a-telling your mother you were on your way. So I won't keep you." Sister Wilkins smiled. "But I hope you'll join my class."

Cyril nodded. "I second that."

"I. . .well, I'll have to see."

"Food for thought, right, Angel?" Cyril's penetrating gaze seemed to pierce the sinews of her soul.

Angel slowly nodded. My, he looked serious. What was he thinking?

⬥

"Well, what do you think, Cyril?"

Cyril looked down at Sister Wilkins but didn't say anything. He was too busy ponderating, as his grandfather liked to say.

"I thought she was a perfect prospect for my class. I thought she'd commit. I really did. . . ."

He couldn't concentrate on what Sister Wilkins was saying as she jabbered on. All he could think of was Angel. She was pretty. Check. And she was single. Check. And she had get-up-and-go. Check. And they'd had such good times together lately. Check.

But she's not interested in Kingdom doings.
Uncheck.

Cyril clearly saw that now. Every time they'd been together

KISS THE ~~COOK~~ *Bride*

in the last few weeks and the subject of God or the church had come up, Angel hadn't had much to say.

Disappointment that was sharper than a hunger pang hit him in the gut. No, the heart.

Chapter 7

Angel sat in her living room, surfing restaurant sites on her laptop on yet another dateless Saturday night, trying to glean ideas.

The proverbial saying, "Absence makes the heart grow fonder," was certainly applicable here. She couldn't keep her thoughts off of Cyril. Apparently, that wasn't the case with him. What was going on? They'd had many Saturday night dates in a row. Now she only saw him in church or downtown when their paths happened to cross.

"Well, I guess that leaves me some free time to devote to the church rebuilding project."

She picked up Pastor Kyle's letter she'd received in today's mail and reread it. He was pleading for volunteers. When she saw the part about the four children in the family and no father, tears came to her eyes. That meant a single mother working her heart out to make a living and raise the children. That sounded familiar. She knew what it was to be in need. And she knew what she had to do.

She put the letter down, picked up her cell phone, and called the pastor. She told him she wanted to sign up for the project and mentioned her areas of expertise. When she found out only nine other people had volunteered, she was flabbergasted. But she didn't say anything.

Their conversation came to a close, and she clicked off her cell phone with more force than necessary. "Ten volunteers for a project this massive? That figures." She was feeling sarcastic tonight—not her usual *modus operandi*. But it couldn't be helped. She'd moved to Nine Cloud with high hopes, only to have them dashed.

The townspeople resisted progress. . . .

Her restaurant wasn't doing well. . . .

And her budding romance had turned out to be no romance at all. She didn't know what had happened with Cyril and her. Whatever had been afloat had sunk like a capsized ship.

On second thought, maybe she *did* know what happened. He was *always* talking about God and church, and it irked her sometimes. Maybe he sensed that about her, and maybe that irked *him*. After all, he was Mr. Evangelist.

Now, when she saw him, she felt awkward and uncomfortable. Before, she'd been so happy every time she was with him. She thought it was the start of a meaningful relationship.

"Relationship? Ha." She closed her laptop, made her way to her desk, and sat down. "Cyril Jackson III, you're too heavenly minded to be any earthly good." *At least any good to me.*

She grabbed a pencil from the penholder and drew a house on the back of Pastor Kyle's letter. She put a front door on it, windows on either side, and flowers out front, all stick drawing, kindergarten-style.

"I don't know what the future holds for me concerning Mr. Right." She couldn't keep the acrimony out of her voice.

"But one thing I *do* know. I'll work my heart out for this poverty-stricken family." She had a strong back and a good eye for righting things. She could hammer nails and paint walls and gather debris. And anything else they requested of her.

Meantime, she would work her heart out for Rue de France, too. She *would* see success, come what may. It was the driving force in her life.

***

"Hi, Cyril. This is Pastor Kyle."

"Well, hello, Pastor Kyle." Cyril pointed the remote and hit the MUTE button. Wonder why the pastor was calling? He would see him in the morning at church. "What can I do for you?"

"I noticed you were the first one to sign up for the church rebuilding project. I wanted to express my thanks."

"I'm looking forward to it. This family. . .what's their name?"

"The Hendersons."

"The Hendersons are going to be mightily blessed. But the ones who work on it will get the biggest blessing. I'm convinced of that."

"You're right, Cyril. It's more blessed to give than receive, the Good Book says."

"Amen. Who's going to head up the project?"

"That's why I'm calling. Will you. . .be the team captain?"

"I. . .uh. . ."

"You have business savvy. . .and Roy Johnson signed up to be a volunteer. . .and he can give you good advice. He's got his contractor's license now. . .and he's—"

"Why don't you make him team captain? He's much more knowledgeable about building than I am."

"I feel like the Lord wants you to do it."

"You do?"

"I do."

"Well, I can't argue with the Lord, can I?" Cyril chuckled.

"No."

"All right. I'll do my best."

"I knew you would."

"Well, I guess I'll see you in church in the morning, Pastor—"

"One other thing, Cyril."

"What's that?"

"Will you give one of the volunteers a call?"

"I'll call all of them, once I figure out a game plan."

"I mean tonight."

"Tonight?"

"Yes."

A pause. A glance at the TV screen. "Sure, Pastor. Who is it?"

"Angel Morgan."

Angel volunteered for the rebuilding project? Well, shut my mouth, as Sister Wilkins would say. Cyril had tried to get Angel to sign up for the project, just as he'd tried to get her to join

74

Sister Wilkins's Sunday school class, to no avail. He said it would please the Lord. No takers. He said it would be rewarding. No takers. He said it would be fun. No takers. He finally got the message. Angel just didn't have her priorities right. That was when he decided to cool things for a while.

"Angel wants to help," Pastor Kyle went on. "She said she can paint walls and trim. And she can drive a pretty good nail. And she said if it's needed, she'd like to help pick out paint colors and things like that. I'd like you to call her tonight, and let her know we appreciate her volunteering."

Cyril quickly summed up the situation. Pastor Kyle must be trying to get him and Angel together. Cyril had had a friend-to-friend conversation with him recently. He'd told the pastor he and Angel had gone on a few dates. He also mentioned he was disappointed in her and hadn't taken her out in several weeks. *The Lord wants you to pray for her*, Pastor Kyle had told him

"Cyril? Did I lose you?"

"No, Pastor."

"I feel—"

"—the Lord wants me to call her?" Cyril interrupted good-naturedly.

Pastor Kyle laughed. "No. This time, I'm the one who feels that way."

Cyril joined in his laughter, for some reason feeling good about the future of his and Angel's relationship. "Okay. I'll do it."

"Keep me posted."

"Oh, I will, Pastor."

Angel heard her cell phone ring. She pushed aside her stick drawing of the house and picked up her phone. She was surprised to see Cyril's number. "Hi, Cyril."

"Hi, Angel. How are you?"

"Fine." *Not really.*

"Pastor Kyle said you signed up for the church rebuilding project."

Angel did a double take. Why'd the pastor call Cyril and tell him she'd volunteered?

"I'm going to be heading up the project. I'm calling it Project Hope."

"My, Pastor Kyle works fast. I just called to tell him I wanted to sign up."

"I'm glad, Angel."

She remembered when he'd tried to get her to volunteer. But that wasn't her reason for doing it. "When I got his letter, I knew I had to help."

"The church appreciates your help. And I know it'll mean a lot to the Henderson family. I've decided to have a planning meeting next Saturday night. Can you make it?"

What used to be our date nights. "What time?"

"I'm firming up plans now. I'm thinking about luring volunteers by providing a meal at my café. If I decide to go that route, I'll probably start it at five thirty."

"That's a great idea. As they say, the way to a man's heart is through his stomach."

A pause ensued.

"Cyril? Are you there?"

"Yes."

"I thought we got cut off." What was going on?

"I'm here." Another pause. "Angel, if I decide to have the eating meeting, would you be willing to make some of your chocolate chip pies for dessert?"

She was caught off guard. Of course she didn't mind bringing dessert. She loved to cook. But his request seemed a little odd to her—

"That's okay. You don't have to. I'll get Mama Edwards to make us something, some kind of cake maybe—"

"I'll be glad to bring the pies. How many are you expecting?"

He let out a smirk-laugh. "We have ten on the volunteer list right now, but we need twenty or twenty-five at least, to pull this off. Pastor Kyle wants the house completed in ten days' time, if possible."

"I'm a positive thinker. I'll bring six pies. Each pie serves eight, so that'll be enough for thirty people and *lots* of seconds for the big eaters."

"Angel. . .you rock, as the middle schoolers say."

The cat had her tongue for a moment. Her heart fluttered. *You rock, Cyril.* "Glad I can help."

"Man, who made this pie?"

"This stuff is pure heaven."

"Oh, that my wife could cook like this. . ."

"Can I have another slice?"

"Whadayacallit?"

"Musty."

"Musty?"

"I *must* have some more." Hand waving in the air. "Seconds, please."

"Is there a name for it?"

"Whoever made it oughta call it Heavenly Pie."

"Oh, man, that's hitting the nail on the head."

"Yep. Heavenly Pie."

"What a divine thought." A geehawing chuckle. A stab in the ribs. "Get it?"

"I sure do." A last bite. A swig of coffee. "And I'm gonna get me some more."

<hr/>

"Ladies and gentlemen." Cyril tapped a fork on his glass, making a *ping* sound. "If you're finished with your dessert, please find a seat on the other side of the café. The busboy will clean our tables while we have our meeting. But before you get to moving about, I'd like to introduce you to Angel Morgan. She's the lady behind the Heavenly Pie."

The crowd applauded.

"Angel, would you stand up?"

Angel stood and smiled.

"She owns Rue de France, the French restaurant down the street."

They applauded again.

"I hope you'll try her fare. Everything I've eaten at her

restaurant is top-notch. She serves entrées. . .and sandwiches
. . .and desserts. . .and Heavenly Pie, of course."

⌧⌧⌧

"There was a motive to your madness." Angel smiled at Cyril as she gathered her empty pie pans while he turned off the lights.

He shrugged then grinned. "Wouldn't you say it was a good one?"

She nodded. "Maybe after tonight, I'll have a few more customers."

"I hope so. They sure loved your Heavenly Pie."

"Heavenly Pie, is it?"

"Somebody came up with that tonight—"

"I know. I heard them."

"I already told you, you should make it your signature pie for Rue de France."

"I really like that name. Heavenly Pie." She'd give his suggestion some consideration. "I think your idea is brilliant, Cyril."

Chapter 8

Angel drove toward the Hendersons' house where she'd been working for a week. Every spare minute away from Rue de France, she spent at Project Hope. She had spread wallboard mud on the new walls, then taped and sanded them—with instructions from one of the volunteers, of course. She carried debris—strips of carpet, pieces of mildewed walls, sections of old cabinets, even a commode—to the trash receptacle outside.

She gave decorating guidance to Ms. Henderson as she made selections of paint colors, cabinets, countertops, and new furniture.

Angel had done everything they'd asked her to do, had been glad to do it. She couldn't wait to hang the curtains and help decide the furniture placement in the rooms. That would be the crowning touch. The icing on the cake.

This evening, she would be painting, so she wore her paint clothes—the same ones she'd worn when she painted Rue de France—a T-shirt, faded cut-off jeans, and old tennis shoes.

She might as well be comfortable.

She pulled into the small grassless front yard. Laying new sod would be the last thing they'd do. She envisioned the heavy snow she saw on last night's news in some other part of the country. Here in Central Florida, it was mild year round, and even though it was October, the sod would be rich and full and green from the day they laid it. She pictured the young Henderson children playing in this filthy dirt pit and then later, their joy at playing on the soft green grass.

To her right and left, she saw rows of houses like the one they were rebuilding, with hardly any space between them. She heard people talking loudly on porches up and down the street. A horn blared in the distance.

Somebody was singing at the top of their lungs, and babies wailed.

Next door, a woman screamed, as if in agony. "You cain't leave me. I cain't stand it if you leave me."

Deeply touched, Angel shook her head. But at least the church was rebuilding one house. She recalled Pastor Kyle's sermon illustration on one of the Sundays he put out a plea for volunteers. It was about a young boy standing on a seashore, throwing back stranded sea creatures that lined the shore by the thousands. A man asked him why bother, and the boy said, "I'm saving this one and this one and this one."

Tears stung her eyes as she got out of her car, her mind on the family they were helping.

"Hiya." A young girl, maybe twelve or thirteen, jumped down from the front porch and made her way to Angel's car.

"Like my new do?" She made a primping gesture.

Angel recognized the girl as a member of the Henderson family. She'd seen her a couple of times during the project. "Looks just like Oprah's hairstyle, Shanika. Or at least the way she was wearing it on her last magazine cover. I think she has a new—what'd you call it?"

" Do—"

"—a new do every day or two."

Shanika nodded. "She has her own private hairdresser."

"That style looks nice on you. And aren't you wearing some makeup?"

Shanika dropped her gaze, shylike. "Yes, ma'am. Part of this program was makeovers for Mama and me. They did me today. Mama gets done Saturday. We got some new clothes, too." She touched the lapel of her crisp white shirt, ran her hand down her stylish new jeans.

"I see that."

"I'm supposed to help you paint tonight. You need a hand with your stuff?"

"Sure." Angel gestured at paint trays and rollers in her backseat and picked up as many as she could hold.

Shanika gathered the rest of the items, and they walked toward the house, picking their way around the huge trash receptacle and various building supplies.

"We sure are glad y'all put a new swing on our porch," Shanika said as they walked up the front steps. "Our old one had some cracked boards down the middle. Kinda caught you in a ticklish spot, if you know what I mean." Shanika's dark brown eyes sparkled. "Thank You, Lawd, for a new swing."

That cracked Angel up—Shanika's cute mannerisms. It took her awhile to quit laughing. "I love a porch swing."

"We do, too. Mama says she doesn't really need to watch soap operas. She can sit right here on the porch and see them day and night."

Angel laughed again. This girl was delightful. She would like to take an interest in Shanika's future, give her guidance and advice, that sort of thing. She'd like to see her make something of her life.

When they got inside the house, Angel could see they were among the first to get there. A quick glance out the kitchen window told her Cyril's car wasn't there yet. Perhaps he'd stopped to pick up something. She was looking forward to seeing him.

While Shanika changed her clothes in the bathroom, Angel made her way into a bedroom and put down her paint supplies. Working on Project Hope had given her a great sense of fulfillment. And it gave her opportunities to be in close proximity to Cyril.

Now *that* was icing on the cake!

Angel glanced at her watch and noticed a smudge of paint on it. She wiped it off. Good thing it was her old one.

Nine o'clock already. The evening had gone by quickly. She and Shanika were finishing up the third bedroom. Shanika was at her side, rolling paint on the wall in fast, even strokes. Though the girl was young, Angel could see she was industrious. She'd go somewhere in life, this girl.

Shanika leaned her paint roller on the side of the tray, opened a can of paint with the special instrument, and then poured more paint into the tray. She closed the can, whisked her roller through the paint, and started painting again.

"Shanika?"

"Yes, ma'am?"

"You're a hard worker."

" 'We'll work till Jesus comes, we'll work,' " Shanika belted out in song. " 'Till Jesus comes, we'll work, till Jesus comes, and we'll be gathered home.' " She giggled. "That's an old hymn Mama likes to sing, especially when she's trying to get us to help her clean house on Saturday mornings."

Angel smiled at her. "You have a dramatic flair, too. That's a winning combination. Hard work and personality." Shanika reminded her of Oprah, with her honey-colored skin and beautiful hair and expressive eyes. "What do you intend to do with your life?"

"Oh, I don't know. . ."

"What're your interests?"

"I love to read."

"That's good. My mother always said reading expands your world. Do you want to go to college?"

Shanika stopped painting. Her eyes lit up. "Someday I'd like to be a teacher. And maybe a principal." She shrugged her shoulders. "I hope I can go to college."

"You hope? Of course you can. If a person puts her mind to it, she can do anything she wants to."

Shanika resumed her painting.

"I guess you know about Oprah's rise to fame?"

"Yes, ma'am. She started out with slim pickings, but now she's got plenty of money. And houses and cars. And TV shows. And she makes movies. And she owns a magazine. And—"

"—and she's smart and. . .generous. . .and gifted. . .it seems like she has the power to do just about anything. I guess you could say she's got it all."

Shanika didn't respond.

"Who knows? Maybe you'll be the next Oprah, Shanika. Now that's what I call success."

"No, ma'am."

Angel was surprised. "What?"

"Oh, I'm not saying Oprah isn't successful. Everybody knows better than that. She's on the"—she paused like she was thinking—"pinnacle—that's one of my spelling words this week. She's on the pinnacle of success. She's riding the high wave. She's not only rich and smart and generous and gifted, it seems like she's got something about her I can't explain. . ."

"I'd say it's an ethereal quality. Whatever it is, it draws people to her."

Shanika nodded vigorously. "But none of that's *real* success, in my book."

"What is *real* success, in your book?"

Shanika held her paint roller in midair. She took on a theatrical stance, putting a hand over her heart and clamping her eyes shut. " 'If I speak in the tongues of men and of angels, but have not love, I am only a resounding gong or a clanging cymbal. If

I have the gift of prophecy and can fathom all mysteries and all knowledge, and if I have a faith that can move mountains, but have not love, I am nothing. If I give all I possess to the poor and surrender my body to the flames, but have not love, I gain nothing.'"

Angel was momentarily stunned. "You're. . .quoting. . . 1 Corinthians 13?"

Shanika opened her eyes. "It's called the Love Chapter."

"I know. Where'd you learn it?"

"At my church. I help teach a children's Sunday school class. I help them memorize scriptures."

"That's amazing."

"No, ma'am." Shanika dipped her paint in the tray and put it to the wall, then kept up with her steady strokes. "It just takes practice." She smiled. "Practice to learn it, and then practice to live it."

Angel swallowed hard. "Shanika. . .you're something. . .you know that?"

Shanika shrugged.

"You didn't answer my question, though."

Shanika gave Angel a sideways glance.

"What is *real* success, in your book?"

"What I just quoted. The love the apostle was talking about is the love for the Lord. Jesus said I am the way, the truth, and the life. Nobody comes to the Father except by me. Putting Jesus, His work, and His Word above all else—*that's* what *real* success is, in my book."

Angel took a deep breath and slowly released it. Rue de

France was the center of her world—not Jesus Christ. And before Rue de France, other things had crowded out the Lord. She'd pushed Him aside in her feverish quest for success.

But you did it for a good reason, came a dark voice. *You wanted to take care of your mother.*

And that's right and good and worthy, Angel responded in her heart.

But what about 1 Corinthians 13? The Love Chapter? An enlightening voice.

Love? I've got plenty of love.

Not the right kind.

A warring seemed to be going on in Angel's soul as thoughts ricocheted through it.

Sure you have love. Look. You're involved in this project.

What's your motive? I'm not only interested in what you do, but why you do it.

But I empathized for the family. A truthful answer. *I identified with them. I gave of myself in this project.*

"If I give all I possess. . .but have not love, I gain nothing."

Angel winced. What had Shanika said about the love 1 Corinthians talked about? That it was referring to the Lord and putting Him first? *That's real love,* Shanika had said.

The nugget of wisdom hit its mark, piercing Angel's heart. *Lord,* she prayed in anguish of spirit. *What should I do?*

Put Me, My work, and My Word first in your life.

I will, Lord, I promise I will.

She was so happy, she hugged Shanika in a sisterly hug. "Thank you, Shanika."

Shanika looked puzzled.

"For bringing me manna from heaven." The manna was light and sweet and good, and Angel envisioned big fluffy dumplings raining down from the sky. The thought made her smile with a newfound joy.

Shanika quietly went back to her painting, as if she possessed the wisdom of the ages.

Angel thought about the irony of the situation. She wanted to give guidance and advice to Shanika, and Shanika ended up giving them to her.

She saw her vision again. Manna. A fitting vision for a cook. *Lord, thank You for speaking to me through this young girl. Forgive me for not putting You at the top of the list in my life. Help me to do better.*

"Please help me achieve *real* success," she said aloud.

"What'd you say?" Shanika stopped painting and looked at her.

"I was. . .well, I was praying."

"That's something I do all the time. Morning, noon, and night. It's what my mother taught me to do."

"Mine, too. And from here on out, I'm going to do more of it."

Chapter 9

Cyril came out on the front porch and restacked building supplies in preparation for tomorrow's work. He saw Angel in the yard cleaning some paintbrushes and rollers under a faucet by the light of the spotlight someone had hung on the eaves. She'd worked hard on this project, and he admired her. He wished—

"Cyril? I need to talk with you." Angel turned off the faucet.

"What's up?" He figured she needed to know something about tomorrow's assignment.

"Can we talk when everyone's gone? I need to tell you something important. I'll meet you here, on the front porch, if that's okay with you?"

"Sure." *This must be serious, by the tone of her voice.* He recalled passing by the room where she and Shanika were painting, and he overheard Shanika quoting a Bible verse. *Hmm. . .*

Fifteen minutes later, when the last person left, Cyril went through the house locking the windows. He stretched his tired muscles as he turned off the lights. He was used to exercise but not this kind of labor. But every ache was worth it. To him, this was a part of working for the Lord. He recalled a scripture where Jesus taught that if we offered a cup of cold water in His name, we were doing it as unto Him.

I've done this project for You, Lord.

He made his way through the front door and locked it behind him, then glanced around and saw Angel sitting on the porch swing.

"Have a seat." She patted the space to her right.

He sat down beside her and pushed hard with his foot, and the swing went back and forth. He laughed. "Reflex, I guess. You sit on a porch swing, and you want to get it going."

She nodded. "You should've heard Shanika tonight. She was telling me her mother would rather sit on the porch than watch TV." She started laughing.

He looked over at her. What did she mean? And why was she laughing?

She stopped laughing and proceeded to explain what Shanika had said about TV and soap operas and porches. "I'm bungling this." She tried again. "I can't seem to capture the essence of what she said." She smiled. "Oh, forget it."

"You wearing on my nerves, girl," hollered someone from next door. "If you don't change them clothes, I'm gonna beat your buns."

"There!" Angel's face was animated. "That's what Shanika was talking about."

He laughed, and she joined in.

"Shanika was so cute, the way she said it."

He sat there, enjoying the moment and enjoying being with her.

"Cyril, I wanted to tell you, I learned something new tonight."

"I did, too. Roy showed me how to lay ceramic tile." From his sideways glance in the dim light cast by a street light, he could see she was itching to talk. But he figured he'd have a little fun with her. "First, you trowel the adhesive on the floor. It's real thick, like peanut butter, and then you lay the tile on top of that, and you put little spacers between them. And then you let it dry for a good twenty-four hours. And then, when it's dry, you go back and put in the grout—"

"I don't mean to interrupt you but—"

"You can't wait to tell me about your conversation with Shanika, right? Other than the one about the porch. . .and soap operas?"

They both laughed.

"Did you hear us talking?"

"I heard her quote from 1 Corinthians 13. That's all. I was on my way outside to get more tile from Roy's truck."

Angel told him how she and Shanika had been teamed together, how impressed she'd been by her, how she wanted to give the young girl guidance and advice. But the tables turned, and Shanika gave Angel the best guidance of all.

"The best guidance?"

"I've got my priorities right, Cyril." Angel looked over at

him, her eyes brighter than the stars that filled the night sky. "Shanika helped me see what's important in life." She continued talking, giving him the details.

"That's wonderful." He'd been praying for Angel ever since Pastor Kyle recommended it, and this was news that thrilled him. Now, maybe they could—

"I've been ministered to tonight, Cyril. By a young girl." She told him about the manna from heaven she'd pictured at Shanika's wise words. "I learned so much from her."

"Sometimes in our Christian walk, we struggle with things, and—"

"*You* have struggles?"

"Of course I do. We all do. We're human. The important thing is to let the Lord speak to us *in* our struggles."

"He sure spoke to me. Out of the mouth of babes. . ."

"When the Lord speaks to us, whether it's through a person, or through His Word, or in prayer, or however He chooses to do it, well, it's like you described. It's like—"

"—manna to our souls." She laughed. "I guess you could say I got some soul food tonight. Food from heaven. And food from Shanika."

"Food for Angel." He took her hand, drew it to his lips, and kissed her fingers. "How about"—his voice grew husky—"angel food?"

Chapter 10

Angel's heart beat a little trill when Cyril tapped on the kitchen doorway of Rue de France at the stroke of noon. Her heart did that every time she saw him. She wanted to be with him every minute, and she was sure he felt the same way, though neither had said the magic words—*I love you*—yet.

"Come on in," she said.

"I figured you were back here." He made his way toward her.

"Shouldn't you be eating at Main Street Cafe?" He had his own restaurant. And this was lunchtime. And business was business. And he'd eaten lunch here for four days in a row.

He drew her to him and put his cheek to hers. "There's a motive to my madness," he said into her hair.

She returned his embrace warmly, longingly. She remembered when Cyril had said that phrase after her pie was such a hit at the Project Hope planning meeting. After that, her business had picked up. Though people weren't lining the sidewalk to get into Rue de France, she was having a better flow of customers.

"A person can eat ham and butter beans just so much." He winked at her.

She smiled, knowing Main Street Café had lots of menu choices, all of them delicious. She led him into the dining room and gestured at a table.

"Okay. I admit it." He pulled out the chair and sat down. "I thought maybe if I eat here a lot, it'll influence more townspeople to try Rue de France."

She handed him a menu, then leaned down and straightened the sweetener packets on his table. "Thanks, Cyril."

"But the real reason I came back today. . .is because I can't stay away from you." He trailed his finger up the back of her hand.

Oh, Cyril. . .I'm sure you're Mr. Right. She almost shouted out *Thank You, Lawd,* Shanika-style but managed to restrain herself.

"What's good today?" He looked down at the menu.

You. She recommended some choices, stumbling over her words, her heart still hammering.

He placed his order.

She headed for the kitchen. *I think True Love just knocked at my door.*

<hr>

The days progressed into weeks, and the weeks into months.

Happy days. . .

Happy weeks. . .

Happy months.

Cyril procured a grant for downtown refurbishment and got the townspeople on board, and Nine Cloud got spiffed up. Paint. New awnings. Flowering shrubs in planters. Benches. Even new streetlights.

"Charming," people were saying.

"Good for business," Cyril always commented. "And no new housing areas yet," he added with a laugh.

Cyril saw the Lord perform spiritual transformations. Ted White from White's Hardware recognized his need of a Savior. Joe Freeman from the funeral home experienced a heart healing and came back to church. Some teenagers found Jesus and gave up their drinking.

Cyril was thrilled for Angel when Rue de France took off. She gave the Lord the credit.

"The Lord blessed me because I put Him first and everything else second," she liked to say.

Besides her hordes of lunchtime customers, she came up with the brilliant idea of teaching French-cooking lessons on Monday and Tuesday nights. She advertised in area newspapers and now had a long waiting list. She'd told him it was fast becoming the mainstay of her business.

"Ideas are spinning in my head like tops on their axes," she frequently said with a smile. "Ideas that are working." She was putting on afternoon dessert hours on Thursdays and Fridays that were a hit with the ladies, where she served a variety of dainty desserts, including tiny wedges of Heavenly Pie. And she catered ladies' events like bridal and baby showers and birthday parties, both at the Rue de France and in private homes.

But the best thing that happened in Nine Cloud was Cyril got to see Angel every day. He went somewhere with her every Saturday—to the shore, the park, the river, a play, a concert. It didn't matter where they went or what they did. They were together. A couple.

He proclaimed his love for her first. He did it the night of their first kiss. . .which happened to be. . .Valentine's Day.

She would never forget the night as long as she lived. . . .

They sat under a full moon on a bench facing the ocean, where people passed by on the boardwalk behind them.

"May I kiss the cook?" he asked.

She felt like laughing at his reference to her apron but nodded instead—vigorously, her heart pounding like the ocean waves.

He kissed her gently at first, and then their lips stayed together for a span of time, both of them seeming to revel in the moment that would stay in their memories forever.

He pulled back and looked deeply into her eyes. "One more question."

"Yes?"

"May I tell the cook I love her?"

"Oh, yes."

"I love you, Angel."

"I love you, too, Cyril." She adored his old-fashioned ways, how he'd waited months to kiss her and tell her he loved her. Thrill shivers coursed through her. And during those months, she'd come to realize she was old-fashioned in some ways. But not quite as much as he was. She reached up, drew his face toward her, and kissed him hungrily, like she didn't ever want to let him go. "I love you, I love you, I love you."

"Now that's the *crème de la crème*," he said, when he came up for air. "Did I say that right?"

Her answer was another kiss.

⚘

The next morning, Cyril called Pastor Kyle. "I want you to be the first to know."

"Know what?" Pastor Kyle had a smile in his voice.

"I told her I loved her."

"Then I'm guessing you'll be needing a preacher?"

"I'm thinking June, if she'll agree."

Chapter 11

The March evening couldn't be any more perfect. Or romantic. Angel took a bite of lobster, then glanced at Cyril. From their table by the window at the superb beachside restaurant, they had a perfect view of the ocean. And the food was nearly indescribable. That was saying a lot from someone who'd studied cooking in France.

Cyril had presented her with a bracelet corsage when he'd picked her up. It was made of lavender and could've been straight from Paris, it was so French looking.

On the drive to the beach, they had enjoyed a pleasant camaraderie. But something scintillating yet sweet had swathed around them like gossamer.

Now, sitting in the restaurant, she felt a draft of cool air from the air-conditioning vent, and pulled her black net shawl around her shoulders. In her movement, their knees touched under the table, and thoughts of love filled her heart.

"A penny for your thoughts?" Cyril squeezed a wedge of lime into his ice water, then placed his hand over hers on the table.

"I. . .um. . ."

"You? Angel Morgan at a loss for words? That kicks in a memory for me. The cat got your tongue the first time we met."

She nodded. "I wanted to meet business owners dressed like a businesswoman. Instead—"

"You were covered in paint—"

"I felt so stupid, I forgot my manners—"

"And I was pretty smug-acting, wasn't I?"

"You could say that. In fact, that night I secretly started calling you Mr. Hooty-Toot."

"You didn't?" He looked playfully thunderstruck.

She nodded, exaggeratedly so. "After I looked up the meaning of your name, I decided Mr. Hooty-Toot was apropos."

"Why? What's it mean?"

"Lord. You were acting so. . .lordly."

He chuckled. "What does *your* name mean? I'm sure it means angelic being. But anything else?"

"Messenger."

He swung his head from side to side, like he was deep in thought. "Couldn't be more appropriate. Angel, you're my messenger of love."

<hr/>

Angel wondered where Cyril was going as he passed the turn to the highway that led back to Nine Cloud. Then she knew. He was taking her to the beach house where they ate her pie on their first date.

He turned onto a narrow private road, then pulled into the

driveway. His headlights showed a refurbished house, the dull weathered boards now painted a crisp sandy beige, the professional landscaping beachy and inviting.

"What happened here?" She was delighted with the changes. When she'd first seen the house, she thought it would make a perfect beach hideaway if only someone would give it some TLC.

"We decided to remodel it when we were making the changes to Nine Cloud."

"It's beautiful, Cyril."

"We knocked down some walls and added a big room on the back. The ocean view is fantastic."

"Can I see the inside?"

"Sure. Come on." In a flash, he was at her door, opening it. "But it's not furnished. Or decorated. That comes next."

At the front door of the house, he stepped inside, found the lights, and flicked them on. "Come on in." He held the door open for her.

She walked into a large room that was big enough for several conversation areas. "This is going to be beautiful when it's all done."

He pointed to a far wall. "That's where the kitchen will be, as soon the cabinetry and countertops are chosen." He pointed to another area. "That'll be the dining room." He walked across the large room and stopped. "This is the addition." He pointed upward, then continued on toward the wall of windows. "Come look out."

She walked over and stood by him in the addition that

couldn't be detected as such. It blended in perfectly with the rest of the house. Through the floor-to-ceiling windows, she saw the ocean that looked like black glass in the moonlight. The sight took her breath away.

"We'll probably have several tables and chairs in this area. We'll use it for casual eating and playing table games, things like that."

She looked around the room. In her mind's eye, she could see a limestone or buffed-marble floor. And beach-type furniture—rattan, maybe, or wicker. And paintings that captured the ocean's beauty. And—

"Care to walk on the beach?"

Her heart did one of its familiar trills. "I—I'd love to."

He unlocked the glass door and slid it aside. "After you."

She stepped out onto an expansive patio, and he followed her out. She looked up into the most spectacular sky she'd ever seen.

"You sure aren't saying much tonight." He whispered the words into her hair from where he stood behind her. "Cat got your tongue again?"

Calm down, my heart. "I—I. . ." She started again. "The beauty of this place. . .the ocean. . ."

"I remember the night you said the ocean made you hug me." His voice was husky as he gently turned her to face him. "You said it had something to do with the moon shining down. . ."

She glanced skyward and saw a full moon.

". . .and the way the waves lapped. . . ."

She heard the ocean behind her, a sound that echoed the beating of her heart.

"Come with me." He took her hand and led her across the patio. "Better take off your shoes."

Shivers danced up her spine, and there wasn't even a slight wind. She knew where they were coming from. Cyril and his nearness. She slipped off her shoes, and he did the same.

He led her into the sand, and they walked down the beach, neither of them saying a word, his arm around her, her arm around him.

After a long while, they turned and headed back toward the beach house, both of them talking in soft tones—words of endearment, *amour*.

Aimer eperdument, Angel thought. Love to distraction.

He stopped and kissed her, and she thought her heart would burst from happiness.

He dropped to his knees in the sand.

Her heart was liquid love. "Cyril. . ."

He took her hand in his. "My darling Angel, will you marry me?"

"Yes, yes, yes." She bent down and kissed him.

"To have and to hold?" he quipped.

"From this day forward."

"Forever and ever?" He stood up and took her in his arms. "Thank You, Lawd!"

Chapter 12

Their June wedding couldn't have been any more perfect.

They had the rehearsal dinner at Main Street Café.

They got married in the white-steepled church in the center of town.

They repeated their vows in front of Pastor Kyle.

They held the reception at Angel Food—formerly known as Rue de France—with the guests spilling out onto the grassy town square.

The wedding cake was a Parisian version, with fondant icing and edible lavender flowers cascading over it.

The groom's cake wasn't a cake at all. It was Heavenly Pie—lots of them—Angel Food's new signature dessert. It was rich like their love but laden with chocolate.

And Nine Cloud was on cloud nine!

And their honeymoon? They spent it at the beach house Angel had just decorated. She named it *Le demeure d'amour*. The abode of love.

HEAVENLY PIE

1 (9 inch) prepared piecrust
1 cup chocolate chips
1/2 cup butter or margarine, melted
2 eggs
1 cup sugar
1/4 cup flour
1 teaspoon vanilla
1 cup pecans, chopped
Whipped topping

Line bottom of piecrust with chocolate chips. (Don't be tempted to use more.) In a separate bowl, mix remaining ingredients with a fork, then pour over chocolate chips. Put foil strips around edges of pie. Bake at 350° for 45 minutes or longer, until brown on top. Inside should be soft but not runny. Serve warm (by oven or microwave) with a dollop of whipped topping. Refrigerate. Stays good several days. (But you probably won't find this out because it'll get eaten before then.)

KRISTY DYKES

A native Floridian, Kristy Dykes is an award-winning author, speaker, and former newspaper columnist. Her novella in *Church in the Wildwood* (Barbour) won Third Place in American Christian Fiction Writers 2004 Book of the Year Contest (novella category). Her novel *The Tender Heart* (Heartsong Presents) was a finalist in the 2004 Golden Quill Awards and won Third Place in the 2004 Barclay Gold Contest. Kristy's novellas have been on the CBA bestseller list and the top-twenty list at Christianbook.com. She was voted as a favorite new author by readers in the 2004 Heartsong Presents Awards. She has written over 600 published articles, worked for two *New York Times* subsidiaries, and taught at many conferences and two colleges. Kristy and her husband, a pastor, live in Florida. She loves hearing from her readers. Write her at kristy-dykes@aol.com, or c/o Author Relations, Barbour Publishing, P.O. Box 719, Uhrichsville, OH 44683. Visit her blog at www. christianlovestories.blogspot.com.

Just Desserts

by Aisha Ford

Dedication

To my family. . .
I love you more than words will ever be able to express.

Chapter 1

Monica Ryan paced her office at her restaurant, The Pie Rack, waiting for Adella to click back over from call waiting. Despite having been on the phone for the past half hour, Monica estimated she and Adella had only clocked about ten minutes of actual talking time.

Thanks to the fantastic technology of Adella's cell-phone service, Monica didn't have to wait in silence. Instead, she got to listen to a nice variety of swoony love songs. Not that she had anything against swoony love songs, but after twenty minutes, Monica was certain the music would start to wear on anybody's nerves!

Impatient, Monica sighed and sat in the rolling chair at her desk. Adella Parker was an old acquaintance from high school, and there was heavy emphasis on the word *acquaintance*.

In the ten years since they'd graduated, Monica had seen Adella around town a few times and generally heard about her appearances at high society parties and benefits.

The closest encounter Monica ever really had with Adella

was running against her for senior-class president. She'd beaten Adella by a huge margin, but Adella hadn't really seemed to care.

Supposedly, her father, the CEO of a multibillion-dollar company, had thought it good leadership practice for Adella to try running for office. However, Adella's ideal job description was more along the lines of carefree heiress rather than serious politician.

Fast-forward ten years later, and Adella still played the role of a carefree heiress, but now she had a new title to add to the list: bride-to-be.

"Hello. Hello?" Adella unexpectedly shouted into the receiver.

"Yes, yes, I'm here."

"Monica?"

"Adella?" Monica cleared her throat and spoke louder. "I'm here—it's me, Monica."

"Oh, good. I thought I'd lost you for a minute. Like I was telling you before, we love everything you sell at the bakery, and we'd want to have you do a dessert buffet at the engagement party—with lots of those sweet potato pies, but we're trying to keep costs down."

"I'm sure we could work out some type of. . .something," Monica said, vaguely wondering if Adella even knew what *keeping the costs down* actually meant.

Nothing in the society news columns of late indicated that Adella's family fortunes were dwindling.

But nonetheless, the job would be great exposure for The Pie Rack, and short of Adella being a bridezilla a million times over, Monica knew there was no good reason she would turn down the job.

"Fantastic," Adella said.

"Well, thanks so much for calling," Monica said, hoping to wrap up the call. Business was business, and there was no way she wanted to get sucked into talking about the "good old days" of high school.

Her old yearbooks and scrapbooks, safely hidden in the attic, were full of the pictorial evidence that the good old days were not that good at all—at least not her senior year.

"Just one more thing," Adella said, interrupting Monica's thoughts. "I was reading one of my bridal magazines the other day, and it says that if possible, I should try to find a caterer who can do both the meal and the dessert. Is there any way you could pull that off?"

Monica sighed as quietly as possible, hoping to reign in the urge to cut a potentially difficult client loose before the situation got too complicated. "Honestly, Adella, we really do only specialize in desserts—"

"But didn't your family own a restaurant when we were in high school?"

"Yes, we did, but due to. . .circumstances, we're only in the dessert business now."

This time it was Adella's turn to sigh. "To tell you the truth, that's not exactly the type of catering setup I was hoping for. Just to make things easier on myself, I'd like all of the food to come from the same vendor."

"You're planning this party yourself?" Monica blurted out

before she could stop herself.

"I am." Adella giggled, then grew serious. "I know everybody thinks I'm a clueless society girl, but the minute Byron proposed, I just knew that I wanted to be in charge of every tiny detail of this entire experience. You get married only once, so I'd like it to be perfect, you know?"

"Wow. I don't think I would have so much fun planning every detail of my own wedding, but I admire your determination."

"Oooh!" Adella squealed. "Are you getting married, too? How come you didn't tell me sooner?"

Why did Adella have such an uncanny ability to turn the conversation to uncomfortable topics? "No, no, I'm not engaged. You sound like one of my relatives now," Monica said, trying to keep the mood light. "I was just saying that if, I mean, *when* I get engaged, I doubt I would enjoy being the sole planner for the event."

"Oh, I understand how you feel," said Adella. "It seemed like it took forever for Byron to propose to me, too. How long have you been waiting for that special someone to pop the question?"

There was no special someone, and there really never had been, unless you counted Gil. "And that won't ever count, at least not now," Monica murmured.

"What was that?" Adella asked.

"Oh, I'm sorry, I guess I was thinking out loud."

"Don't worry about that, I know you're probably having a busy day—oops! Call waiting—it's Byron, let me put you on hold for one tiny little second."

Before Monica could protest, Adella placed her on hold again—with more swoony love songs!

❦

"That's fantastic, honey. It might be just what The Pie Rack needs to get us back on the map."

This was all the encouragement Monica needed to hear. Spending the better part of an hour listening to Adella ramble on and on had been worth it just for this.

"Thanks, Dad. The only catch is, her parents want to keep the costs down so they can splurge on the wedding."

"No problem there; we can give them a good deal. The exposure alone will be worth it."

Monica shifted her cell phone to the other ear and pondered how to tell her dad the second part of the agreement. A gust of wind blew so hard that her car veered slightly into the next lane. Monica tightened her grip on the wheel and wondered how she would break the rest of the news to her dad.

"Did you sign papers yet?"

"Not exactly. We talked over the phone, but the contract will be contingent on us providing the entire menu for the party."

"What do you mean?"

"It means, we get top billing, but we have to provide all of the food for the party."

"And how are we supposed to do that, since we only serve desserts?"

Monica could hear the frustration building in her father's voice and instantly regretted telling him the news over the phone. She should have told her mom first, and then they could have broken the news together.

"Well, I'll be. . .that Amos Butler got the best of me again, didn't he?"

"Bob. . .calm down," Monica heard her mother saying in the background. Usually, when her father got started about Amos Butler, his former business partner, there was no stopping him.

"Dad, it's not a lost cause. It'll be okay. She's given me three days to find a caterer who will provide the entrees, and we can still do the dessert, and everything will be fine."

"And how are you supposed to do that?"

"I'm totally capable of finding someone. Remember the National Restaurateurs' Convention I went to last summer? I made some good contacts there and got to know some local restaurateurs better. I'm sure I can find someone local who'll be willing to agree to this deal."

"I don't like the sound of it, but I trust you. Do what you can do. If not, we'll do fine without the job."

"Thanks for understanding, Dad. Any other time I might have turned the offer down flat, but for some reason I couldn't say no."

"Humph. Three days is a ridiculous deadline, so you'd better get on the phone and start calling folks now."

"I will do my best just as soon as I get home from the gym."

"The gym? You're not even at work?"

"Actually, I'm on my way to the gym now, but I'll call you

later with an update about how the search is going."

"Monica, I know you're in charge of the company, but maybe this is something you should have discussed with me first. After all, if it doesn't work out, then you're putting the company name on the line."

Monica could see his point, but part of being in charge was making mistakes, wasn't it? And what about taking risks? Didn't all the entrepreneurs who prospered take big risks at one time or another? She could tell this conversation was not going to end well or soon, if her dad had his way. The best course of action for now would be to get off the phone.

"Okay, Dad, I promise we can talk about this later. But right now isn't the best time. It's really windy outside, and I'm having a hard time steering the car, so I probably shouldn't be talking on the phone."

Bob grunted in reply, but Monica knew he wouldn't protest further. One of his pet peeves was driving near people who seemed to be distracted because they were talking on the phone. Both of her parents constantly lectured her about her habit of driving and chatting. Their remedy for the situation had been to buy her an earpiece for the phone, but Monica usually forgot to put it in the car.

"All right. Get off the phone and call me later. Even though I wonder if going to the gym when you've got so much to do is a good use of your time."

"Love you, Dad." Monica hung up quickly, before her dad could give her a speech on the virtue of diligence at work.

How could a man who never took a day off from work in

over forty years possibly understand her need to blow off steam by doing something other than standing over a stove, concocting new recipes?

Just over a year ago, when her mother had finally convinced him to retire, Monica and her mom were both at their wits' end, because her father found a way to come into the office nearly every day.

Over the past few months, she'd managed to convince him that the place was in good hands, but the last thing she needed was for this deal with Adella to fail. If that happened, she might as well move right out of her office, because her dad would be back at work quicker than Adella could click over to the other line.

Pulling into an empty parking space, Monica decided now was a good time for a quick prayer.

"Lord, looking back, it feels like maybe I did the wrong thing to say yes to the deal with Adella. If it was a mistake, please show me a graceful way to bow out before I get in over my head. But if this is something that will be good for business, then I'm asking You to help me with all of the details—and please keep my dad calm in the process."

A loud, forceful bang on the passenger-side door of the car interrupted her thoughts. Monica quickly glanced over to see what was going on.

The man parked next to her had opened his door and rammed his door into hers. With an apologetic look on his face, he mouthed, "Sorry," and bent down to examine the damage.

"Great, just what I need. Instead of getting my cardio

in, I get to sit here and haggle with this guy over insurance information."

She yanked her gym bag out of the backseat and steeled herself to get down to business. Tall and handsome, with an air of confidence, he looked like the type of guy who would try to convince her that any damage wasn't his fault, and then brag to his friends about how he'd put one over on some naive woman at the gym. He almost reminded her of Gil, but underneath that borderline arrogant exterior, Gil was truly a nice guy. At least, he had *seemed* nice—he and his backstabbing family.

"Well, no one's going to walk all over me today," Monica muttered, stepping out of the car and hefting the bag over her shoulder. "I already messed up with Adella, but this pushover is reformed as of right now."

Feeling mildly disgusted that she had thought about Gil twice today, when she'd gone years without even saying his name, Monica had a feeling her dad was right. She should have stayed at work and skipped the workout today, but since she found herself in this situation, she was determined to get a satisfactory resolution, no matter what antics this guy tried to pull.

As Monica walked to the other side of the car, the man stood up and grinned. "Amazingly, it looks fine to me."

"Are you kidding? It sounded like you hit the door with a sledgehammer." *Don't back down,* she told herself.

He shook his head and motioned to the door. "Nope, not even a scratch. And, for the record, I didn't hit it on *purpose*. It's this January weather," he said, gesturing midair. "Right when I got out of the car, the wind picked up and took the door with it."

As Monica reached the door, he stepped back so she could examine it for herself. Bending over, she saw no sign of scratches or dents.

Embarrassed for being so nitpicky, she stood up, feeling a sheepish grin spread over her face. "I guess you're right. So no harm done."

"Right. . .right," he said, speaking slowly and staring at her so intently that she grew uncomfortable under his scrutiny.

Her first impulse was to jump in the car and drive away, but she recognized something distantly familiar about this stranger.

Forgetting her manners, Monica stared back, straining to get a better look at him, despite the dim light outside.

"Monica?" he said.

Was it really? No way.

"Monica!" he said again, this time, more assured.

"Gil?" Monica wondered if the long day at work had stressed her to the point where she was merely imagining him. What if other people in the parking lot were watching her converse with nothing but air. Or maybe she had simply fallen asleep at her desk.

Before she could ponder more possibilities, the man presumed to be Gil took a step forward and enveloped her in a hug.

It was Gil. This was not a dream.

Chapter 2

I t really has been a long time, hasn't it?"

Monica nodded, sipping her banana-berry yogurt smoothie. "Part of me can't even believe we're sitting here together." She quickly considered how that might have sounded and tried to think of a way to clarify her thoughts. "Not. . .together, together. Just, together. . .here. . .you and me, you know?"

The corner of Gil's mouth twitched, but if he found her statement uncomfortable, he hid it well.

"I know. I mean, it almost feels like I'm meeting you for the first time."

Except for the hug. Nobody would hug a stranger like that. Monica pushed the memory of his cologne aside and tried to concentrate on her smoothie instead.

"So tell me everything that's been going on with you," he said.

Monica chuckled. "How much time do you have? Because recapping ten years is going to take more than a few minutes.

"I've got time," he said, a glint of laughter in his eyes.

"No, you don't," she protested. "Besides, that would leave no time for you to talk. What have you been up to?"

He shrugged. "This, that, and everything. I went away to college while I was getting my business management degree, and I came back and worked at the restaurant during the summer. By way of an interesting turn of events, I discovered I was just as good at managing talent as I was at managing in the food business, so I moved away for good, became a talent manager for gospel musicians, and then came back a year ago to pick up where I left off. It seems that my dad heard your dad was retiring and decided to play copycat."

The mention of their fathers gave Monica pause. Suddenly, her smoothie wasn't as appetizing. What would her dad say if he knew she was sitting in the café at the gym, sipping a banana-berry smoothie across from the son of the man who had almost ruined all that he had worked to build?

As she glanced around to see if she saw any familiar faces, Monica felt a like a criminal.

She pushed her smoothie aside and stood up. "Well, it was nice seeing you again."

Gil stood, too. "Wait, that's not fair. You didn't tell me what you've been up to."

Monica lifted her gym bag and took a step away from the table.

"Hey, I know what happened with our parents wasn't. . . ideal. But I think we can at least make the decision to be friends with each other, can't we?"

Monica took a step back toward the table but kept her keys in her hand, ready to escape at a moment's notice. Yes, she wanted to befriend Gil again, but she didn't want to disappoint her family. There was a fine line here; she didn't want to cross it. Especially not now. The last thing she needed on her already-full plate was an old family feud.

"You know what? I think my dad was wrong." Gil stood and took a step closer. "And honestly, ever since then, business hasn't been the same."

"And you connect that to what happened between our dads?"

Gil shrugged. "I can't say for sure, but I know things have been tough. Right now I don't know how much longer we. . . My dad begged me to come back and see if there's a way to keep from shutting the place down."

"Oh, Gil, I'm sorry." Ashamed at her own selfish thoughts, Monica sat back down. "I. . .I didn't know. Really, I didn't. My dad doesn't even like to talk about your family."

Gil sat down across from her. "I really didn't want this conversation to be the Butler-family sob story. That's why I asked what was going on with you."

Monica hesitated, wanting to be honest but not seem as if she were bragging.

"It was tough in the beginning, right after our parents split the company. But my dad was determined to make a dessert café succeed. It's been hard work, but we're finally getting to a place where things are starting to look up. We're actually shooting a commercial in a few weeks, and we have a spot scheduled on a local TV show soon."

KISS THE ~~COOK~~ *Bride*

"That's great. You guys deserve it."

"We've worked hard for it."

A long silence passed between them, and finally Monica broke it.

"So what are your plans for your dad's business?"

Gil shook his head. "My honest opinion is that we should close it before we lose too much more, but he's got it in his head that we can hold on until we can get some kind of breakthrough. I don't have the heart to tell him it's not that probable. The big chains are just chipping away at our profits, day by day." He looked down at the table and was quiet.

Monica put her hand over his. "I'm so sorry. I know what it feels like to keep advertising and hoping word of mouth will spread and seeing nothing happen."

"Brainstorming for hours on end, looking for the one elusive idea that might change the course of things—and not finding it and feeling helpless," Gil spoke up, finishing her thoughts.

All at once, she remembered her situation with Adella and realized that she could solve her problem and extend an olive branch to Gil and his family in their time of need.

Quickly, she explained the terms of the deal and asked if he might be interested in partnering together to fulfill the terms of the contract.

"I still can't believe you're even asking me, I mean, after everything."

"Maybe this opportunity will give our families the boost in business we need and provide us all with the chance to heal," she answered.

"Are you sure? Really? Catering Adella Parker's engagement party with you?"

"Do you think you can do it?"

"At this point, I'm willing to try anything to make my dad happy," said Gil.

"Then that's it. We'll work at it together and hopefully. . ." Monica paused, not knowing exactly how to finish her thoughts.

"Hopefully," Gil said, breaking the silence, "our families will be friends again."

Chapter 3

Gil went straight to his family's restaurant, Amos's Smokehouse, office as soon as he left the gym and spent the next several hours poring over his parents' old recipes, hoping to find some dishes that would work for Adella's party.

He couldn't wait to tell his family about this exciting venture, but he dreaded the look on his father's face when he found out that partnering with Bob Ryan's company was part of the deal.

Gil slumped over the desk, resting his hands in his forehead. Maybe this wasn't such a good idea after all.

Should I call Monica and tell her this isn't the good fit I thought it would be?

Gil picked up his phone but couldn't bring himself to dial her number. If he had to cancel the deal, he should at least do it in person, right?

And then what would she think of him? After he'd failed her in their relationship so long ago, how could he go back on his word now?

There was also the undeniable fact that she was still just as beautiful as she had ever been, if not more. Following through on this deal would also give him the chance to reconnect with her and maybe rekindle the romance that had just budded when the spilt happened.

Most people who had known the Butler and Ryan families for many years always speculated that one day he and Monica would get married and expand the family business.

He and Monica had grown up as best friends by circumstance, spending most of their free time at the restaurant, simply because their parents were there. As they grew older and entered the phase where they began noticing the opposite sex, they both dated other people but remained close friends.

Then, the summer before the last year of high school, after their parents decided to open a second location, things changed. It was as if all of a sudden, a curtain was lifted, and they saw each other in a different light.

Their families were elated that the two of them were finally dating, and deep down inside, Gil felt he had found the woman he wanted to spend the rest of his life with. He never told Monica how serious he felt, partially because it would have been awkward at their young ages, and partially because just after Christmas, their parents had the big disagreement.

At first, he and Monica had continued to date, because their fathers often disagreed on how to run the business. Despite their many arguments, Amos and Bob always came to some kind of compromise. But this time had been different.

First, the problems increased when Gil's father issued the

ultimatum—either sell the struggling second location or part ways. Monica's father had refused, because he felt that they hadn't given the second restaurant a chance to build a clientele.

Gil's father saw dwindling dollar signs and worried that the place was losing too much too fast, and wanted out immediately.

Suddenly, they no longer ate family dinners together, their fathers stopped speaking to each other at work unless it was absolutely necessary, and then Monica's father did the unthinkable—he quit.

Gil didn't blame Monica's dad for his gumption. While he loved his own father, Amos Butler had a tendency to run his household and his business like a bully—his way or no way. Most of the time it worked, but it seemed that now his heavy-handed tactics had backfired.

After Amos realized Bob was serious, he decided to make sure Bob knew he was making a big mistake by legally and permanently severing ties with him.

Lawyers were called in to organize the deal, and it was agreed that the Butlers would keep the original restaurant location, the original recipes, and the well-recognized name, while Bob Ryan decided he would assume ownership of the not-so-successful location, taking only the sweet potato pie recipe.

Amos had openly mocked Bob for not putting up more of a fight and demanding more. Bob refused to argue any longer and moved across town to be closer to his business.

Gil and Monica continued to date, but the situation grew increasingly awkward as Gil's father looked for a way to wield more control over Bob Ryan.

Out of sheer frustration that he had been unable to get Bob to change his mind, Amos Butler forbade his family to have contact with any of the Ryans—and for Gil, that meant no more dating Monica.

He remembered the day he had gone over to her house to explain the situation. He promised her it was temporary, and soon enough, things would be back to normal.

But soon enough never came. They saw each other at school and different social events but didn't really talk. After a couple of months with no change in the atmosphere, Gil had an argument with his father and decided he didn't care about the rule any longer. In a huff, he drove to Monica's house, only to have her father answer the door and inform him that now Monica was forbidden to talk to him.

By that time, graduation was coming up and when Gil heard Monica was going to the prom with one of their mutual friends, he gave up on the relationship.

Instead, he spent his last few months of high school with an eye to the future, hoping to move as far away from St. Louis as possible.

But now that he had the authority to make decisions like this for the company, along with the chance to see where this relationship might go, there was no way he was going to let his dad talk him out if it.

❧

Monica paced the floor of her living room late that night, wondering how in the world she would explain this new turn of events to her parents.

At least half a dozen times since her chance encounter with Gil, she had picked up her phone to call them but always lost her nerve before she could fully dial the number.

"Lord, did I mess this up even worse?"

She turned on the TV to try to mask the growing rumble of doubts running through her mind, but that did little to help.

Despite the impulse to back out of the agreement with Gil, she couldn't help but wonder how things might have been between them had their fathers not had that argument ten years ago.

Would they have remained high school sweethearts and gotten married after college and stayed on to manage the restaurant together? Would they have had children by now?

"Stop it," Monica said, turning off the TV. "You just ran into the man; stop imagining what could have been and focus on what is."

She picked up her phone again, this time, wondering if she should just call Gil and cancel the whole deal.

No. She wouldn't do it. She couldn't, not after the way she had run into him under such unusual circumstances. Maybe it was more than coincidence they had met today. Wasn't partnering with Gil the best idea after she had prayed and asked for a solution to catering Adella's party?

Yes, if nothing else, God had provided an answer to her prayers. As for their families reconciling, Monica didn't have the same high hopes Gil had expressed, so there was no use in letting her mind wander to the what-ifs of what might have been.

Yes, he was still just as good-looking, but that had nothing to do with their deal. From the way he talked, he had been able to put the family business aside long enough to establish a life away from work, something Monica had never really been able to do.

While his family had the benefit of working with an established restaurant, Monica's family had been working overtime for the last ten years to play catch up. Though he had been cordial and very friendly today, he had given no indication that he was interested in more than a work relationship. And why should he? Monica couldn't imagine why he wouldn't have a girlfriend or even be nearly married right now.

Monica turned on her laptop and started typing out preliminary notes for the party menu. She and Gil had agreed to meet again tomorrow afternoon to compile their ideas and finalize the menu before she met with Adella again.

While she typed, Monica thought about how her father would take the news. There was really no way to case into such a potentially inflammatory announcement.

Thinking back to the days after the split, Monica remembered her father spending hours working overtime and even taking a second job just to keep The Pie Rack afloat, just to prove to himself that Amos Butler was wrong.

Would the news be a bit more bearable if he knew how desperately Gil's family needed this job, or would he remember how alone they felt after Amos had laughed and told him that a dessert café was a ridiculous idea?

And worse yet, would her father be angry with her for even

speaking to Gil? Not long after Gil's dad had stopped him from seeing Monica, Gil had come over to visit, but Monica's dad had refused to let her see him, and told her she wasn't allowed to speak to Gil any longer.

That decree had been uncomfortable back when she was seventeen, but out of respect to her parents, she'd obeyed and considered her romance with Gil to be over.

Now that she was almost twenty-eight, she doubted the rule still held, but if her dad remembered, explaining her way out of it would be uncomfortable to say the least.

"I'll tell them first thing in the morning," Monica decided, turning off her computer.

It was no use trying to work right now. Too much had happened today, and she couldn't see a real rhyme or reason to any of it.

Her new plan for the evening didn't get much attention. Monica decided she would go to bed early, get a full eight hours of sleep, and deal with all of the pesky little details in the morning.

Chapter 4

Monica's dad slapped the arm of his easy chair for emphasis. "There is no way The Pie Rack will do business with Amos Butler."

Monica slumped on the sofa in her parents' living room. So far, not so good. "Dad, please, just give it a chance. Remember, yesterday you told me to do whatever I needed to do to make this catering job a reality. Maybe this is a good thing."

"I don't even want to discuss this further," Bob said, crossing his arms over his chest. "Get on the phone right now and call that boy and tell him I said no."

"I can't do that, Dad. They need this job just as badly as we do, if not more."

"No. No, and what are you even doing talking to him? Didn't I tell you not to associate with them any more?"

Monica chuckled nervously, hoping she could make her dad calm down. "That was ten years ago, Dad. I think I might be able to make a few decisions on my own."

"No good can come of this."

"If we don't take this deal with the Butler's, we can kiss the engagement party good-bye. Where else am I going to find someone to partner with before tomorrow?"

"That's what I told you yesterday. Three days is a ridiculous deadline." He shrugged then continued. "Just call Adella and tell her we can only do dessert. If she says no, then we can't do it."

"Dad, it's been ten years since we've spoken to this family, and I just ran into Gil out of nowhere yesterday. Do you think this is God's way of telling us it's time to bury the hatchet?"

"Or maybe this is God's way of telling us we're not supposed to be catering this party." He held up his hands in protest. "Don't bring God into this. I've forgiven the Butlers, and I'm not holding any grudges. But that doesn't mean I'm going to sit back and let his son break my daughter's heart again. Who knows what they're up to this time?"

"Dad, I'll be fine. This isn't about me and Gil."

"I know that's right, because I won't let it be about that. How do you think I felt when my best friend stooped low enough to tell his son he couldn't see my daughter any more. You cried for two weeks straight."

"I was seventeen. Everything was a big deal then."

"No. That's the end of it. I'm the boss, and I say no. This won't work. We can't trust those people."

"Bob," her mom said, speaking for the first time since Monica had explained the situation. "Since you're officially retired, Monica is technically the boss, and I think you should let her make the final decision."

Both Monica and her dad turned to stare at her mom.

Monica was surprised because her mother generally deferred to her father's final decision in all things business related.

"Phyllis, please let me handle this," Bob said. "I know what I'm doing."

"I'm not saying you can't handle it, but think about how you've taught Monica how to run the company. You've always said you wanted her to be prepared to do this on her own, and now when she has the chance to prove herself, you swoop in and take over again."

"I'm not taking over, I'm providing business advice."

"You gave her an ultimatum, not advice. It was an order. Don't you remember last week when Reverend Molson preached about casting your cares on the Lord?"

"Yes, but that has nothing to do with this situation."

"In a way it does. If you cast your cares on God to fix a situation, then you trust Him to do it. You give it to Him, and you don't keep taking it back just so you can make sure He's doing things right."

"Monica is not God, Phyllis."

"I didn't say she is. My point is that if you trust her to run The Pie Rack all by herself one of these days, you should trust her to make decisions you don't necessarily agree with without jumping in to stop her."

"Monica, I understand what your mother's saying, and I do trust you, but I can't allow this to happen while I sit here twiddling my thumbs. It's too risky."

Monica felt a surge of courage and spoke up again. "Dad, isn't that what Amos Butler told you about the second restaurant? And didn't he say the same thing when you took the pie recipe and decided to open a dessert café?"

"That was different."

"Was it really?" Monica asked.

"How so?" asked her mom.

Bob shook his head. "No, Phyllis. I just don't trust them. They have to be up to something else."

"I honestly don't feel like that, Bob," said her mother. "If nothing else, I think we should go ahead and do this. If it doesn't work, then we cut our losses, but I don't want us to teach Monica that she should never take chances. Most things worth anything involve taking a chance."

"Like what?"

Phyllis grinned. "Like you asking me out back in college when you thought I would turn you down."

Bob nodded in agreement. "Now you're right about that. It took me two months to work up the nerve."

"Like I didn't notice that you followed me around all the time and just happened to turn up at every event I went to."

Bob laughed. "So I wasn't exactly as subtle as I thought."

He grew quiet, and Monica didn't interrupt his thoughts, even though she felt like she could come up with a hundred reasons why she should be allowed to make the final decision.

"All right, Monica," he said finally. "You decide. Like your mother said, we do trust you, and even though we might not agree with every decision you make, you will eventually be the sole owner of The Pie Rack, and I know you'll do a good job. If you think this is a good risk to take, we stand behind you."

"Oh, thanks, you guys!" Monica exclaimed, and hugged both of her parents. "I promise this will be the best risk I ever take."

"You think so, honey?" her mom asked, smiling. "You know marriage is a big risk, too. So is starting a family."

Bob frowned. "Who said anything about marriage?" He cleared his throat. "Monica, honey, you can make all the business decisions you want, but just don't get any ideas about marrying that boy. I can barely stomach the idea of doing business with a Butler, but I draw the line at being related to them."

Phyllis grabbed his arm, pulled him up out of his chair, and led him toward the kitchen. "Bob, you're cranky because you haven't eaten. Let me fix you some breakfast."

"You're trying to change the subject, but I'm too hungry to argue," he said.

"Guys, I wish I could stay and eat with you, but I've got to get to work. I've got a lot to do today," Monica said.

"Just remember," her dad said, "this is strictly business. Don't come in here announcing you're engaged to Gil Butler."

Phyllis laughed. "Monica, have a good day at work, honey." To her husband she said, "And, Bob, stop being ridiculous. Who said anything about marriage?"

Bob rolled his eyes. "You did, and don't think I forgot."

Phyllis winked at Monica. "Don't pay any attention to him, honey. Go to work and do a good job."

***

"Out of the question. Absolutely not. How can you think of

joining forces with the enemy?" Amos Butler jumped out of his seat and paced the floor of Gil's office.

Gil laughed out loud. When he needed to, his dad could certainly turn on the dramatics. Sometimes he wondered if his father hadn't gone into the wrong profession. Amos Butler, Oscar-winning performer, sometimes seemed far more accurate than Amos Butler, restaurateur.

"Dad, calm down. This is current day St. Louis, not some old western film. The Ryans are not the enemy. If anything, they could say the same thing about us."

"They're not the enemy to you? So how do you see it?"

"What they are right now is a welcome breath of fresh air for our struggling restaurant. We need them more than they need us for this deal. If we say no, Monica will find another company to fill the void."

"I'm not that desperate."

Gil pushed away from the desk and stood up. "Okay, fine. You may not be that desperate, but I am. You dragged me back here to run this place, but you won't let me fully utilize the managing skills I learned in school. Every time I have an idea, you shoot it down. Too frivolous, too risky, too bold, not bold enough."

"I'm the one who built this business."

"Yeah, you built it with the help of your best friend who you ditched in order to save a few dollars. And where did it get us?"

Amos said nothing but stared out the window, his jawline twitching.

"I'll tell you where it got us." Gil pulled up the monthly balance sheet on his computer and swiveled the screen so his father could see it. "In the red." Gil instantly regretted doing so, because he had managed to sidestep the question of how much money they *hadn't* made for the past couple of months.

The corner of Amos's mouth twitched, but no emotion filtered through his stoic gaze. He shook his head. "It's a mistake. Stop doing the bookkeeping on the computer and go back to paper."

"No. It's not a mistake."

"You got that. . .Internet on this computer?" Amos asked, tapping the screen with his finger.

"Well, yeah, but. . ."

"That's the problem," his dad interrupted. "You probably got some kind of virus. That's what's messing up the numbers."

"No, Dad, there's no virus on this computer. The antivirus program works just fine. And I've double- and triple-checked the numbers. There's no way around it. We can't blame the computer."

Amos folded his arms over his chest. "Go back to paper. Pencil, paper, and calculator are all you need. I did it that way, and it worked just fine before you insisted on having computers. I put you through college doing the bookkeeping on paper."

Gil sat down in the chair across from his dad. "Dad, I'm sorry to break the news like that. I was angry and trying to prove my point. But I have double- and triple-checked those numbers, on the computer and on paper. We've been in the red for a little over a month, and I don't see a way out. If anything, this job will give us what we need to get back on stable footing again."

"It'll put us in the black again?"

Gil nodded slowly. "If we're very careful with our spending, yes. In the meantime, we need to start exploring more options to either make more or spend less."

"I won't sacrifice quality!" Amos barked.

"That's not what I'm asking you to do."

His dad sighed loudly and leaned back in his chair. "Then what *are* you asking?"

"Just for your permission to work on this project with Monica. It doesn't mean you're bound by contract to do anything else with the Ryans, but it could mean the difference between us having what we need to stay open long enough to turn things around."

Amos stood up and looked at the ground.

Gil's heart ached for his dad. Over thirty years of running his own business and the man had very little to show for it.

When Gil had been away, he could push this reality aside, but now that he lived here, he, too, felt the burden of wondering how to turn things around.

He wished desperately he had the perfect formula to bring in more customers and revenue, and with every passing day, he felt less and less confident in his own abilities to get the job done.

The bright moment in all his time here recently had been running into Monica. Yesterday, after they parted, he'd been full of optimism and hope about where their relationship might go, but this morning he'd awakened to more realistic thoughts. Now, just thinking about her brought on such a flood of emotion that he found himself pushing the thoughts aside rather than processing them, simply because the memories filled him with such regret.

Where would they be now had their parents not parted ways? Would they be married, maybe even have kids?

But the more pressing question was, why would Monica want anything beyond a business relationship with him? His father had almost ruined her family financially. Now the shoe was on the other foot.

Why would she want to date a man who had nothing to offer but a failing business? True, his music-management projects had been successful, but she didn't know that.

All she saw when she looked at him was a business failure. He had seen it in her eyes when he'd tried to explain why he had come back to St. Louis. She'd probably only offered the job because she felt sorry for them.

And yet, as desperately as he wanted to reject the work if her offer was out of pity, there was no way he could turn her down. Plain and simple, his family needed the money. If only his father could agree and give his blessing.

As if overhearing his thoughts, Amos spoke up. "Monica, huh?"

"Excuse me?"

"Is this more about getting your old girlfriend back or saving the restaurant?"

Gil shrugged. "I don't know. Both, I guess, but if I had to

make an educated guess, I'd say that after everything that happened, there's no way she'd even think about dating me again."

"You're probably right about that," his father agreed. "But if you promise to put as much energy into fixing the business as you will into winning this girl back, then I won't stand in your way."

"You're sure about that? You're not going to change your mind and make me look like I was trying to sabotage them? I know how hard it is for you to stay away from work, even though you're supposed to be retired. Do I have your guarantee that you will not ruin this for me?"

Amos shrugged. "A few months ago, I might've, but now that I got a look at those spreadsheets, it doesn't look like I have much of a choice, do I?"

"Not necessarily, Dad. I want more than anything to try this, but I will let you make the decision."

Amos moved to the door. "I gotta get over to the YMCA and meet your mother for this spinning class, and if I'm late, I won't hear the end of it for days. As far as the deal with the Ryans, you make the choice. I trust you."

"Thanks, Dad. I promise that I will give this my all."

"I know you will. But leave some energy for pursuing that girl, too." He laughed softly. "Because if she *is* interested in you, it's not going to be for money."

Chapter 5

"So we're done?" Gil wanted to know.

Monica glanced around the restaurant where they had met for a late lunch. The dinner crowd was starting to trickle in, and their waitress would probably love for her and Gil to leave so she could seat someone else at their table.

"I believe we are. And, hey, look at it this way, this was probably the longest lunch meeting on record. We started at two, and it's almost five o'clock," Monica answered.

Gil stretched his arms over his head and yawned. "It has been a long meeting, but the time seemed to fly by. Now what's the next step?"

"Tomorrow evening, I'll run this by Adella, and if she likes it, we're all set."

"And. . .you'll keep me updated?"

Before Monica could answer, her cell phone rang. Checking the caller ID, she saw it was Penny Phelps, the host of a local TV show that was widely watched. In two weeks, they would come by to profile The Pie Rack for the "Hidden Treasures" segment they showed each day.

"I need to take this," she told Gil. "Do you mind?"

"Not at all." He pushed the papers they'd been working on aside and took a bite of his salad.

"Thanks," Monica said, flipping the phone open. "Hello?" She angled slightly away from Gil so as not to be rude.

"Monica? Penny Phelps here, calling about your appearance on *St. Louis Morning*."

"Yes, yes, I got a confirmation from the camera-crew assistant a few days ago, and we're all set for the Thursday after next."

"Yes, I know," Penny said. "But I have another opportunity for you, if you'd be interested."

"Really? I guess I'm definitely interested," Monica said. "What does it involve?"

"Funny you should ask," Penny said. "We just learned our guest for tomorrow's taping of the 'Daily Recipe' segment has a nasty flu and won't be able to make it. Apparently, baked potato soup is not something she can even *think* about without tossing her. . .well, you get the picture."

"So. . .you want me to make the soup for her?" Monica asked, puzzled.

"Not exactly. I was looking through the upcoming features segments and saw that you guys are famous for your signature sweet potato pie. I'm wondering if you'd be willing to come on and demonstrate it for the viewers. If anything, it'll drive more customers to your place in advance of your 'Hidden Treasures' segment."

"I'd love to. Just name the time and place."

"And you don't mind giving up your recipe?" Penny probed.

"Honestly, I can't give them the *exact* recipe we use, but we do have a good recipe we give to our patrons all the time. I could definitely use that one."

"Perfect," said Penny. "Now, you should be at the studio at 7:00 a.m. tomorrow, and bring all the ingredients for your recipe, as well as a couple of already prepared pies—one to display and one for us to taste after we finish the demo. Anything else you need to know?"

Monica racked her brain to search for additional questions but couldn't think of any. "Nothing off the top of my head, but if I think of something, is it okay to call you at this number?"

"Sure, it's my cell, so I always have it on me. I believe we're set. Thanks for the favor, and I'll see you in the morning."

"Great. See you then." Monica hung up the phone and turned to face Gil, who was looking at her expectantly.

"You sound like some kind of big shot," he teased. "What's going on?"

"Oh, wow, this is the most exciting thing!"

"Really? Was it Adella calling to say she wants us to cater the wedding, too?"

"No," Monica answered, shaking her head. She instantly remembered that Gil's business wasn't doing so well, so she reigned in her exuberance in order to not seem like she was rubbing her company's success in his face.

"Penny Phelps just asked me to demonstrate a pie recipe on her show tomorrow."

Gil grinned widely. "That's fantastic. When will it be on?"

"I'm pretty sure it's live. Oh, wow. I'm going to be on live TV. I wonder if I need to come with hair and makeup done or will they do it for me?" Monica sighed in frustration. "Of course I would come up with questions like this after she hangs up."

"If it's live, I guess I'll be getting up early to watch you. It's not every day you see a good friend on TV."

Good friend. His words jarred her a bit, but she determined not to show it. What right did she have to be disappointed? Their short-lived romance had been finished for a decade. At least he still wanted to be friends. That said a lot, considering how he could actually be content to never talk to her again.

Besides, her parents were counting on her to not let her judgment be clouded by emotions while she and Gil worked on this project. So he was making it very clear he was just her friend.

Fine, I can deal with that, she decided. *But why does he have to be so blunt about it? At least have a little compassion for a girl's feelings, huh?*

"Earth to Monica," Gil said, laughing. "Is it just me, or have you gone into full-speed brain fog since Penny called?"

"Sorry about that. I guess I'm trying to mentally pull together everything I need to get done for tomorrow."

"Let me help you," Gil said, opening to a blank page in his notebook. "Here's your 'to-do' list. Just say whatever you need to get done, and I'll write it down. That way, you won't lose track of any thoughts while you're trying to get your list together."

"You're volunteering to be my scribe?" she teased. "I have to warn you, I can be a little long-winded sometimes."

"Oh really?" he asked, arching his eyebrows. "That's funny. Must be my luck, because my favorite girlfriend was also very talkative."

Monica was taken aback. Was this his way of telling her he was in a relationship?

Gil must have sensed her confusion, because he hurriedly continued speaking. "Yeah, actually you remind me of her a lot. I dated her my senior year of high school, and we haven't really talked since then. Well, actually, I ran into her yesterday, but I didn't get to ask her anything important, like whether or not she was dating anyone. . .or if she would let me take her out to dinner tonight?"

"Dinner?" Monica echoed, feeling pleased that he actually seemed to be showing some interest in her. He was certainly taking an indirect route to asking her out, but she couldn't help but find it kind of cute.

"Yeah. Apparently, she got some really exciting news about her job today, and I wanted to take her out to celebrate." Gil leaned a little closer to her. "Give me some advice. Should I ask or do you think she would laugh in my face?" In a stage whisper, he added, "We didn't break up in a very ideal way."

"Since when have you ever seen an ideal breakup?" Monica countered.

"So I should go for it? Do you think she would say yes?"

Monica tilted her head to the side and pretended to be thinking. "I think she would definitely say yes, except she might not have time—at least not tonight."

Gil frowned in an exaggerated fashion. "So that's a no?"

"I wish I could, but I have so much to do. I have to be at the studio at 7:00 a.m. But I've got stuff to finish at the office this afternoon, and I've got to bake a couple of pies and then get ingredients together for the demo, find something to wear, and make sure I have everything together for the meeting with Adella tomorrow night."

"I can think of one item you can strike from the list," Gil said triumphantly.

"Really? Which one?"

"Baking pies. The last I heard, the bakers at The Pie Rack make several dozen pies every day. Just pick up a couple from the restaurant."

Monica shook her head. "I can't. I know I'm probably being too hands-on, but I feel like if I'm going to demonstrate it, I need to bring pies I actually did myself."

"Then let me bring takeout over, and I can eat it while I watch you cook."

"Gil, are you inviting yourself over to my house?" she asked, pleased that he wanted to spend more time with her.

"Guilty as charged."

"I heard that girl you wanted to take to dinner really, really likes sesame chicken."

"Then I will be at her house at seven on the dot with sesame chicken."

Monica quickly jotted down the directions to her condo, then gathered up her notes and headed back to work. If her dad had been less than thrilled about this morning's announcement, the call she was about to make would more than make up for the shock of having to work with the Butlers for the engagement party.

Chapter 6

W ow, do you have like an army of kids in the neighborhood, or is cooking for hundreds of people just a hobby of yours?" Gil asked, taking in the sight of Monica's kitchen.

"Excuse me?"

Gil pointed to the kitchen table and countertops, which held industrial-sized packages of baking ingredients. "Do you bake cookies for your neighbors in your spare time? I can't think of any other reason why a single woman would need this much flour."

Monica laughed and walked to her refrigerator. Swinging the door open to reveal a nearly empty interior, she said, "Ha, ha, my comedian. No, I don't have all this stuff just sitting around every day. I brought these ingredients home from the bakery so I could work on the pies tonight."

"Well, that makes much more sense," he said.

"I can't believe you thought I have all that stuff just sitting around. You should see my cabinets—they're even more empty than my fridge."

"What do you eat? Air?"

Monica put a finger to chin and feigned deep thought. "Let's see. . .my weekday dinner preparation usually consists of stopping at the grocery store on my way home from work to pick up a frozen dinner."

He pointed to a pot resting on the stovetop. "What's cooking now?"

"I just peeled a bunch of potatoes for the pies I have to bake tonight. Hopefully they'll be boiling soon."

"Smells good." Gil held up the bags he'd carried in. "Well, rest assured, this sesame chicken is not from a box in the freezer section. Should I plate it up?"

"No, no, you're the company. Why don't you sit down in the living room, and I'll get dinner on the table."

"Are you sure there isn't anything I can help you do?" he wanted to know. "Can I help you get your ingredients together?"

Monica shook her head. "I was going to do that really quick before dinner. Just make yourself at home, turn on the TV, whatever."

Monica put the takeout into the microwave to heat and began transferring the ingredients into smaller canisters.

"Hey, I have the same laptop!" Gil called from the living room. "Mind if I check my e-mail?"

"Go right ahead. Dinner in about five minutes."

Monica transferred flour into a smaller canister, then pulled dinner out of the microwave and fixed plates for her and Gil.

Walking into the living room to let him know dinner was

served, she watched as he clicked on her laptop. To her surprise, she watched in amazement as her bookkeeping program popped up on the screen.

Why in the world was he looking in that program? Wasn't he supposed to be checking his e-mail?

Monica cleared her throat. Gil turned abruptly and closed the cover of the laptop.

"How's the e-mail?" she asked, trying to keep her voice level.

"Well. . .honestly, I didn't quite make it there yet. I. . .I accidentally pulled up some other program."

Monica put the plates down on the dinette table and headed over to where Gil sat with her computer.

"Really? What other program?"

"It looks like your bookkeeping program. I must have accidentally clicked on a different icon, and it just opened." He stood up and walked to the table where their dinner sat. "But don't worry," he added. "I wasn't snooping."

Monica followed him to the table and noticed she'd forgotten silverware. "Let me run back into the kitchen for a minute."

As soon as she entered the kitchen, Monica realized she'd forgotten to finish transferring the salt and sugar to the canisters, so she took Gil the flatware and explained that she would join him in a few minutes.

"I started this job in the kitchen, and I know I won't be able to relax and eat dinner if I leave things undone."

Gil nodded and kept eating as Monica made her escape.

She was vaguely aware of the fact that it was probably rude to make Gil sit and eat by himself, but she needed to do something to keep herself busy and refrain from jumping to conclusions. If she were sitting across from him right now, she would have a hard time reining in her imagination.

While she transferred the ingredients, Monica prayed silently.

Lord, if my dad was right and Gil really is up to something wrong, please show me before something goes wrong for The Pie Rack.

Monica hoped against all hope that he had been telling the truth—that he'd opened the program accidentally and he wasn't snooping.

She pressed the lid back on the sugar jar and took a deep breath before returning to the table.

Gil looked up and smiled. "It was starting to feel a little uncomfortable, sitting here eating by myself. Glad you came back. And I do hope you believed me when I said I wasn't snooping. The last thing I want to do is give you a reason not to trust me."

"Oh, you know me, I have a one-track mind when it comes to my 'to-do' list," Monica said, sidestepping the question.

"Are you baking the pies after we finish?"

"Probably. The longer they sit after you bake them, the better they taste."

"I remember. Our dads took six months to perfect that recipe."

Monica laughed. "I remember that after they finally agreed

on the recipe I was so tired of sweet potato pie I could hardly stand to look at one, let alone taste it, for at least a good year."

Gil shook his head. "I never had that problem. And after we stopped selling it, I had to rely on going to friends' houses to taste it."

Monica stopped eating, her fork midair. "You stopped selling the pie?"

"Yeah. After the whole. . .fiasco, my dad got the idea that he didn't want to have anything in common with your dad, so we stopped selling sweet potato pie, and he refused to even have it in the house."

"You're kidding."

"I am not. I remember once, when I was home for Christmas break during my sophomore year of college, I was at my friend Eddie's house. They had a couple of pies from The Pie Rack, and I think I ate an entire pie by myself."

Monica couldn't help but laugh out loud. "Did anyone notice or say anything?"

"I doubt it. A bunch of people were there hanging out, going in and out of the kitchen, and I just knocked that whole pie off, piece by piece."

"That's a great story. How would you feel about taking a pie home with you tonight?"

"I would be eternally grateful."

"Then it's settled." Since they were finished eating, Monica stood and began clearing the table. "If you don't mind hanging around while I make these pies for the show, I'll make one for you, too."

"Absolutely no problem for me. Can I help?"

Monica shook her head. "I work best if nobody is standing over my shoulder when I cook. You can either watch TV or check your e-mail while I get the pie into the oven, and we can talk while it's baking."

"I'll go for the TV, since I already had a difficult time checking e-mail. But hurry up and finish so I don't feel like I'm just sitting around doing nothing while you do all the work."

"I'll try." Monica went to the kitchen, drained the now soft potatoes and began mashing them and adding the other ingredients.

She felt a sense of relief that he had turned down the opportunity to get his hands on her computer again. Surely that meant he really had opened The Pie Rack's financial files by accident.

At any rate, she was also glad that he wanted to stick around and talk to her. Of course, the promise of pie had something to do with that, but wasn't the way to a man's heart supposedly through his stomach?

In record time, Monica mashed, blended, and whipped the ingredients and got the pies ready to bake.

Gil came in the kitchen just as she slid the last pan in the oven.

He walked over to the bowl where she'd mixed everything. "Can I have a taste?"

"No—that's another one of my kitchen rules. No eating anything with raw egg in it."

Gil frowned. "I'm sure I'll be fine. Everything smells

good, and it's going to be hard to wait until it's done baking."
"You are worse than a little kid," she teased. "Let me see if I can find you something to tide you over until these are done."

Monica checked the drawers in her refrigerator and found she had a couple of single slices of pie she'd brought home from work yesterday.

"Can I interest you in a slice now?" she asked, waving the container under Gil's nose.

"As long as I can warm it up in the microwave, yes."

"It's hot now, but you have to promise me you'll let it sit overnight before you cut it."

"Are you serious?" Gil wanted to know.

"Yes, I'm serious. And if you don't promise me, I will be forced to keep it here tonight, and you can come pick it up tomorrow."

"I don't recall having this rule back when our dads made the pie."

"That's because my dad did a little retweaking of the recipe and the cooking procedure. We discovered that even though it tastes fine right out of the oven, if you let the flavors set up while it cools for several hours, it tastes even better."

"I don't like the idea because I want a piece right now, but I'll do what you said."

"Great."

"So what time can I cut into this masterpiece?"

"Well. . .I'm getting to the studio around seven, and I think we'll be going on the air shortly afterward, so I guess after seven, seven thirty, you can eat it."

"I'll do that. Maybe I'll even get up, cut a piece, and then taste it while you're doing your segment. I'll have to make sure I don't feel superior over the other viewers, since I have a pie that was personally prepared by the beautiful woman showing Penny how to make it."

"You can call me beautiful all you want, but that won't let you cut the pie sooner."

Gil hung his head in mock shame. "I guess you saw right through my attempt to butter you up?"

Laughing, Monica put her hand on his shoulder and steered him toward the door. "Enough about cutting the pie right now. It's not ready yet. Now go home before I change my mind and take it back."

Gil opened the door and paused. "Thanks for the pie and for a great evening. I had fun catching up on old times with you."

"Me, too."

"We should. . .do this again, sometime?"

Monica tilted her head to the side. "Are you trying to get me to bake you more pies?"

"No. I mean, anytime you want to give me a pie, I won't turn it down, but I'm saying I have fun with you. I can't talk to a pie. I miss you a lot more than I realized."

"Same here."

A long silence passed while neither of the two moved.

Was he going to try to kiss her good night? Monica couldn't

decide if she should push the door open to signal that the evening was over or lean in to invite a kiss.

Gil moved a step closer and hugged her. It wasn't a terribly romantic embrace, since he was balancing a still-warm pie in one of his gloved hands, but it worked for Monica.

She inhaled the scent of his cologne, mixed with the aroma of pie, and relaxed.

She didn't know how he felt, but she wouldn't mind giving the relationship another chance.

He ended the hug, waved good-bye, and left Monica standing there, watching him get into his car and drive away.

Monica reluctantly closed the door and got ready for bed. She would have liked to call her mom or a friend and analyze her evening with Gil to determine if he had given any indication that he wanted more than friendship right now, but she didn't have time.

If she wanted to do a good job in the morning, she needed lots of rest tonight. The analysis would have to wait.

Chapter 7

G il got up an hour earlier than usual to get ready for work and watch Monica on *St. Louis Morning*.

Keeping his word, Gil had not touched the pie last night, but his mouth watered as he went to the kitchen to cut a slice.

Gil put the pie on a saucer and turned on the TV just as Penny Phelps introduced Monica.

He watched as Monica went through the motions of mixing the ingredients and Penny chatted and asked questions.

I am so fortunate to know her, and even more fortunate that she wants to be friends again after all that happened, Gil decided.

Remembering back to their hug from the night before, Gil wondered how she would have reacted if he had kissed her. The thought had crossed his mind, and he had almost followed through with action. But at the last moment, Gil had ruled out more than a hug, mostly because it would have been incredibly awkward to attempt a kiss while he held a pie in one hand. But the next time he saw her, there wouldn't be any pie. . . .

When they reached the part of the recipe where Monica produced an already-cooked pie out of the oven twenty seconds after putting in an uncooked one, Gil chuckled. Having grown up around the restaurant business, he had always found the illusion of speedy cooking on TV shows quite funny.

Finally, Monica cut slices of pie for herself and Penny.

"Oh, I can't wait to taste the famous Pie Rack sweet potato pie," Penny gushed. "I've always heard so much about it, but this is my first time to actually have some."

Gil mirrored Penny as she put some on her fork and took a generous bite.

As soon as the dessert hit his taste buds, he realized that the grimace Penny had on her face was involuntary—because he was making the same face.

Spitting the pie onto the plate, Gil tried to figure out what had gone wrong with the recipe.

Penny didn't fare much better. "Water!" she croaked, as Monica looked on with a stricken expression on her face. Utterly confused, Gil watched as Monica finally tasted the pie herself. Unlike him and Penny, Monica did manage to swallow the bite, but it appeared to take a great deal of effort.

Gil took the uneaten pie back to the kitchen and got ready to leave. He didn't know how long Monica would remain at the studio, but wherever she was, he planned to find her and do what he could to help.

Monica rested her head on the steering wheel and cried, not

caring if anyone saw her. Penny Phelps had been good-natured about the whole situation, and she assured Monica that the "Hidden Treasures" segment would still air. In fact, the crews were coming in two days to get some footage.

"Mistakes happen," Penny said. "I'm just sorry it was live and I wasn't able to pull it off more convincingly."

As soon as she had tasted the pie, Monica understood exactly what was wrong. Mentally retracing her steps, she realized that in her haste to transfer the ingredients to smaller canisters, she had poured salt into the sugar container.

Any other day, she probably would have caught the mistake before it went too far, but because she was so flustered after catching Gil in her bookkeeping files, she hadn't even noticed.

Gil.

Monica sat up and wiped her eyes, remembering her dad's warning.

"No good can come of this."

He had been right. Now Monica even doubted that Gil was telling the truth last night. Accidentally. "Ha! The big liar," she said bitterly.

Her cell phone rang, and the caller ID read GILBERT.

"Calling to rejoice in my failure?" she said to the phone. "Forget it. Pretending to help me and then trying to sabotage me behind my back does not count for friendship." She turned the ringer to silent mode and ignored the call.

Thoroughly embarrassed, Monica pulled herself together and drove to her parents' house.

Chapter 8

An hour later, having been comforted by her mother and encouraged by her father, who diplomatically refrained from any I-told-you-so statements, Monica headed to The Pie Rack, feeling better emotionally, but mentally more confused than she had ever been when she'd arrived.

Looking in the rearview mirror and noticing that her makeup was a little less than pristine, Monica realized she'd been so flustered after the recipe demonstration that she left her makeup bag at the TV station.

There was no way she felt like showing her face there any time soon, so she decided to make a stop at the pharmacy to replace a few basics.

A woman on a mission, Monica swiftly gathered up mascara, lipstick, powder, neutral eye shadow, and headed to the checkout line.

All of the lanes were crowded, with at least four people waiting. Monica quickly perused the customers' shopping baskets and moved to the line where people were purchasing the fewest items.

While she waited, she thought about the conversation she'd just had with her parents. Strangely, they both found the pie-tasting mishap quite comical, and despite the potential image problem the appearance might cause for The Pie Rack, they both seemed to doubt Gil had deliberately tried to make her ruin the recipe. Though they both seemed concerned that he had accessed The Pie Rack budget spreadsheets, they both agreed to give him the benefit of the doubt that it had truly been an accident.

"But he took a pie home, too," Monica protested. "If he was really my friend, he could have at least tried to warn me before I went on the air."

"I thought you told him to let it sit overnight. Maybe he still has yet to taste it," her mother suggested.

Gil's repeated calls to her cell phone also polished her parents' opinion of his character.

"At least give him a chance to explain himself," her dad advised. "If he's as wonderful as you described him the other day, he just might be feeling pretty terrible right about now."

"I doubt he would keep calling if he'd done something untoward. About now is the time you'd expect someone like that to quietly slink out of sight."

Monica had agreed to give him a chance to explain, but right now she didn't want to think about it. All she wanted right now was to hurry up and get out of the store, so she could reapply her makeup and go to work without looking as bad as she felt.

KISS THE ~~COOK~~ *Bride*

The woman in front of her in line turned around and said, "I can't believe this is taking so long. What are they doing up there, anyway?"

"Tell me about it," Monica nodded in agreement. "I have to get to work pretty soon."

The woman shook her head and turned back around. With nothing better to do, Monica examined all of the impulse-buy items strategically placed on both sides of where she stood.

The lady in front of her turned around again, as if she wanted to continue the conversation, but Monica pretended to be engrossed in reading the copy on a package of scented hand sanitizer. She wasn't trying to be rude, but neither did she feel much like making small talk.

Although Monica made no move to converse with her, the woman still kept turning around intermittently to glance at her, and she wondered if there was something hanging out of her nose. There was nothing worse than having people stare at you without saying anything.

"Monica, isn't it?" the woman said.

Startled, Monica looked up at her. "I'm sorry?"

"Your name is Monica, isn't it?"

Monica nodded, although she couldn't ever recall having met this woman before in her life.

"I knew I had seen you somewhere before. I'm Leeda Adams."

Monica blinked. The name didn't ring a bell, either.

The woman must have realized that Monica had no recollection of ever meeting her.

"I'm Gil Butler's cousin. We met once when he brought you to a family dinner."

Monica could remember the event itself, but not Leeda in particular. Ten years had passed since then, and Gil had about a million cousins. Well, not really a million, but at least twenty or thirty.

"So how's business for you? Pretty good, I hear, ever since your family ran off with the better location and left Uncle Amos and Aunt Melinda in the lurch."

Monica felt herself growing angrier by the second. First, Gil had indirectly ruined her TV appearance, and now his cousin wanted to accuse her family of initiating the dissolution of the partnership.

Monica didn't have a chance to defend herself because Leeda kept going. "You know, Uncle Amos always said your family would get what you deserved someday, and if it hasn't happened yet, it will sooner or later, because God don't like ugly, that's for sure."

Monica was taken aback by such a harsh statement. Had Gil's family really told people that her family cheated them? The nerve of them! The exact opposite was more honest.

Trying to keep composed, she answered, "I really don't think you should be commenting on matters you don't know anything about."

The line was finally moving now, and thankfully, Leeda's items were already being scanned.

But that didn't stop her from throwing out another nugget of wisdom. "Oh, I know enough, all right, and I know one thing for sure, as long as you let it keep festering, it'll just get worse. What you reap is what you're gonna sow. What you need to do is get together and at least talk it out. And it seems to me a little apologizing might be in order."

Likewise, Monica thought. *Wouldn't it be nice to hear Amos say sorry to Dad for greedily taking the most profit and leaving us to start over financially? Or maybe Gil would like to explain why he was* really *snooping in my files.*

The checker moved swiftly, and within moments, Leeda and her platitudes were gone. And not a moment too soon. Monica didn't know how much longer she could remain civil.

As soon as she finished paying for her purchases, Monica went to her car, reapplied makeup, and thought about her promise to let Gil explain himself.

For the rest of the short drive to The Pie Rack, she fussed under her breath about the nerve of Gil's cousin.

By the time Monica pulled into the parking lot at work, she had calmed down considerably, but there was no way she was calling Gil right now. Leeda had told her that Amos wished The Pie Rack would fail. Was he bitter enough that he'd stoop so low as to send Gil to make it happen?

No, she wasn't going to be calling Gil back anytime soon. The last thing she wanted to do was hear his smug voice right now.

Monica entered the building and graciously accepted the sympathetic glances and pep talks from The Pie Rack employees.

On a normal day, she might stick around out front and chitchat with the waitresses or go back to the kitchen to make small talk with the bakers, but today she did neither. Instead, she went straight to her office.

No sooner than she had gotten situated at her desk, someone knocked on the door.

"Come in!" she called.

The door swung open, and Gil stood in the doorway.

Chapter 9

A long silence passed between them. Monica wondered who had sent him back to her office. As soon as Gil was gone, she intended to find out and have a long talk with that individual about respecting her privacy.

Gil held a vase of roses and he stood still. His usual confidence was gone, as if he could sense that she didn't want him there. "Can I come in?"

Monica wanted nothing more than to tear into him about the accusations his cousin had just made, but just before she opened her mouth, she remembered her parents' advice and pushed aside the impulse to jump to conclusions.

He'd better do some pretty fancy explaining, she told herself.

Gil came in, and Monica fully expected him to take a seat in one of the chairs in front of the desk.

He surprised her completely by putting the vase on her desk, then coming around to her side of the desk and bending down to give her a hug. Although at first she wanted to pull away, Monica didn't. She rested her head on his shoulder and hoped he was being sincere. All of the old feelings she'd experienced after their breakup came flooding back, and Monica realized that what she really wanted was to find a way to make sense of this whole mess.

Despite what had transpired ten years ago, and regardless of what his cousin said, the last thing she wanted was to lose him again.

"How are you?" he asked quietly, pulling away from the hug and taking a seat in a chair.

"Completely mortified. It's not every day you make a pie so nasty that Penny Phelps spits it out on live TV."

"I wish I'd tasted the pie last night. At least I could have warned you about it."

Monica could tell he was sincere, and her earlier misgivings melted away. "At least you kept your promise."

"Is there anything I can do to help remedy—" Gil was interrupted by Monica's cell phone ringing.

Monica checked the caller ID and groaned. It was Adella. Her menu presentation was later this afternoon, and Monica didn't know if she had the resolve to handle Adella's personality after all that had already happened. She wondered if Gil might be willing to handle that meeting by himself. All he really had to do was show Adella a list of potential dish choices.

"Hello?"

"Monica, this is Adella." Her tone was clipped and very somber.

Monica wondered if the room was abnormally hot, or if she was just getting nervous. "Hi, Adella. We're still on for the meeting this afternoon? Three o'clock?"

"I don't think so."

"Excuse me?"

"This morning, I was awakened by several phone calls from friends who saw you on *St. Louis Morning* and told me I was making a big mistake to let you cater my engagement party."

"Adella, I can explain that. We had a mix up with some ingredients, and that's why the pie I used this morning didn't taste right. I can assure you that nothing like that will happen for your event."

"Well. . ." Adella hesitated, and Monica glanced at Gil.

He seemed to be getting the gist of the conversation, and he looked worried. Now that he was counting on this job, Monica wanted to do everything she could to make sure it didn't get pulled out from under them.

"You do realize our contract was contingent upon you finding another company to provide the dinner menu, right?"

"Yes, I'm aware of that, and I have found a partner. We've actually written out several sample menus that we were going to show you this afternoon, and I think you'll be more than happy with—"

"Hold on, that's my other line." Adella clicked over and left Monica on hold. But today's music was more along the lines of contemporary jazz rather than the swoony love songs of a few days ago.

Although Adella's frequent switching to another line annoyed her to no end, Monica took the opportunity to quickly explain the seriousness of the situation to Gil.

"I'm sorry I was such a klutz. The last thing I wanted to do was lose this job for us," she told him.

"Don't worry, I doubt she'll actually fire us, because that would mean she'll have to go back to the drawing board."

Monica nodded in agreement. "You're right. But now she'll feel like she can ask for ridiculous concessions, and we'll have to give them to her."

Gil shrugged. "That's the beauty of this business. The customer is always right, so you have to be willing to go the extra mile."

"Your dad always said that," Monica said, remembering.

"Yeah. He still does. I think it's his motto. My mom says she's surprised those weren't my first words."

Adella clicked back over. "Here's the deal. I will be willing to reconsider if you set up a complete menu tasting for me and Byron."

"So you'll come in this afternoon and pick a sample menu, and then we'll set up another date for you to taste everything?" Monica clarified.

"No, the meeting for this afternoon is cancelled. I want you to cook all of your sample menus, and then we'll come in and taste everything and *then* pick the menu we want for the party."

Monica held back a retort. There were easily sixty to seventy dishes on those sample menus. She couldn't ask her staff to work that much overtime, and she doubted Gil wanted to ask the same of his employees.

For once, it was her turn to put Adella on hold. "Could you

wait just a moment while I check on something?" she asked.

Adella agreed, and Monica put the phone on mute to discuss the situation with Gil.

"She wants us to cook every item on the sample menus, and then she'll taste everything and decide if she still wants us for the party. Is it still worth it to you?"

"I'm in if you are."

"If you're in, I guess I have to be." Monica picked up her phone again.

"Adella, I think we can arrange what you've requested. When would you like to schedule this tasting?"

"How about tomorrow?"

Monica sat up very straight in her chair, indignant that Adella even thought something so complicated could be arranged in a mere day. Trying to remain diplomatic, she spoke quietly. "I'm sorry, but that would be impossible for us. I was thinking more along the lines of a week from now."

"That's too late for me. The party is in three weeks, so if this doesn't work out, I'll have to find another caterer in record time."

Monica hated to agree with Adella, but she made a lot of sense. She would feel the same way if she were in Adella's shoes.

"Okay, I understand. Tomorrow is still impossible for us, but is there another day you would like?"

"Let me check. . ." Monica could hear Adella turning pages, presumably in her appointment book, and she hoped Adella would pick a reasonable time frame.

"Quite honestly, I'm really booked right now. The only other day I have is this Friday."

"We'll take it," Monica said, hoping Gil would be in agreement.

"How does two o'clock sound?" Adella wanted to know.

As if I really have a choice, Monica thought. "Two o'clock is great. We'll see you then."

She hung up the phone and turned to Gil.

"How did it go? Did we save the deal?"

"Maybe. We'll find out on Friday."

"Friday? That's three days away. I thought you were going to insist on more time."

"It was the best I could do. She was this far from canceling the whole thing," said Monica, holding her thumb and forefinger a mere fraction of a millimeter apart.

"Then I guess we'd better get in gear to get all of this stuff ready."

"Yeah." Monica pulled her planner out of her purse and started mentally noting what she would be able to put off in order to make time to get ready for the tasting. She and Gil would have to set up shop at The Pie Rack and work evenings to get the dishes ready.

This time, there would be no room for mishaps. She would taste anything that went to the table before Adella could even lay eyes on it.

Then she realized that two days from now, the crew from the TV station was coming to get footage for the "Hidden Treasures" segment. She'd planned to spend the next two

KISS THE ~~COOK~~ *Bride*

days getting The Pie Rack into tip-top shape. There was no way she could have the kitchen being used as catering central with cameras coming. Everything had to be beautiful and flawless—especially after what had happened this morning. And if she were busy getting The Pie Rack to look immaculate, where would she find time to help Gil?

"Monica? What's wrong?" he asked. "I think you just paled several shades," he said, resting his hand on hers.

"We have a slight emergency on our hands," she told him.

Chapter 10

"A re you sure this is a good idea?" Monica asked. She and Gil were in the kitchen at her condo, warming up finger foods.

"It's not ideal, but we don't really have a choice. And it's about time. This needed to happen eventually."

"Convincing them to help us will be harder than trying to nail Jell-O to a tree."

"In theory, yes. But they are our parents, and they want us to succeed, so they really are our only hope right now. Besides, I know my dad, and ever since he retired, he's been itching to get back into the kitchen."

"My dad, too. But doesn't your dad ever cook at home?"

"My mom lets him in there sometimes, but he prefers the hustle and bustle of a deadline—hungry customers waiting for their food." Gil took the lid off a simmering saucepan full of spinach and artichoke dip.

"Hey, mister, hands off. What did I tell you about messing around with stuff while I'm cooking?" Monica warned, waving a wooden spoon at him.

"I forgot you like to be the queen of the kitchen without anybody 'hovering' over you."

"Exactly. If you want to help, go in the living room and see if anything needs to be picked up."

"That would be fine, except you and I both know the living room is spotless. You're just giving me busy work," he protested.

"Yes, I am. So get out of the kitchen," she said, grinning at him.

A few moments later, Gil returned with a handful of envelopes and a large package. "What should I do with the mail?" he wanted to know.

"Actually, you can give it to me." She'd been so preoccupied over the past few days that she'd let the mail build up and hadn't had a chance to look at it.

Monica took the mail, and gave Gil her spoon in exchange. "Keep an eye on that spinach dip for me? Don't let it stick or burn."

"Oh, so now you let me cook. But only when it's convenient for you."

"Hey, it is *my* kitchen," Monica retorted, taking a seat at the table to look through the mail.

Most of it was the usual, junk mail and bills, but the package caught her eye. It was from Angel Morgan, a friend she'd met at the National Restaurateurs' Convention last summer.

She, Angel, Haley, and Allison had met and bonded when the elevator they were all riding at the convention got stuck.

Monica shook open that package and an envelope fell out, along with an apron.

Angel had purchased the last apron but hinted that she might share it if she found romance.

Monica tore open the envelope and read the letter. It was chatty, highlighting some of the recent happenings in Angel's life.

The last few sentences caught Monica's attention:

> *Remember the apron I bought? And how you and the girls told me I needed to share it if it brought a man into my life??? Well, God sent a certain gentleman by the name of Cyril Jackson III (and boy is he dreamy!) my way, and we're about as cozy as two peas in a pod. No engagement ring yet, but I have every reason to believe one will be forthcoming!*
>
> *This cook is getting plenty of kisses nowadays, so I thought I'd send it your way. Keep in touch, girl, and let me know how the restaurant business is treating you.*
>
> *Lots of Love,*
> *Angel*

Monica held up the apron and laughed at the red lips next to words that proclaimed KISS THE COOK.

It was a little gutsy for Monica's taste—not exactly something she'd normally purchase for herself, but just seeing it brought back the memories of time spent with Angel, Haley, and Allison.

She smiled as she carried the apron into the kitchen with her. She would have to wear it a few times before she sent it on to Allison or Haley.

Gil was still busily stirring away at the spinach dip. He looked up at her and waved her over to where he stood.

"I didn't let it stick," he said, waving the spoon in the air.

Monica looked down at the stovetop and gasped. "Yeah, but you're dripping cream sauce all over my flat-top range. Do you know how hard it is to clean these things?"

She put the apron on the counter and grabbed a sponge, intending to do some damage control.

As she scrubbed away, she sensed Gil standing right next to her. Irritated, she scrubbed even harder. Couldn't he find anything better to do than *watch* her clean?

Sighing loudly, Monica stopped scrubbing and turned to face Gil. "What? Isn't there something else you can do?"

He grinned. "Well. . .if you insist." Before she realized what was happening, he took her in his arms and kissed her.

It was probably the most unromantic time for a kiss, but Monica didn't want it to end. Suddenly, the stress factors of the day—the salty pie, Adella's demands, and the meeting with their families—didn't seem as troubling.

When the kiss ended, Monica and Gil stood silently, not speaking, just looking at each other.

Monica racked her brain to think of something to end the awkward pause and could only come up with, "What was that for?"

Gil shrugged and pointed to the apron. "I was just following the instructions."

At that moment the doorbell rang. Monica hurried to the entryway to find her parents standing on the front porch.

Gil's parents were making their way up the walk, warily eyeing the Ryans.

Monica motioned everyone inside and took their coats. An eerie silence filled the room once again, until Gil's dad spoke over the quiet.

"This better be good."

Gil put his arm around Monica and smiled. "Trust me, Dad, you'll love it."

Chapter 11

Monica stood next to Gil, who was peeking out the hallway window into the dining room. They were at Amos's Smokehouse, watching Adella and Byron sample the food.

He smiled down at her. "How is everything in the kitchen?" he whispered.

"Like a dream. They're in heaven. It almost seems like old times."

"Really? No problems whatsoever?"

"Well, your dad and my dad had a minor 'discussion' about how to season the barbeque sauce—sweet or spicy—but they compromised. How are Adella and Byron liking the spread?"

"They love it, from what I can tell. They're going back for seconds and thirds for some of the dishes."

"Looks like this job is in the bag," she said. "And all because you're such a genius."

"More like our mothers are geniuses," he corrected her.

"How did you figure it out?" she asked again. "The entire

time you were talking, I kept praying silently that our dads wouldn't argue. The only thing is, I missed pretty much everything you said. Since then, everything has been such a blur that we haven't even had a quiet moment to talk."

"I know," he said, rubbing her shoulder. "You spent all your time at The Pie Rack and left me here at our restaurant to supervise our parents cooking. I missed you. . .and your kiss-me apron."

"It's not a kiss-me apron. It's a kiss-the-cook apron."

"And you're the cook," he retorted. "So how did the taping for 'Hidden Treasures' go? I got home too late to call you last night."

"Beautifully. The place was spotless, we had a nice crowd of customers, the weather was great, so everything looked sunny and bright on camera, and Penny sat down and ate an entire piece of pie. Before she left, the staff took a picture with her, and they're going to put it up on the wall."

"I'm proud of you," he said. "You didn't let the salty pie keep you down. You got right back up and kept going."

"You're not as proud of me as I am of you," said Monica. "Now finish telling me how you figured out our moms had been communicating all these years." Monica chuckled softly. "I still can't get over the looks on their faces when you said, 'Mom, Mrs. Ryan, is there something you'd like to share about money that only the two of you know about?' "

Gil shrugged. "It wasn't that hard. I was searching desperately for any accounting mistakes in the hope that there might be more money in some other account somewhere. I didn't find another account, but I found several instances of unexplained disappearances of money not long after the split. Then, in this past year, I kept seeing unexplained appearances of money. For a while I got nervous because I thought either my parents were sloppy at balancing the checkbook, or they were cooking the books."

Monica shook her head. "Our dads were stunned, but they couldn't protest so loudly when our moms admitted to sending each other money secretly when things got tough. It was pretty humbling to watch."

"Yeah, all of a sudden, they realized that friendship was about more than who won the argument. The money your mom sent definitely kept us afloat for several months."

"Your mom did the same for us, too. I remember those first few years after the split as being pretty lean, but things could have been a lot worse if she hadn't been helping."

A sudden eruption of laughter sounded from the kitchen.

"Sounds like everything is fine back there," Monica said.

"Yeah, the only thing is, now they're talking about coming out of retirement to work together again."

Monica put a hand to her forehead. "I was just getting used to my little office."

"Actually, they're thinking more along the lines of a catering company. The moms don't want them at a restaurant all hours of the day and night, but all agreed that cooking for different functions now and then might be fun."

Monica shrugged. "As long as they can keep it fun." She peeked out to look at Adella and Bryon again.

"If this goes well, Adella hinted that we might be able to cater her actual wedding. Wouldn't that be fun for our parents?"

"Yeah. I think wedding catering is a good place to start," he agreed. "Maybe one day they can even cater ours."

Monica stepped back and looked at him in amazement. "Gilbert Butler, I know you are not proposing to me right now. For one thing, this is not even a *remotely* romantic setting. We're in the middle of the hallway between the kitchen and the dining room, peeking out of a window."

Gil took a step closer, but Monica kept talking. "Plus, we've only been reacquainted for a few days, we haven't even gone out on an official date, and our parents are just coming off of ten years of not speaking to each other. Not exactly ideal conditions for getting engaged, don't you think?"

"I agree, and that's why I'm not proposing."

Monica suddenly felt embarrassed. Talk about jumping to conclusions. She looked away so he couldn't see her face.

He moved closer and put his arms around her. "I'm not proposing *yet*. But I'm pretty sure I'm falling pretty hard for this girl I broke up with back in high school."

"Really?" Monica said, not caring that she was grinning from ear to ear. "What's she like?"

"She's a little shorter than me, has really pretty, light brown eyes, sometimes she panics when she gets stressed out, and she has this cute little apron that keeps telling me to kiss her."

"A talking apron, hmm?"

"Not really. But, now that you mention it, I think I hear it calling right now."

Gil pulled her closer and kissed her.

When the kiss ended, Monica rested her head on his shoulder. "That's some apron," she said, smiling.

SWEET POTATO PIE RECIPE

1 (9 inch) deep-dish pie shell, frozen
2 1/4 pounds sweet potatoes
Pinch baking soda
4 tablespoons margarine
1 cup sugar
1/2 tablespoon nutmeg
1/2 tablespoon cinnamon
1/4 cup whole milk
1 egg
1/2 tablespoon vanilla

Thaw pie shell for 10 minutes; then poke sides and bottom with a fork. Bake at the temperature indicated on packaging for 7 minutes or until very lightly browned, then remove from oven. Peel and quarter sweet potatoes. Place in pot and cover with at least two inches of water. Add baking soda to water, and boil potatoes for 25 to 30 minutes or until soft enough to mash. Drain and mash potatoes. While potatoes are still hot, mix in margarine. Add sugar, nutmeg, cinnamon, milk, egg, and vanilla, one at a time, mixing well to fully incorporate after each addition. Pour entire mixture into blender or food processor and blend for 20 to 30 seconds or until mixture has a smooth consistency. Pour filling into pie shell and bake at 400° for 40 minutes or until mixture is well set. Cool for at least one hour before slicing.

AISHA FORD

Aisha lives in the beautiful state of Missouri, a place that gets to experience all four seasons—sometimes in the same day. She likes to interpret these seasons as winter (also known as ice and snow), spring (allergies and thunderstorms), summer (blistering heat and humidity), and fall (more allergies and an occasional early snowstorm). Despite the weather and sinus-related challenges, Aisha thinks Missouri is a great place to live!

She's been an avid reader since she was a kid. One of the great things about reading is that when the weather isn't so great, reading is something she can do regardless of the conditions outdoors. Besides great novels, another one of her favorite things to read is the newspaper. She can also read a novel and watch TV at the same time, which is a good thing, because there are only so many hours in the day to enjoy the adventures of the characters of great books, reality shows, and cable news channels.

She went to college with the intent of majoring in English, but changed her mind and studied dance instead. Somehow, she ended up "write" back where she started—writing!

Aisha's hobbies include playing tennis (at least running

around on the court with a racket in her hand), knitting (sort of), and as of late, reading blogs.

She also enjoys cooking and will admit that creating edible items in a kitchen is one of her more accomplished hobbies, especially in the area of baking. She didn't go to culinary school (although she really thought about it, sometime in between majoring in English and studying ballet), so she watches cooking shows to feed her never-ending curiosity about the chemistry and how-tos of cooking. However, she has resigned herself to the fact that she will probably never be able to make those incredible melted-sugar sculptures or do anything productive with phyllo dough. If you have any phyllo dough tips, feel free to drop her a line at her Web site, www.aishaford.com!

A Recipe for Romance

by Vickie McDonough

Dedication

This story is dedicated to my dad, Harold Robinson, who graduated to heaven on February 11, 2005. Dad loved to feed people. No one ever visited our home and left without eating something.

We used to go over to my parents' home every Sunday after church for dinner when my boys were little. Along with his roast beef meal, Dad would cook fried okra because he knew we all loved it, but every week he'd burn it. One day I finally asked him about it, and he told me he thought he was supposed to cook it until the okra turned brown. We got a good laugh out of that for a long time. I miss you, Dad, but I imagine you're playing your trumpet in heaven and cooking up some mischief there.

Also to my Aunt Mildred, who always served me her delicious "pink stuff" whenever I visited her.

*But now that you have been set free from sin
and have become slaves to God,
the benefit you reap leads to holiness,
and the result is eternal life.
For the wages of sin is death,
but the gift of God is eternal life in Christ Jesus our Lord.*
ROMANS 6:22–23

Chapter 1

E-mail Glossary

<G>—big grin
BTW—by the way
JFTR—just for the record
LOL—laugh out loud
TTFN—ta-ta for now
TTYL—talk to you later
VBG—very big grin

April 6
E-mail from hammer_king:
Dear Miss Tannehill,

My name is Sergeant Scott Jantzen. I'm a friend of your brother Brent. He thought we might like e-mailing each other.

I met you once in high school. You were a sophomore when I was a senior. You probably don't remember, since there were so many students there.

I live in Tulsa and do construction work but am currently stationed in Kuwait with the Army National Guard.

Would you be interested in exchanging e-mails with a lonely soldier?

Scott Jantzen

P.S. I hope this doesn't get marked as spam.

Haley stared at the computer screen. Was this on the level? She'd never once heard her brother mention this Jantzen guy. If her high school yearbooks weren't at her parents' home in Tulsa, she'd have a peek at this Scott guy. Instead, she reached for the cordless phone lying beside her mouse pad and called Brent at the restaurant he owned and where she worked.

"Tannehills."

"Brent, tell me you didn't actually give my e-mail to some soldier."

"Sorry, guilty as charged."

"I can't believe you'd give my e-mail to a stranger." She glanced at the message again.

"He's not a stranger. He's a friend from high school."

Haley's grip tightened on the handset. "He's a stranger to me."

"Oh, lighten up, Sis. He's a nice guy."

"How come I never heard of him before?" She reached over, picked up her glass, and took a sip of water, hoping it would take the warbling out of her voice.

"He didn't start at our high school until the middle of his

junior year. I think he worked a lot after school, so he didn't attend ball games and other activities."

"So how do you know him then?"

"He was in a couple of my classes, and we were paired up on a physics project. C'mon, you know I wouldn't put some weirdo in contact with you. Give the guy a chance."

"I guess I could. It's not like he can ask me out since he's clear on the other side of the world."

"That's right, though it wouldn't hurt you to work a little less and go out once in a while."

"I can date after I pay off my student loans. I don't like being in debt."

"I'll give you a raise if you'll e-mail Scott."

Haley laughed at her brother's teasing tone. She could imagine him waggling his brown eyebrows. "Is he so desperate that you'd pay me to write him?"

"No, not desperate, just a bit homesick."

"All right, I'll do it. A raise would be nice, but I don't want to be paid for e-mailing Scott. Just consider it serving my country in some small way. So, is he cute?"

Her brother's loud laugh forced her to pull the phone away from her ear. "You're asking me if I think a guy is cute? Sorry, I'm not the best source for that particular information. Listen, gotta go. A deliveryman needs to be paid. See you later."

Haley hung up and glanced at the clock. Two hours until she had to be at Tannehills. Time enough to e-mail a lonely soldier and still grab a quick meal and a shower.

April 7

E-mail from out_to_lunch

Hey Scott,

   Haley Tannehill here. I talked to Brent, and he told me a little about you. I'd be happy to swap e-mails, though I admit, I'm not on my computer all that often, because I'm working long hours to pay off my college debts and to get experience so I can run my own restaurant one day.

   I used to live in Tulsa but am currently helping at Brent's restaurant in Oklahoma City. My parents still own a small café in Tulsa, and I get up that way about once a month.

Stay safe,
Haley

April 9

E-mail from hammer_king:

Haley,

   Glad you want to swap e-mails. Brent told me a lot about you. <G>

   Kuwait is an interesting country. I'm fortunate to be here instead of Iraq but am looking forward to coming home next month. But enough of the army talk.

   Where's your parents' café? I'd like to eat there sometime when I get back home next month.

Scott

A RECIPE FOR ROMANCE

April 12

E-mail from out_to_lunch:

Brent's been talking about me? Oh no! What did he say? I can only imagine.

Hey, isn't that a song title?

Guess what, I'm going to be a bridesmaid in a wedding next weekend. I've never done that before and hope I don't mess up. My dress is a pretty periwinkle color.

JFTR—you're not married, are you?

I bet you're really excited about coming home soon.

Haley

Haley's heart ricocheted in her chest. She almost wished she hadn't asked Scott if he was married. Surely Brent wouldn't have a married guy e-mail her. If he was already spoken for, she'd have to find a polite way to stop writing him.

She stretched and crossed the room, wondering what it was like to be a world away from your family. As she flipped down the bedcovers, she wondered if she'd hear back from Scott tomorrow.

April 15

E-mail from hammer_king:

LOL—No, I'm not married. What kind of guy do you take me for? And in case you're wondering, I'm not currently dating anyone, either. I'm strictly a one-woman man. I'm a Christian and believe in waiting for the one special gal God has for me.

Yes, I can't wait to get back home and see my family

and get back to working construction. I really like building things and seeing projects come together.

What do you like to do for fun? I like sports, video games, movies, just about anything outdoors. Have you ever gone rock climbing?

Scott

April 22
E-mail from out_to_lunch

Sorry I haven't written in a while. Been working lots.

You asked what I like to do. Read. Watch movies, especially romantic comedies. Gardening. Not much of a sports fan. My brother holds that title.

You mentioned you're a Christian. I used to go to church but got busy in college, studying and working, and finally quit going. I know I should start going again, but it's hard getting up on Sunday morning when I've worked until midnight or later on Saturday.

Do you still want to e-mail me since you know now that I'm not attending church?

Haley

April 23
E-mail from hammer_king:

Of course I still want to e-mail you. The first thing I do when I get back to my barracks is look to see if

I have a message from you.

I've been helping build a school that was bombed out a few years ago. Being outside so much helps with that manly tan, you know. 'Course, it does get hot in the summer—120 degrees in the shade.

You'd be amazed at how friendly the children are here. They're probably hoping for some American candy or other treats. Most of us share stuff with them if we have it. These kids have been through so much in their young lives.

BTW—You never did tell me the name of your parents' café or where it is.

Scott

April 22

E-mail from out_to_lunch

Arg! Are you going to force me to name my folks' café? It's just a little place down on Peoria. Even though the food is great, I hated going there as a kid—even worse was working there. We had to go in before school and roll hundreds of yeast rolls every morning. Then after school, we had to go back to the café until it closed. We did our homework during the afternoon lull, sitting in a booth. After I turned sixteen and got a car, I got a job at a movie theater so I didn't have to work at the café. I even talked my parents into having my high school graduation dinner at a different restaurant.

I feel bad about it now. But back then I was just a

spoiled teenager who only thought of myself.

If you only knew which café I was talking about, you'd understand how I feel.

You probably think I'm awful. I've grown up being embarrassed by my parents' old café. I'm grateful, though, that it helped fund my college education and provided my parents with a living.

Kids at school used to tease me about the café. But that's past history. Now I'm working at my brother's upscale restaurant called Tannehills. I hostess sometimes, work in the office, and even cook. As much as I despised my parents' place and hated working there, I guess the restaurant business is in my blood. My degree is in restaurant management.

TTFN
Haley

April 24
Email from hammer_king:
I noticed you avoided naming the café again. Am I going to have to drive the length of North and South Peoria, stopping at every café until I find yours?

That's interesting how you got a degree in restaurant management when you hated working in your parents' café so much. Didn't someone once say, "We love the things we hate?"

I bet you make a pretty hostess. Okay, I should probably confess that Brent e-mailed me a picture of you last week.

Maybe sometime when I get back I'll drive down to

*OK City and have dinner at Tannehills. I could sit there
and watch you hostessing all night, and you wouldn't even
know I was there. VBG + evil laugh. Bwahahahaha!*

Scott

Haley shivered. Could Scott really sit in Tannehills
without her recognizing him? His short military haircut would be a clue, but then lots of guys wore their
hair short these days. Still, Brent would know him.

Would she really mind meeting Scott in person?
This time the shiver that coursed through her was of
excitement, not fear. Time would tell. For now, she
couldn't resist teasing him a bit.

April 25
E-mail from out_to_lunch

*You wouldn't dare! I believe that's called stalking, and
it's illegal. Not to mention very creepy.*

*Guess I'll have to hit Brent up for a picture of you. Um...
let me guess...brown hair, blue eyes, tall. Am I close?*

Haley

April 27
E-mail from hammer_king:
Haley,

*I hope you know that I was joking about hiding out at
Tannehills. Besides, Brent would recognize me.*

Close, but no cigar on my description. Tall—six-two.

Blue eyes. But black hair—though there's not much of it at the moment. Thanks to Uncle Sam's military hairstyle. <G>

Okay, my turn. I know you have honey blond hair. Couldn't make out your eye color from the picture. I'm guessing brown like Brent's. No idea on your height, since you were sitting down.

If you're not going to tell me the name of your parents' café, at least give me a hint.

Hey, have you ever seen a picture of a camel spider?

Scott

May 1
E-mail from out_to_lunch

Sorry I haven't emailed lately. Some friends asked me on the spur of the moment to drive down to Dallas with them to go to that King Arthur dinner club. It was awesome! Wish you could have been there to see all the cool stuff. Knights dressed in armor fought with real swords and did jousting. One knight got knocked off his horse. Bet that hurt.

Yep, you're right about my eyes. They're dark brown. Nothing fancy—just plain old brown. Wanna swap? I always wanted blue eyes. Sigh.

And no thanks, I don't want to see a picture of a spider. Ewww!

Okay, a café clue, huh? How about flashing-neon cowboy boots?

TTYL,
Haley

May 2

E-mail from hammer_king:

Good to hear from you, Haley. I wondered if you were gone or if there was a glitch in the e-mail. Sometimes we have connection problems over here. I'm glad you had a good time. I've heard of that place in Dallas but haven't been there. Went to a similar place in Branson once— though it was a western show rather than medieval.

Would you believe I figured out where your parents place is? It's <u>the</u> Cowpoke Café, right? I've actually been there before and remembered those neon boots. A friend I worked with back home is a big-time cowboy, and he took me. You're right about the food. It was awesome! Mmm. . . gotta love home-cooked chicken-fried steak, mashed potatoes and gravy, homemade rolls. Mmmmmmm. Way better than MREs. Know what those are? Meals Ready to Eat. That's three lies in a row. LOL

I guess I can understand why the place would embarrass a teenager. It's a bit on the country side and needs a coat of paint. Yeehaw!

So, you wanna get together for dinner and a movie when I get back home? Only three more weeks.

Scott

Chapter 2

Haley Tannehill stared at the e-mail she'd just read. Her finger trembled over the left mouse button. Scott wanted to meet? In person?

And he'd be back home in only three weeks! Yikes!

She pressed her hand to her chest, willing her heartbeat to slow down. While she enjoyed e-mailing Scott, she wasn't sure if she was ready to meet face-to-face. She enjoyed having a friend with whom she could chat, without worrying about how she looked or if they were compatible. Meeting would take their relationship to a whole different level. Scott seemed like a nice guy, very polite, and had a great sense of humor. Brent would never have given him her e-mail address if he hadn't known he was a decent guy. Though her brother could be irritating at times, he was still protective of his little sister.

Unsure how to reply to Scott's question, Haley rose from her chair, crossed the room of her one-bedroom apartment, and flopped onto the bed. She had to admit she liked Scott and looked forward to coming home after a long evening at work and finding his e-mail. It was almost as if someone were waiting at home for her.

She reached over to her nightstand and picked up the picture of Scott that Brent had e-mailed to her and she'd printed off. His brown army T-shirt stretched nicely over the muscles he'd gotten from working in construction. Loose-fitting camouflage pants hid his long legs. A garrison cap covered his hair, which he'd said was black. His eyes squinted in a narrow line, probably from the glare of the sun.

Haley sighed. She'd always thought squinty eyes looked manly. The cowboys in the shows she and her brother had watched when they were kids had eyes like that.

Her gaze was drawn to Scott's smile. His white teeth showed up well against his "manly tan," as he'd put it. So how come a guy this good-looking and so nice wasn't married? There had to be a story there somewhere.

Haley yawned and glanced at the clock. While she enjoyed hostessing at Tannehills, being on her feet for hours and hours made them ache. She rubbed her toes and looked up as Gidget, her white cat, sauntered in and rubbed against the door frame. The cat stretched her legs out in front of her, yawned, and then hopped onto the bed, where she normally slept.

Gidget moseyed over and nudged up against her. Grinning, Haley scooped up the cat and hugged her. She scratched Gidget's head and looked at Scott's picture again. It had been a long time since she had dated, or had a guy friend, for that matter. She didn't plan to go back to Tulsa for a while, so that would give her more time to get to know Scott long distance before a meeting could take place. Deep in her heart, she thought maybe she'd like to take a chance with him. Time would tell.

Yawning again, Haley laid Scott's picture back on her nightstand and turned off the lamp. She set Gidget down, then fluffed her pillow and scooted under the sheets.

It would be nice to have a guy to hang around with sometimes. She thought about the few times she'd dated in college, but she'd been too focused on her studies to get serious with anyone. She'd pretty much isolated herself by working such long hours now—but she *was* chipping away at her school debts. Normally she was too busy to think about being lonely, but she realized that she really was.

"So what do you think, Gidget? Do I take a chance on a handsome soldier?"

A loud *purr* was all the response she got.

Haley allowed her body to relax. Morning would come too soon. And she'd have to answer Scott's e-mail. Maybe she'd quiz Brent again and see just how well he really knew Scott before she agreed to meet.

She slid her hand under her pillow and pulled it snug against her head. As she drifted off into a fog of sleep, a blaring noise suddenly jarred her back. It took her a moment to realize the phone was ringing. Her hand groped in the dark, finally finding the cordless phone.

"Hello?"

"Hi, honey. It's Mom."

Haley's gaze darted to the alarm clock on her nightstand. It was after eleven thirty. Her mother never called this late.

"Is something wrong, Mom? Is Daddy okay?"

"Your dad is fine. Nothing's wrong. It's just that I have some exciting news that I *had* to share. I figured you'd still be up since you work late, and I just couldn't sleep until I told you."

Haley scooted up, rearranged her pillow, and then leaned against it. "What's so exciting that it couldn't wait 'til morning?"

"You'll be so proud of us. Your dad and I have decided to quit working and move to a retirement village out on Grand Lake. Your grandmother left your father enough money when she passed that we no longer need to work so hard. Can you believe it?"

Haley's heart jolted. No, she didn't believe her parents would ever quit working at the café, even though they'd recently received a sizeable inheritance. A flicker of excitement ignited a kindling of hope. If her parents were retiring, that meant they'd be selling the Cowpoke Café! She'd finally be rid of her nemesis, once and for all. Yes! She wanted to shout *yahoo*!

"Haley, did you hear me?"

She shook herself out of her cloud of stunned delight. "That's wonderful, Mom. You and Daddy have worked so hard all these years, you deserve to relax and have some fun. So are you going to sell the house *and* the café?"

"Oh no, we thought you'd want to live in the house. Brent doesn't need it since he already has a home in Oklahoma City. We'll leave it in our name, but you can stay there as long as you like."

Confused, Haley reached out and petted her cat. "How can

I work for Brent and live in Tulsa? Oklahoma City is too far away to commute."

"I wasn't finished, sweetie. There's more. Are you sitting down?"

A knot of pending doom suddenly twisted in Haley's stomach. "Yes, I'm sitting."

"Since Brent is tied up with Tannehills, we didn't see any reason to leave him the café, so we're giving it to you. You'll finally be able to manage your own restaurant. Isn't that great?"

A Titanic moment. That's all this could be. Haley pinched herself to make sure she wasn't having a nightmare.

"Haley? Are you still there? Did I shock you to death?"

"Yeah, Mom, it's a shocker all right." Haley's heart pounded, and sweat broke out on her forehead.

"Aren't you excited? You'll finally have your own restaurant to run and won't have to work for Brent any more."

Numb. Stunned. Bewildered. Yes, but excited wasn't on the list. "I'm speechless."

"I knew you'd be thrilled. Can you believe it?" She could hear her mother's smile in her voice.

"No. . .no. . .I can't quite grasp it yet." A cloud of dread settled around her as she thought of whiling away her life, making thousands of homemade rolls until she was old and gray. Her eyes stung with unshed tears, and she reached over and pulled Gidget onto her lap, needing the closeness of her friend.

"Well, I'm glad you're happy about it. Your dad had his doubts."

How could her mother be so clueless? Had she been so busy

working all those years that she'd never noticed how much her daughter hated being at the café?

"I can't wait to get moved in at the lake. You'll have to come up and go boating with us. The retirement center has several boats the members can use."

For the life of her, Haley couldn't imagine her landlubber, workaholic parents riding around in a boat. Had they gone crazy? Were they having a midlife crisis?

"Well, good night, dear. You must be very tired or just shocked at your good fortune. I love you. Call your dad tomorrow so you and he can work out the details and transfer ownership of the café. I'll talk to you in a day or two."

Haley hung up. Right! Shocked didn't begin to explain how she felt. She curled onto her side and cuddled up with Gidget. Tears burned her eyes and made her throat ache.

How could she have ended up owner of the café she had despised all of her life?

⟡

Haley stood outside the Cowpoke Café and stared at the façade. For some reason, it didn't look as bad as she'd remembered. The country blue and tan paint job looked only a month or two old. When had that happened? Even the parking lot looked better with its dark black coat of new tar and freshly painted white lines to mark the parking slots. Her parents must have decided to fix up the café for her.

She'd wrestled for a week, hoping and struggling for a way out. But gradually, a spark of excitement took hold. It had taken

Brent another week to find two new people to do all the work she had done. Now she was here, and her parents had already moved to the lake. They had only come back this week to finish the paperwork.

Staring across the street, she realized even the grocery store had been spiffed up on the outside. This part of midtown Tulsa had recently gone through a renovation, and the whole area looked fresh and alive. New businesses had replaced older ones, and down the road a few blocks, new buildings were being constructed.

If she truly owned the café, there was no reason she couldn't renovate it and turn it into a trendy deli with a salad bar. Anticipation tickled her stomach. Yes, she could do this. It would be fun. No more neon cowboy boots or yellowed menu covers. No more signed Hank Williams photos in cheap gold frames.

She hoisted her purse strap over her shoulder and stepped inside. The scent of home-cooked rolls still lingered in the air and made her stomach growl. Familiar knotty-pine walls still held the crooked photos of famous country music stars and local celebrities who had eaten there over the years. The quietness of the empty café sent a wave of melancholy coursing through her. Though she hadn't cared much for the café, seeing it die made her sadder than she'd expected. Her parents had put more than thirty years of hard work into this place.

Well, now it was time for the Cowpoke Café to move into the twenty-first century.

"Haley!" Her mother stepped through the swinging doors

that separated the dining area from the kitchen. "It's about time you got here."

"I had to arrange for someone to keep Gidget, and Brent took forever to hire a replacement for me." Haley accepted her mom's hug, noting a spark in her eyes that she hadn't seen lately. Retiring would be good for her.

"Why didn't you bring that fat cat with you? You're moving into the house."

Haley held up her hand. "We'll see, Mom. I haven't made that decision yet. I think it would be better for you and Dad to sell the house and get the money. It's too big for one person."

"Well, talk to your dad about it. He just wants to make sure you're provided for."

Haley chuckled. "I'm twenty-three, Mom. Time I provided for myself."

Her mother shook her head. "You always were so independent. What you need is a good man."

Ignoring her mother's last comment, Haley glanced at the flashing-neon cowboy boots hanging on the inside of the front window. She was so anxious to be rid of them, she felt like rubbing her palms together in glee. "I think y'all should take the boots with you. Dad would miss them too much. You could use them on your porch for a night-light."

Pam Tannehill's hand flew up to her chest. "Oh no. They need to stay here. They're the icon of the Cowpoke Café."

Haley laid her hand on her mom's arm. "Mom, I have big plans for this place, and they don't include those neon boots or all the pictures. You can have them. Since they're all autographed, you could probably sell them for a tidy sum on eBay. I'm planning to gut this place and start over. No more knotty-pine walls, either."

Her mother gasped and stared at her, eyes wide. "No! You can't change a thing. It would kill your father."

Anxiety charged up Haley's spine. "Mom, surely you can't expect me to leave everything the same. This place is so run-down. I really don't think Dad would care. Where is he, anyway?"

Her mother glanced toward the kitchen and nodded her head in that direction. She leaned closer. "I didn't want to tell you on the phone, but your father isn't well."

The hairs on Haley's arms stood up, and her heart skipped a beat. "W—what's wrong with him?" A wave of guilt washed over her. Why hadn't she visited them more often?

Tears glimmered in her mother's brown eyes. "He has a heart condition. The doctor believes it can be treated with medicines, but Dad needs to relax more and not work like he has been. That's why we decided to retire even though we're not really retirement age. So you can see why he couldn't handle the stress of you redoing the restaurant he loves so much."

All her hopes and dreams sank like a ship going down for that last time. Her father wasn't well, and she would have to run the café just as it was. She couldn't refuse to accept her parents' gift. That might upset her father. And just how sick was he?

"Pam?" Robert Tannehill moseyed through the swinging

doors, and a grin lit his face when he saw her. "Howdy, sweetheart. Long time no see."

Tears blurred her eyes at the thought of never seeing him again. She threw herself in his arms. "Oh, Daddy."

Chapter 3

Scott stepped out of his truck and stared at the Cowpoke Café, certain that it had been painted recently. The outside looked much better than he remembered.

"So this is the place you were so anxious to eat at? Don't look all that great to me." Chip scratched his head and slammed his car door.

"Trust me," Scott glanced at his army buddy who'd agreed to meet him for lunch, "you haven't eaten anything as good as the food here since before you went to Kuwait."

"Aw, I don't know 'bout that. My mom's meatloaf sure was good. Had it the night we got back in town." Chip ambled around the front of his blue Cavalier. "Don't look like it's open to me."

Scott figured his friend was right since there weren't any other cars in the lot. He walked to the front door and found it locked. Ever since he started e-mailing Haley and learned about her Cowpoke Café connection, he'd had a hankering to eat at her parents' restaurant again. The sign on the door said the place was closed Sundays and Mondays. He peeked inside, saddened to see it empty.

Disappointed, he turned to face Chip. "You're right. They aren't open on Sundays—or Monday, for that matter. Where to now?"

"Doesn't matter to me. One thing's good as another, just so we don't have to eat MREs." Chip's exaggerated shudder made Scott smile.

"You want to follow me, and I'll stop somewhere?"

"Sure. Okay."

They headed to their vehicles. The moment Scott reached his pickup truck, a blue Volkswagen Beetle whipped into the parking lot. His heart skittered. The driver resembled the picture of Haley that Brent had sent him, but he thought she was still in Oklahoma City. At least that's where she was when he received her last e-mail before he'd returned home from Kuwait. Since he'd been back, he hadn't heard from her. Intrigued, he watched the Bug pull up right in front of the door.

A pair of sandal-clad feet—attached to trim, tan ankles—appeared below the open door. A women with honey blond hair stood and slammed the car door.

Chip whistled through his teeth.

Scott's pulse revved up a notch. Stylish sunglasses blocked the woman's eyes from view, but Scott was certain they were brown. He wiped his palms on his tan pants and cleared his throat. His heart pounded like it had right before his unit left on a mission. This must be Haley. She looked so different from their high school days. Different in a very nice way.

She whipped around to face them. "Sorry, guys, we're always closed on Sundays. And we'll be closed this whole week, because I'm in the middle of a major clean-up." Haley slipped her glasses up onto that golden mass of hair and smiled. She started to turn away, then stopped and stared at him. Slowly, her mouth dropped open, and her dark eyes widened.

Scott couldn't help grinning. *Yes!* She'd recognized him.

"Scott?"

"You know this babe?" Chip's brows lifted in surprise. "You've been holding out on your ole buddy."

Scott nodded and stared.

Haley walked toward them, a soft smile on her lips.

He wasn't prepared to see her today, not like this. At least he was dressed decently, having just come from church. He ran his hand over the prickles of his military haircut. What should he say? Talking to a woman via e-mail was different than in person. He took a step forward and held out his hand in greeting.

Haley started to shake his hand but hesitated. "You *are* Scott Jantzen, right?"

"No, that would be me," Chip teased. "You don't want him, honey. He's much too quiet. You want a tough, talkative soldier like me." Chip thumped his chest.

Haley's questioning gaze darted to Chip and back.

"Don't listen to him. He's just jealous because I know you and he doesn't. And yes, I'm Scott."

A slow smile curved her lips. Her eyes were such a dark brown he could hardly make out her pupils. She stepped closer, and this time she stuck out her hand. "Nice to finally meet you in person."

He reached out and grasped her palm, hoping she wouldn't notice his was damp. "Yeah, uh. . .same here." Great! Here he was staring into the eyes of the woman he'd longed to meet again for years, and he was tongue-tied. Realizing he still held her hand, he suddenly let go.

"So when did you get home?" Haley's gaze ping-ponged from him to Chip and back.

"Three days ago."

"And you came to eat at the café already?"

"He's been filling my ears with how good the food is here, so I had to try it." Chip's hands moved animatedly as he spoke.

"Really?" Haley's thick lashes flew up, and her golden brows lifted. A soft giggle slipped past her slightly full lips. "Well, sorry. You'll have to wait till next week."

"So, what are you doing here?" Scott asked. "I thought you were in Oklahoma City."

Haley rolled her eyes. "It's a long story—too long to tell standing out here in the hot sun. You want to come in and have a Coke?"

Scott glanced at Chip, hoping his buddy wouldn't mind. He didn't want to miss this chance to talk with Haley face-to-face, even though he was more nervous than when he'd endured his first sandstorm overseas.

"Listen, I have some things to do this afternoon, so why don't I take a rain check on that lunch. You need to visit with this babe while she's still willing to chat with you." Chip grinned and tipped an imaginary hat at Haley. "By the way, I'm Chip Cooper. Scott and I are in the same National Guard unit."

Haley smiled. "Nice to meet you."

"Same here. See you around." Chip sauntered back to his car.

Scott almost wished his buddy had stayed. Conversation was never a problem when Chip was around. Anxiety—or maybe just hunger—churned in Scott's stomach.

"You still want to come in?" Haley peeked at him, then watched Chip's car slip out of the lot and merge into the traffic onto South Peoria.

"Sure. If you don't mind."

"No, it's fine."

She pivoted so fast, her skirt swished around her shapely legs. He couldn't help watching her stroll toward the door. It reminded him of the first time he saw her, way back in high school. She'd been talking with Brent and then swirled around and walked down the long hallway, chatting with a girlfriend. He'd never had the guts to talk to her back then. His unrequited crush had lasted a long time—until after he'd graduated.

Shaking himself, he followed Haley into the dim café and back to the kitchen, where she flipped on a light switch. The fluorescent bulbs flickered and buzzed, then finally decided to light up. Professional stainless-steel appliances glimmered as if they'd just been polished.

"Don't look too hard. I'm only halfway done cleaning." Haley grabbed two clear plastic cups and filled them with ice from a machine.

She handed one to him, and he tried to ignore the way his fingers tingled when they touched hers.

She pointed to the soda-pop fountain. "Help yourself."

As he stepped past her, his stomach gurgled loud enough he could hear. Mortified, he rammed his cup under the root-beer sign, hoping the swooshing soda pop would mask the noise. With his cup full and foaming at the top, he turned to face Haley.

A wide smile brightened her face. "Maybe I should fix you something to eat."

Busted. He could feel his cheeks getting warm. "Uh. . .no, that isn't necessary."

She giggled again and waved a hand in the air. "No problem. I'm hungry, too."

Scott sighed. This wasn't at all how he'd planned for their first meeting to go. She'd probably never want to see him again after today.

⚜

Haley opened a loaf of bread, then grabbed a spatula from a drawer, as she tried to analyze her feelings. Scott had surprised her. She knew he was on his way home from Iraq, because they'd had to quit e-mailing each other for a time. But why hadn't he e-mailed since he returned home? She turned to face him, hoping to mask her emotions. "Mayo or mustard?"

"Mayo."

"Ham, turkey, or roast beef."

"Mmmm, roast beef. I can't seem to get enough beef since

coming home." Scott smiled and looked around the room. "Can I help?"

"No, I can get it." Haley grinned. She enjoyed watching his mannerisms and how he moved, after only talking via e-mail for so long. He was really tall, and no picture could do those deep blue eyes justice. After taking a breath to calm her jittery nerves, she laid the bread on the shiny stainless-steel countertop and spread mayo on all four slices. Okay, she had to admit she was glad to finally meet Scott face-to-face, but she only wished it had been on her own terms.

She slapped some meat onto both sandwiches and added some leaf lettuce. "Cheese? Tomatoes?" she asked, glancing over her shoulders.

He shook his head, looking a bit like a lost puppy. Haley bit back a smile as she turned around. Chip was right; Scott *was* awfully quiet. She added chips and a pickle to both plates, then went into the dining area, with him following.

"You don't mind if I leave the lights off, do you? I wouldn't want folks to think we're open." He shook his head. She set the plates down and slid onto the faded-aqua vinyl seat, scraping her calf on a sharp vinyl tear. *Ow.* She should have stopped by the house and put on some jeans before coming here.

Oh, how she wished she could update this whole place. For now, a little duct tape would have to do on the seat. Too bad duct tape didn't come in a twenty-year-old teal color.

"Looks good. Thanks." Scott slid into the seat across from her and looked up. "Mind if I pray before we eat?"

She shook her head, feeling a shaft of guilt for not regularly asking God's blessing over her meals. Her heart skipped a beat when Scott slid his hand across the table.

"We hold hands at home when we pray."

No question or demand, just a fact, although his ears did look a bit redder than they had been. Haley slipped her hand into his, marveling in its warm, calloused feel, then closed her eyes.

"Father, we thank You for this food and the hands that prepared it. Thank You for allowing Haley and me to finally meet in person. Bless us this day. Amen."

They both took a bite of their sandwich and chewed for a moment. Haley wondered how Scott could be so chatty via e-mail but so quiet in person.

"So, uh. . .where are your parents? Home, I guess?—since it's Sunday." His eyes darted everywhere except at her.

Haley pressed her lips together to keep from smiling. How could a big, tough soldier/construction worker be so shy? "Well, I told you that was a long story. About three weeks ago, I got a call from Mom telling me they'd decided to retire. . . ."

When she finished the story, Scott looked around and said, "Wow, I don't know whether to say congratulations or sorry."

"Both would probably fit. I think I'm still in a state of shock." She laid down her half-eaten sandwich and looked up. "At first, I was actually angry that they'd saddle me with this place. You know how I feel about it."

He nodded and gave her a sympathetic grin.

"But then I got to thinking about it. This part of town is being revitalized. Maybe I could be a part of that by updating this place and turning it into a deli with a salad bar."

"But your Mom put a stop to that, huh?"

"Yeah. Big-time."

"They really won't let you fix up the place at all? Seems like it would help business to have the place looking fresh instead of run-down." His gaze darted up, as if he'd said something that might offend her.

"You'd think so. I guess they were so caught up in the every-day work that they couldn't see the café the way I do. Having been away for a while, I notice the uglies more. She looked up at the stained-ceiling tiles. One of the light fixtures hung at a precarious angle, and cobwebs danced on the breeze from the air conditioner.

"After talking with Mom, I didn't think they'd let me make *any* changes." Haley took a sip of her soda. "But I chatted with my dad later, and he doesn't mind if I paint and do minor repairs. He just doesn't want me to 'cut the heart out of the place,' as he said it."

"Too bad—I mean, I know how much you disliked this place." He took a swig of his root beer and bit his pickle in two. "Mmm. . .good pickles."

What was that old saying? The way to a man's heart was through his stomach? She paused. Did she really hope to make her way into Scott's heart?

She picked up her sandwich and glanced at him as she took a bite. He was easy on the eyes and would look even bet-ter once his dark shadow of hair grew longer. His deep blue eyes reminded her of sapphires, and she'd caught the flash of a dimple in his right cheek when he smiled earlier.

"What?" He held his sandwich away from himself and looked down at his shirt.

"I'll get some more pickles. I like them, too." She eased out of her seat and hurried to the kitchen, mortified that he'd caught her staring. *Yikes!*

She grabbed a bowl and put several pickle spears in it, then slowly made her way back. "Ummm. . .let me top off your drink." Without giving him a chance to respond, she set down the bowl, grabbed his cup, and hurried to the kitchen again. Maybe by the time she returned, her cheeks wouldn't be burning.

When she sat back down, Scott had finished off his sandwich and was munching another pickle. "You know, there's a lot you could do here, without tearing the heart out."

She looked around, trying to see the place from his eyes. "I thought I'd paint after I finish cleaning. And one thing for sure, those faded-yellow menu covers have to go. I've been toying with the idea of using paper menus, but they get dirty so fast. The good thing, though, is you can change them whenever you want—just print off some new ones."

Okay, she was rambling.

He stared at her, eyes wide and dark brows lifted. "You don't mean to paint the knotty pine, do you?"

Well, she'd considered it. If she could get away with it. "It's all scratched and the shine has come off in places. Besides, if I did paint the walls, it would brighten up this whole area."

"Yeah, but that's the real deal. It would cost big bucks to put up a knotty-pine wall now." He walked across the room and ran his hand over the wall. "I can sand down most of these scratches and refinish the wood. As for the lighting, I don't remember it being too dark, but you could get some of those stylish drop-down lights if you think you need them."

Well, she'd learned one thing: If she wanted Scott to talk, all she had to do was talk shop. He moseyed around the room with his hands in his back pockets, looking nice, dressed in that hunter green polo shirt and tan khakis.

"I could replace those broken-ceiling tiles and paint them, and do whatever other repairs you need." He turned and looked at her.

She hadn't expected him to offer his help. She blinked. "I—wouldn't you rather be relaxing or doing something fun? I mean you just got back home."

He shook his head. "I like to keep busy. 'Course, I wouldn't mind doing something fun, too, if you came along."

Chapter 4

Did he just ask Haley for a date? Scott wondered if that would scare her off. He'd already offered to help her fix up the café. Was he pushing too hard?

After eating across the table from her for half an hour, he knew his old high-school crush had never fully gone away.

"I wouldn't mind doing something sometime. But what's your idea of fun?" She stood and walked across the dining area toward where he'd been examining the knotty pine, her hair swishing with each step.

He could think of lots of fun things to do with her, like walking around a lake and holding hands, touching her hair, which had to be soft and silky, or maybe kissing her— "I—uh. . .like sports, movies, getting together with friends. The normal stuff." He willed his pulse to slow down. He didn't want to push her away because of his strong desire to be with her.

"Yeah, me, too. Except for maybe the sports stuff. I never was too good at those. Plus, I never got a chance to play sports since I had to be here each afternoon." She grabbed the plates off the table and headed toward the kitchen.

He reached for the cups and followed.

"You're lucky you caught me here. I just stopped by on my way home from church to grab a sandwich, since my groceries supplies are low at home. It's not like I could do any work dressed like this." The plates clinked when she set them in the metal sink.

He put the cups beside the plates and turned, leaning back against the sink. "You look nice."

An embarrassed smile tilted her lips. "Thanks. I went to church because you made me realize I needed to stop making excuses for not attending."

His chest swelled with happiness. Brent had told him Haley had drifted away from church while in college. One of the reasons Scott had contacted her was to try to help her find her way back to God. And nothing serious could come of their friendship unless Haley made a commitment to the Lord. That was important to him. He couldn't see himself with anyone who didn't feel the same way about it.

"I'm happy to hear you went to church. Life's hard enough, even *with* God on our side. I'd hate to see you go it alone."

"Yeah, you're right. I'm learning that. Maybe if I'd stayed in church my folks wouldn't have dumped this place on me. You think God would punish me like that?" Haley shrugged, then raised a hand when Scott started to speak. "Sorry. I didn't mean that. I have to believe there's a plus side to owning the café. My parents made a good living at it, though they worked all the time. I just don't want my whole life tied up here."

"It's hard to see the positive when you're in the middle of the storm."

Haley nodded. She wet a rag, returned to the dining area, and washed off their table, then came back into the kitchen.

Scott chuckled. "I bet you've washed a few tables in your day."

"Oh! If I only had a nickel for each one." Haley smiled and waggled her eyebrows.

Her wide grin took his breath away. For years, he'd longed to have that smile turned his way—and now it was. *I'm a goner*.

"So, how much more cleaning do you have to do? I have the next week off. Maybe I could help."

She crossed her arms and walked back into the dining room, studying the area. "I still need to clean out the refrigerator and the supply room. After that, we can paint the kitchen, then start in here." She whirled around like a dancer. "How are your painting skills?"

He flexed a muscle and grinned. "Hey, I'm a carpenter, remember? And I also wield a mean hammer."

"Ah, so that's how you got your e-mail name? You're the hammer king?"

"That's right. And don't you forget it." He put his hands on his hips and puffed out his chest.

Haley grinned. "So, macho man, how about I fix breakfast tomorrow in exchange for some elbow grease?"

"It's a date." He held out his hand to shake on the deal, but he wasn't prepared for the jolt of electricity that bolted up his arm when Haley grasped his hand.

KISS THE ~~COOK~~ *Bride*

Lord, help me keep things in perspective. Make it clear to me if You want me to just be a friend to Haley. And give me the grace to obey if that's Your desire.

⬥

Monday morning, Haley rolled up her sleeves, ready to tackle cleaning out the industrial refrigerator as soon as she and Scott had breakfast. She dragged a huge trash can over and put in a new liner, then washed her hands.

She pulled some bacon and four eggs out of the fridge and checked on the biscuits already baking. A knock on the front door reverberated in the empty dining room. Her heart jumped, not from fear, but from the excitement of seeing Scott again. What was it about him? She actually liked the guy. He was so different from the self-centered boys who'd tried to snag her interest in college. And why couldn't she remember him from high school? If he'd been Brent's friend, then she probably would have met him at some point. She needed to drag out her old yearbook and look him up. Maybe that would jog her memory.

Of course as a teen, she was in her own little world, focused on her friends and getting her own way. She shuddered at the memory of her bad attitude. Those guys in college had nothing on her. *I sure hope I'm not that way anymore.*

As she walked through the dining room, she saw Scott's tall form outside, and her stomach tingled. Was there such a thing as love at second sight?

Being somewhat tall herself, she'd always hoped to marry a guy who was over six feet.

Whoa! Love? Marriage? Where had those thoughts come from?

She shook her head, trying to remember the last time she'd thought about getting married. Probably several months back when she'd gotten an e-mail from Angel Morgan, telling her she had gotten married. She was excited for her friend, but knew it would change the dynamics of their group when they met again at the National Restaurateurs' Convention in Dallas next year. At least the other two friends she'd met when she'd gotten stuck in an elevator at last year's convention were still unattached.

As she neared the door, she noticed a cardboard sign Scott held up against his chest. WILL WORK FOR FOOD. She couldn't help laughing. After flipping the dead bolt, she pulled the door open. "Hey."

"Mornin'." A shy smile graced his lips, and he jiggled the sign.

"I saw it." Haley took it from him, grinning. "Made me laugh. You're so silly."

"That's what my friends tell me." He stepped across the threshold and shoved his hands in his pockets. "I, uh. . .tend to be shy until you get to know me—in case you hadn't noticed."

"Well, I'm not shy." She looped her arm through his, pulled him out of the entryway, and then locked the door. "C'mon. The biscuits are almost ready, and we need to finish cooking the rest of the food."

"Mmm. . .smells good. Do you ever get tired of smelling food cooking?"

She waved her free hand in the air, trying to ignore how nice *he* smelled and how good it felt to hang onto his arm. "After awhile you don't even notice. I guess it's the same with any job. Seems to me the noise of working construction would drive someone batty."

Scott's chest vibrated against her arm as he chuckled. "I guess you're right. That makes sense. 'Course, earplugs do help on occasion, when things get really noisy."

Reluctantly, she released his arm as they moved into the kitchen area. "Can you crack eggs?"

"Duh! Who can't? I just can't guarantee I'll get them in the pan."

Smiling, she pulled a small glass bowl from the cabinet overhead and set it on the counter. "Crack them in this, one at a time. It's easier to get the shells out, plus if you get a bad egg, it doesn't ruin the whole batch."

"Smart idea. D'you ever actually get a bad egg?"

He picked one up and gently cracked it against the side of the bowl, barely making a dent in the shell. She held back a smile. How could such a macho guy be so gentle?

"Uh. . .yeah, had one egg that had a dead chick in it. Ewww! Talk about a shock!"

"Sounds kind of gross."

"It was. Yuck! I don't like to think about it. I didn't eat eggs for two years after that." She shuddered at the memory.

He smacked the egg again, this time getting it in the bowl. He grinned like he'd succeeded at something huge.

"Do you cook at home?"

His gaze darted in her direction, and his ears turned red. "I'm embarrassed to say I'm currently living with my folks. I got rid of my apartment when I went to Kuwait, but I plan to get another one soon. My mom or the maid does pretty much all the cooking."

"You have a maid? How nice is that?" She stifled a stab of envy. Her life would have been *so* much easier if they'd had a maid. And her parents probably could have afforded one, but her mother would never have let a stranger clean her home. Most times their house was a fairly clean but cluttered mess. There wasn't time to do much. Everyone was so tired when they got home from the café they crashed until bedtime, taking the opportunity to relax.

"I guess having a maid is okay. I don't really like her cleaning my room, so I do it myself—except the bathroom."

Haley sighed. Was this guy not the greatest thing since microwave ovens?

"So what kind of work do your parents do?"

His gaze darted sideways again; then he picked up another egg. "Dad owns a construction company, but he does other things, too."

Haley turned on the fire and laid the bacon strips in the skillet. She picked up a pancake turner and looked at him. "You work for your dad?"

Scott nodded. "But he made me start at the bottom. He believes people in management need to know how to do all aspects of the business."

"How long have you worked for him?"

"Ever since I was fifteen. I worked summers and sometimes on Saturday."

The bacon sizzled, and as the edges puffed up, she pressed them down with a spatula. She grabbed a smaller skillet, dabbed a little butter into it, and set it on the stove. "That's for the eggs. Did you go to college?"

He dumped the eggs into the pan and nodded. "Two years at the community college and one at OSU–Tulsa, studying business. I would have finished by now, but we got deployed for a year. I'll go back next semester."

Haley enjoyed their easy camaraderie. She'd never done anything this domestic with the few guys she dated. For one, she didn't trust them enough to bring them home. Scott was different. Comfortable, like an old pair of sweats. She could get used to this.

While he scrambled the eggs, she removed the bacon and whipped up some gravy. Her mouth watered at the thought of the cholesterol-laden meal. *Enjoy today. Diet tomorrow.*

After breakfast, they tackled the huge refrigerator. Scott had offered to start sanding the knotty pine, but she wanted to work together and vetoed his suggestion.

"We'll never get this bleach smell off our hands." She sniffed her fist and grimaced.

"It'll wash off. The fridge sure looks better."

"Yeah. And empty. I've got to inventory everything and place orders, so I'll have the supplies I need for when I reopen next Tuesday."

Scott straightened and pressed his fist into the small of his back. Obviously, bending over all morning made his back ache as much as hers did.

"Where are the people who work here? How come they aren't helping you?"

She dumped the dirty water down the drain and set the bucket in the closet. "Dad wanted them to have a break. He gave them the choice of helping me at full pay or taking the week off at half pay."

"Guess they all took the easy way out, huh? A vacation at half pay's better than none." He gave her a sympathetic grin. "Well, I'm glad I don't have to share you with them."

Haley's heart skipped a beat. She was glad to have Scott all to herself, too, but she couldn't tell him that.

Chapter 5

On Friday afternoon, Haley sat down in one of the booths, ready for a break. Scott had worked by her side every day this week so far, and she was ahead of schedule. "You know, if you hadn't helped me, I'm sure I wouldn't have been done in time to reopen on Tuesday."

Scott swiped his screwdriver through the air in a wave of dismissal. "Glad to do it."

Haley smiled and looked through the doorway into the kitchen. They'd done far more than she had planned. The kitchen shimmered in its new coat of pale yellow. All the appliances gleamed, the refrigerator was cleaned, stocked, and ready to go.

She watched Scott screw in the last of the new drop-down lights. The pendant lights with their multicolored globes added subtle illumination and character over the booths lining the inner walls. She unwrapped the last globe and crossed the room to hand it to him. "You were right about these lights. It's not nearly so dark in here. And they're so colorful and cute!"

He screwed in the bulb and then attached the globe. She flipped the light switch, and a soft dark blue, much like the color of Scott's eyes, glowed through it. All around her, mellow red, green, yellow, and blue pendant lights hung at different levels in groups of two or three over the tables along the wall.

He stepped down off the booth seat and turned to face her. "Do you think your parents will be okay with this?" He swung his hand toward the lights.

She shrugged. "I hope so. I, for one, love it."

"What now?"

Haley couldn't help smiling. "We're done! And here I thought I'd have to work all weekend to get finished on time. How can I ever thank you?"

His eyes flashed, as if he knew the answer; then he glanced down at her lips. Tingles of excitement charged through her body at his nearness. Last night she'd dreamed of kissing Scott, but so far, he'd done nothing physical like holding her hand, other than in play when he'd nudged her hip with his or tickled her once.

She licked her lips, and his gaze flew up to meet hers. For a long time, she lost herself in his stare. Heart pounding, she stepped closer, doubting he'd have the nerve to make the first move. His beautiful eyes sparked with something intriguing, and he leaned forward.

Haley moved closer and could feel his warm breath on her lips. One more inch.

A loud pounding on the door made them both jump back.

Haley shook off her disappointment and went to let the mailman in. Rats. She'd come *so* close.

"Howdy, Miss Tannehill." Ronn, her regular mail carrier stepped inside and looked around. "Hey, I like what you've done here. Looks great."

"Thanks. We're hoping people will think it's an improvement." She looked around the room but purposely avoided looking at Scott. Could anything be more awkward than a near-kiss?

Ronn handed her some letters and a padded-manila envelope. "I'll have to stop in for lunch soon. When do you reopen?"

"Next Tuesday, but Wednesday is fried chicken day. If I remember, that's your favorite."

Ronn grinned and nodded. "Yep. I've got a hankerin' for some Cowpoke Café's crispy chicken. Oh, man, you're making my mouth water."

Haley chuckled and waved good-bye as he left. She laid the envelopes on the counter and stared at the package. "It's from Monica."

"Isn't she one of the women you met at that convention you went to in Dallas?"

Curious, she nodded and ripped off the end of the envelope. Some kind of cloth was folded up inside. She pulled it out and a paper fluttered to the floor.

Scott crossed the room, picked up the paper, and handed it to her.

Haley flipped it open and began reading the note out loud.

Dear Haley,

Remember this apron? Angel bought it at the convention, and we all tried to steal it from her. Angel wore it, and now she's married. And guess what! Remember me telling you about Gil? Well, he's back in my life—and we're getting married! No date set, but it will be soon. I've waited too long for him already.

I'm passing the apron on to you. Maybe you can keep it awhile and then share it with Allison. I hope you enjoy it as much as I have. Every time I wore it, Gil tried to steal a kiss. Not that I minded, you know.

Anyway, hope you enjoy this. Maybe—

Haley stopped reading and glanced at Scott, then finished the rest of the note silently.

—love will come your way soon. Wouldn't that be awesome!

Monica Ryan—soon to be Monica Butler

Haley gulped, wishing she'd chosen to read the whole letter to herself. Would Scott think she was rude because she didn't read the rest of it out loud? Avoiding his gaze, she set the note on the counter and shook open the apron, remembering how she and her friends had raved over it.

The apron flipped open, facing Scott. He grinned, revealing his dimple and making his eyes squint the way she loved. She remembered the apron had big red lips on the bib—but what had it said? Turning it around, she wished she could melt into the tiny cracks between the tiles on the floor.

KISS THE COOK.

She peeked up at Scott.

He shrugged. "Well, I tried."

They stared at each other for a moment, then erupted in a gale of laughter. A few moments later, Haley regained her composure enough to fold up the apron. She stuck it back in the envelope, and shoved it under the cashier's counter. *Talk about timing.*

<hr />

"That was a great dinner. Thanks." Haley held on to Scott's arm as they climbed the steps up to the pedestrian bridge, which crossed over the Arkansas River.

"Bet it's nice not to have to cook."

"Sure is. I'm glad I won't be cooking at the café. Dad had been training a man, and I didn't even know it. This way I can concentrate on the business end, which is what I like best."

Scott helped her up the final step, and they strolled across the old railroad bridge, their steps muffled as they walked on the aging railroad ties. The sound of gushing water below and lights overhead made for a romantic setting. If only there weren't so many other people around—and they weren't up so high.

About halfway across, Scott stopped, took hold of her elbow, and led her over to the side of the bridge. She halted three feet from the railing, and he looked down with his brows raised.

"I—I'm afraid of heights." Her heart pounded as if she'd run a marathon. She hoped Scott didn't think she was a wimp for being scared.

He held out his hand. "Trust me, Haley. I'll take care of you."

She closed her eyes, wishing for nothing else. She could imagine Scott being there, taking care of her the rest of her life.

Okay, maybe her imagination was running rampant. But she knew him to be an honorable, capable man she could trust. He'd never once done anything to make her doubt that. She looked up. His steady gaze pleaded with her to have faith in him.

Finally, she heaved a sigh and placed her trembling hand in his. Scott's lips tilted up in a pleased smile, revealing his dimple. He pulled her close to his side and wrapped his arm around her shoulders. Together they moved to the side of the bridge.

Haley trembled as she looked down at the swift-running water below. She forced her gaze away and off to the right where the low-water dam created a mini-waterfall.

Just breathe deeply and don't look down.

"Are you okay?" Scott rubbed his hand up and down her arm.

Maybe if she looked at him, she'd feel better. She turned in his arms to face him. "I'm sorry. I've always been afraid of heights. Ever since I was seven. I followed Brent up a tree and fell out, breaking my arm."

"You want to leave?"

"No—I don't want to spoil the nice evening you planned."

He smiled, turning her insides to tapioca pudding. "That's not going to happen."

The warm evening breeze lifted and tossed a strand of hair

into her face. Before she could raise a hand to move it, Scott did it for her. Softly. Gently. This time she trembled from his nearness, not from her fear. He leaned forward, kissing her forehead, then pulled her against his chest. She closed her eyes and wrapped her arms around his waist, feeling as contented and protected as she could ever remember.

"So, did you think about what we talked about over the phone?" The words vibrated his chest against her cheek.

She'd thought long and hard about what he'd said about being a Christian when he'd called the night before. That just attending church didn't make you one, but you needed a personal relationship with Christ. She remembered him telling her about Mary and Martha in the Bible. Rather than being like Mary, she was like Martha—always running about, staying busy with daily chores instead of focusing on a relationship with Christ. She needed to change that—wanted to change it—but didn't know how.

"Yes," she answered. "What you said makes sense, though being so practical minded, it's hard for me to understand it all. Martha was tending to the Lord's physical needs. Wasn't that important?"

She felt him nod against her head. "Sure. But not to the point that she stayed so busy she ignored all her spiritual needs. You see?"

She still wasn't 100 percent clear on it but knew that sometimes you had to take things by faith. Scott had told her as she read the Bible and gave her heart to God, she'd begin to understand these things better, and she believed that was true.

He leaned back but kept a firm hold on her. "Haley, what you really need to do is give your heart totally to God. You can't please Him by simply going to church, singing a few worship songs, and giving an offering. You need Him in here"—he tapped his chest—"to help you through your daily struggles. You don't have to go it alone. God can even make you grateful for the Cowpoke Café."

She couldn't help grinning at that comment. "Uh-huh. That would truly be a miracle."

He smoothed the hair from her face again. "Miracles still happen."

She looked into his handsome face and wondered if it was a miracle that had brought Scott into her life. Though she knew her brother would gloat and tease her, she needed to thank Brent for introducing them.

Scott looked as if he wanted to kiss her, but something was holding him back. Maybe the topic of their conversation. Or maybe the number of people around. She glanced at a couple with three boys, jostling and tugging each other along. As she passed by, the woman glanced at her, a twinkle making her eyes dance. Haley wondered if she was thinking back to when she had dated her husband.

Haley pulled her attention back to Scott. She knew she was ready to give her heart to God, but she didn't want to do it here. "So, you ready for that dessert I promised you?"

Scott smiled, his dimple peeking out, doing odd things to her insides. "You bet. I'm always ready to be a guinea pig for a new dessert."

She gladly stepped away from the bridge railing to the safer middle and tugged him along with her. "I didn't say it was new. In fact, it's something I've been eating all my life—Aunt Mildred's Icebox Cake. Mmmm!"

Scott wrapped his arm around her shoulders. "Can't say I've ever eaten an icebox cake. Sounds interesting."

"It is. Every time we visited Aunt Mildred, Dad's sister, I'd ask her if she'd made any of that pink stuff. I still don't know if it ever had a real name." She looped her arm around Scott's trim waist, reveling in being so close to him.

Be still, my beating heart.

Twenty minutes later, they sat in the kitchen of her parents' home with two bowls of pink stuff in front of them. Scott lifted a spoon, and she watched with anticipation as he tasted her aunt's dessert.

"Oh, wow! This stuff should be illegal."

He wolfed down his helping and turned pleading eyes on her, waggling his dark brows up and down.

Haley giggled at his boyish behavior but spooned some more pink stuff into his bowl. It thrilled her to be able to do a little something for him after all the help he'd been to her.

After a few minutes, he shoved his bowl aside and leaned back in his chair. "That's some of the best stuff I've ever tasted. You gonna serve it at the café?"

"I'm thinking about it. Just not sure how to classify it, since it's not really pie or cake."

"Classify it sinfully delicious."

He stretched, and Haley tried not to notice how his knit shirt tightened over his chest muscles. She still didn't understand why some woman hadn't snagged him up and married him, but she was glad no one had. Maybe—like her—he'd just been too busy to get serious with someone. She hoped once the café opened that she'd still have time to spend with him.

He glanced at his watch. "I'd like to stay longer, but I promised Dad I'd help him work on his latest project. We're getting an early start tomorrow."

Haley set their bowls in the sink and ran some water in them. She found a plastic container and spooned a generous supply of the pink stuff into it, then handed it to Scott.

His eyes lit up like a Christmas tree. "For me?"

Her lips tugged up in a smile. "It has bananas in it, so it doesn't stay fresh more than a couple of days."

"Not a problem. I'll eat it for breakfast."

Haley giggled at his enthusiasm. "It's not a very healthy breakfast. In fact, it's not a healthy anything."

"Hey now, bananas are good for you. So is the pineapple." He stuck out his lower lip in mock offense.

Haley ignored him and put the remaining pink stuff in the refrigerator, thinking she might have to have some for breakfast, too—but she wouldn't confess that to him.

Her stomach twitched with nervousness, and she wondered how to broach the topic that had been spinning in her mind since they'd left the bridge.

Scott headed for the door, and she realized it was now or never.

"Wait. Don't go yet."

Scott paused and turned to face her, his brows lifted.

"I—I want you to pray with me. I want to give my heart to God."

Chapter 6

Haley unlocked the café door, wondering if this would be the week business picked up. Since she'd opened three weeks ago, things had been slower than she'd expected. She'd been reconsidering closing on Mondays and wished now that she'd waited to purchase all those pendants lights, although the customers raved about them.

She'd been praying hard, trying to give her concerns to God ever since she gave Him her heart, but she couldn't shake the feeling that she was failing her parents by not being more successful. What if after decades of thriving, the Cowpoke Café died under her supervision?

She tucked her purse away in a drawer in the tiny office behind the cashier's counter and stretched, pushing away her negative thoughts. She'd spent Saturday evening with Scott and stayed home Sunday after church to do laundry and work on the house. It was a lot easier to keep clean with only her and Gidget there. But today was Monday, and she needed to get some things done while the café was closed.

A knock sounded on the front door, and she slipped out of her office and noticed an elderly couple standing outside. She twisted the lock and opened the door, recognizing Harvey and Edith Hamilton, longtime customers. Haley smiled, wondering what they wanted on a Monday.

"Hello, Haley. We're glad you came back to work." Mr. Hamilton flashed a smile of teeth so straight and even that they could only be dentures. "Why are you closed today? More remodeling?"

"I told you, Harvey, they're closed now on Mondays." His wife rolled her eyes, but her tone was gentle.

"Nah. Hogwash. The Cowpoke Café's not closed on Mondays. Never has been."

"Just look at the sign right there, Harv. It says they're closed. Do you see any other people in there?"

Haley bit back a smile as the elderly couple argued good-naturedly. Finally, she thought she'd better intervene. "I'm sorry, Mr. Hamilton. We didn't used to be closed on Mondays, but I changed the hours when I took over. I don't want to work myself silly like my parents did. I want to have a life."

"See." Edith nudged her plump elbow in Harvey's skinny side. *Told you so* was written all over her face, but she didn't voice the words.

"Well, shucks. I had me a yearning for some of her chicken-fried steak."

"That's the Friday special, Harv. Let's go home. I'll fix you a bologna sandwich."

"I'd be happy to offer you a soda pop and some pie." Haley

said, just to be courteous.

Harvey's eyes lit up, but Edith responded. "No, thank you, darling. If Harv eats pie, his blood sugar goes too high."

Edith turned her disappointed husband away from the door and pointed him toward the car. She swung back around to face Haley. "Stubborn old coot won't listen to me, even after fifty-two years of marriage. I told him you weren't open today, but he had to see for himself." She hurried to catch up with her husband, shaking her head the whole time.

Haley locked the door and chuckled. What would it be like to be married to the same man for so long? Would she and Scott be like that after they'd been married fifty-two years? She had no doubt she'd fallen fast and hard for him and hoped and prayed he felt the same way.

Lately, he'd been a bit freer in holding her hand or putting his arm around her. Haley's pulse kicked up a notch as she remembered his chaste good night kisses, but she longed for him to loosen his restraints and give her a real, heart-stopping kiss. Was his shyness holding him back? Or was it something else?

She crossed the dining area to the photo wall. What would it be like to be married to Scott? He'd pretty much gotten over his shyness—except for the kissing part—around her and was funny and a tease. She loved the way his eyes sparkled right before he'd joke about something. And she loved how safe she felt walking down the street with him. It didn't hurt that women would often look their way. *Probably wondering what a hottie like him is doing with someone like me.*

But most of all, she loved his character and his total dedication to God.

Haley shook her head. If she dreamed of Scott all day, she wouldn't get a thing done. He said he'd be busy this week, helping his dad with their new business, so they might not see each other as much. She tried to remember what kind of business it was but couldn't actually remember if he'd ever told her.

Oh, rats. Forgot my camera. She jogged back into the office and retrieved her digital camera, and then snapped several shots of the wall holding the pictures autographed by famous people. Over the years, local politicians, movie stars from Oklahoma, country western singers, and others had visited the Cowpoke Café and left their autographed photos. Each one had been framed and hung on the wall where they'd remained for decades.

Haley lifted the Hank Williams picture off the wall and tried not to smile too hard. She remembered the phone call from her mother last night with joy. Her father missed his pictures. Her mother had explained how he used to go in each morning and afternoon and take a break, sip his coffee or pop, and look at the photos, remembering all the good times.

When Haley suggested that she take down the pictures and put them in a photo album for her dad's upcoming birthday, her mother was ecstatic. But then she'd asked Haley if she was sure she didn't want to keep them.

"No way, José!" Haley shouted the words out loud that she'd wanted to say last night.

She grinned and removed another picture—one of an ex-Oklahoma governor. "No, Mom," she said to herself, "I sure don't want to keep these. Not for one more second."

She'd reassured her mother that it was fine with her and then had gotten off the phone and whooped with joy and done a little celebration jig with Gidget looking at her as if she were crazy.

She tugged another photo off the wall. Wouldn't Scott be surprised the next time he came into the café and saw the bare knotty pine?

She spent the next four hours listening to a Christian music station on the radio and taking down photos, removing them from their cheap gold metal frames, and then chucking the glass and dusty frames in the trash. All that was left was a pile of aging photos, which she put in a box she'd brought from home.

As she stared at the big blank wall, her mind danced with ideas of what to put there. Maybe she'd go shopping later. If only her dad wanted those old neon boots, too.

Half an hour later, Haley walked down the sidewalk on her way to the post office, a few blocks from the cafe. She thought about the three weeks she'd been open. Business had been good for breakfast but slower at noon than she'd remembered. She wondered if her parents' longtime customers would quit coming now that her folks were no longer running the café. Fighting feelings of being a failure, she couldn't help wondering if her business would pick up if she put in a salad bar.

Her heart skipped a beat. Maybe that's what she could do along the back wall where the pictures had hung. Her mind raced, catching the vision and filling her with excitement. It could work. She'd lose a couple of tables, but that shouldn't be a problem since they had yet to be filled to capacity. Maybe she could e-mail Angel, Monica, and Allison and see if one of them knew of a reputable dealer to buy a salad bar setup from. Probably though, her dad had a catalog or two in the office.

With traffic whizzing past and the warm summer sun bearing down on her, she rounded the corner and noticed a parking lot overflowing with cars. Her gaze lifted to the shiny new sign that read: GRANNY'S COUNTRY KITCHEN. FAMILY DINING AT ITS BEST. Her heart plunged clear down to her socks, and she nearly stumbled. Another family-style restaurant? Only two blocks from her café? No wonder business had slacked off.

This was the opposite direction from how she normally drove home every night, otherwise she would have known before now about this new competition. When she saw the place being built a month ago, she'd thought it was a store of some sort. Never once had she considered the possibility that it might be an eating establishment.

Disappointment weighed her down, and her legs felt sluggish. How could she compete with a place so new and shiny?

She lifted a prayer heavenward. Scott had told her just because she was a Christian now didn't mean she wouldn't have hard times. But in those difficult times, she needed to pray and ask God to help her. Well, this was a biggie—and she sure needed His strength.

She finished her business at the post office, then trudged back to the café. As she passed by Granny's Country Kitchen again, she studied the wide brick building. Blue and white checkered curtains hung in the windows, anchored with tiebacks. A three-foot tall white picket fence lined the sidewalks and kept little hands away from the gorgeous array of multicolored flowers. White high-back rocking chairs sat on a covered porch. Inside, it looked as if there might be a store of some kind where customers could shop while waiting for a table.

Haley hurried away, fighting the tears burning her eyes. How could she compete with this awesome place?

As she contemplated her problem, an idea formed. She couldn't fight her competition unless she knew more about it. Yes, that's it. She'd go home, clean up, and visit Granny's Country Kitchen for dinner tonight. Then she'd know what she was up against.

⚜

Scott glanced at his watch. He should have been off work an hour ago. Even though his father's new restaurant was now open, there had been little things he needed to finish.

His hopes to call Haley and see if she could eat dinner with him dwindled with each passing minute. She'd probably already eaten by now anyway.

It had been nearly twenty-four hours since he last saw her—and he missed her like crazy. He didn't know exactly when his schoolboy crush had grown to full-fledged love, but it had. Once Haley gave her heart to God, Scott felt as if the last barrier to their relationship had disintegrated. He'd kept his kisses chaste, because he didn't want to get caught up in his passion. There would be plenty of time for that—once they were married. *If* Haley would have him.

He tightened the screw, hung a framed, decorative landscape on it, and then looked around the manager's office. It was six times bigger than Haley's tiny office. What would she think about his dad's place? He dreaded telling her about the restaurant and had just kind of skipped over mentioning it whenever they talked about his family. Now he wished he'd told her straight out.

He wished there was something he could have done to get his father to locate the restaurant somewhere else, but when he returned from Kuwait and found out about Granny's Country Kitchen, the building was over halfway finished. And he had no idea until he saw the location that it was only two blocks from the Cowpoke Café.

When Haley learned who the owner of the new restaurant was, she'd probably never speak to him again—much less want to marry him.

Somehow he had to tell her. Soon.

He hated how he sometimes avoided things, because he didn't like confrontation. He'd never lied to Haley—and wouldn't. But wasn't avoiding the inevitable a lie of sorts?

Scott shook his head and dropped his screwdriver into his tool belt. Maybe he'd drive by her house and see if she was there.

He left the manager's office and made a beeline for the exit, hoping nobody had anything else for him to do. The dining area was nearly filled to capacity, which made him thankful Haley didn't stay open for evening dinner. He rounded a corner and headed toward the cashier.

"Scott. Hold on." He winced and slowed his steps at his father's voice. Turning, he saw his dad coming toward him.

"You're mother is here, and we'd like you to join us for dinner."

Scott heaved a sigh. "I'm not really dressed for dinner, Dad." He glanced down at his dirty jeans and T-shirt. His tool belt still hung around his waist.

His father eyed him up and down. "Nonsense. This is a family restaurant. It's come as you are."

He knew there was no point arguing. Besides, that would be disrespectful. It didn't matter that he ate dinner with his parents nearly every night he wasn't with Halcy. They'd been clingy like that—ever since he'd returned from Kuwait, but he couldn't really blame them.

He followed his dad and then smiled as his mother scooted over in the booth, which smelled of brand-new vinyl. His dad scrunched in across from him.

"You've done a wonderful job on this place, sweetie." His mother patted his hand.

"I didn't do it alone."

"I know, dear. You didn't have plans with Haley tonight?" His mother's bright blue eyes sparked with curiosity. "We really would like to meet her soon."

"You will before too long." He wasn't quite sure if Haley was ready to meet his parents. They were great but could be smothering. If he weren't considering getting married in the near future, he'd move out and get his own place.

He reached for one of the homemade dinner rolls, whose smell had taunted him all afternoon, but noticed his grimy hands. "Gotta wash up. I'll be back in a minute."

Scott exited the dining area and noticed that a line was already starting to form in the gift shop. He locked his tool belt in his truck and went back inside to wash his hands. As he exited the restroom, his gaze landed on the back of a woman who looked just like Haley. Her teal-colored Capri pants fitted her slim frame perfectly, and a thin-striped, multicolored top molded to her tiny waist. His heart revved up like a jackhammer.

She turned to look at something, and he realized it *was* her. His first thought was to dash back into the bathroom unseen. But he was more of a man than that—at least he hoped he was.

"Scott!" Haley's face brightened as her gaze landed on him.

Scoundrel. Lowlife. That's what she'd think of him soon.

"What are you doing here?"

He moved forward and took her outstretched hand. "I just finished working."

"Here?" Her golden eyebrows dipped in confusion. "I thought you said you were working for your dad."

He tugged her back to the entryway of the restrooms to give them a little privacy. "I am."

She blinked, and her pretty lips pressed into a thin line. "I don't understand."

Scott ran his hand through his inch-high hair. "My dad owns this restaurant." He heaved a sigh, glad that she finally knew the truth.

Chapter 7

Placing her palm on a hot grill wouldn't have hurt as much as Scott's confession. "*Your* dad owns Granny's Country Kitchen? You can't be serious."

He nodded, but she could see the regret in his eyes. But was it regret because he'd been spying on her business so he could report back to his dad, or did his regret stem from something else? She fell back against the wall, weak with disbelief. Had he purposely tricked her?

"Haley, it's not what you're thinking."

"How do you know what I'm thinking?" She allowed her angry gaze to pierce his and tried to ignore the pain she saw in his eyes.

"I wanted to tell you, but I was afraid it would mess up things."

"Well, you were right. Did you get the information out of me that *Daddy* wanted?"

"No! It wasn't like that." He held his hands up in defense.

"Is that why you started e-mailing me?" People turned their

251

direction at her raised voice. Tears pooled in her eyes, blurring her view of Scott. Her throat tightened.

"Haley, you know that's not true. I've had feelings for you since I first saw you sashaying down the halls in high school. I was too shy back then to do anything about it. When Brent found out I was in Kuwait, he started e-mailing me. After awhile, I got up my nerve to ask if I could e-mail you. And the rest is history."

Haley just wanted to get out of there and away from all the people. She stabbed a finger in Scott's chest. "*We're* history."

She darted around him, ignoring the way his mouth dropped open and the pain lacing his eyes.

"Haley, wait!" He reached for her.

His fingers slipped off her arm as he tried to stop her. She dodged around curious people, displays of "homemade" candies, candles, and embroidered shirts as she made a beeline for the exit. The scent of cinnamon mixed with country-style food teased her nose and hungry stomach. As she reached the door, she fumbled around in her purse for her keys, hoping Scott wouldn't follow her. Thankfully, as she hurried outside, a busload of people entered.

She tried not to cry as she drove away, but tears streamed down her face in spite of her efforts. She never should have trusted a guy. They always messed up everything and made her feel worse than before she'd met them.

All her hopes and dreams melted away like a forgotten bowl of ice cream.

Scott rolled over in his bed and looked at the clock through dry, gritty eyes. Five a.m. Even during sandstorms in Kuwait, he'd never been this miserable. Seven days had passed since Haley had stormed out of his dad's restaurant.

He'd made a huge mistake not telling her about Granny's Country Kitchen. If he could only go back and change things. He hadn't been honest with the woman he loved, and now he was paying the price.

Sitting on the side of the bed, he could make out the first faint signs of daylight on the horizon. Haley hadn't answered his e-mails, and whenever she answered the phone and realized it was him, she hung up. She could be stubborn like that, but then tenacity was what would make her a success in the restaurant business—if Granny's Country Kitchen didn't steal too many of her customers.

What could he do to fix this? Prayer was all he could think of—but it was the best thing anyway.

He slipped to his knees and leaned his forehead against his mattress.

"Dear Lord, I'm sorry for not telling Haley the truth sooner. Forgive me for not trusting You to be in control. I should have let You work things out instead of trying to do it in my own power. Please, if there's a way You can fix the breach between Haley and me, I'd forever appreciate it. Give me wisdom, Lord, to know what to say to her next time I see her."

He swatted at the sting in his eyes and stood; then he walked over to his laptop and opened it, hoping Haley had e-mailed him. When he saw no message from her, he sat down in his desk chair, thinking hard what to say. After a few minutes, he began to type.

> *Dear Haley,*
>
> *—And you are very dear to me. Do you have any idea how much?*
>
> *I hope and pray you can forgive me for not being totally honest with you. I was afraid if I told you about Dad's restaurant you wouldn't want to have anything to do with me. PLEASE forgive me for not telling you sooner. I tried but just couldn't get the words out. I didn't want to see the hurt it would cause on your pretty face.*
>
> *Can we get together and discuss this? Please?*
>
> *Groveling,*
> *Scott*

He pressed the SEND button and prayed this would be the e-mail Haley chose to answer. Yawning, he rubbed his whiskery chin. He had just enough time to get dressed and grab some breakfast before being at work at six. He'd be glad when the weather cooled down, so he wouldn't have to go to work so early.

Crossing the room to the window, he marveled at the colorful sunrise. The neon pink and orange colors reminded him of the old cowboy-boot sign in Haley's café window.

Oh, how he longed to see her. But he felt she needed time to cool down. He'd wait another week or two, and if he didn't hear from her, he'd track her down. Somehow she had to understand how sorry he was for hurting her. And he'd do his best to never hurt her again.

Haley pushed her foot against the wooden floorboards, and the porch swing glided back and forth in a gentle sway. The warm morning air made the back of her legs sweat, and it was only 8:00 a.m. She slammed shut the devotional book she'd been reading and stared across the street at the prolific honeysuckle vine that had woven itself all through the chain-link fence dividing her two neighbors' yards. Her anger with Scott resembled that vine. It had entwined itself in her heart and threatened to tear her apart.

Why couldn't he have just told her the truth as soon as he became aware how closely located the two restaurants were?

She knew the reason—and he was probably right. If she *had* known sooner, she might have been too upset to e-mail him or get to know him.

When she'd read Scott's latest e-mail, she'd struggled with what to do. Until now, she'd been so upset she'd just deleted his previous e-mails. But this one made her heart ache. She missed him so much, but if he truly cared for her, wouldn't he have been honest?

Oh, why was she being so stubborn? Tears burned her eyes and blurred the view. Because she loved him. And he'd hurt her deeply.

Why had everything fallen apart after she rededicated her heart to God?

The devotional said that problems came to everyone. It is how we handle those problems that can give us character and mold us into the person God wants us to be.

Haley knew she'd blown it—both with God and Scott.

She'd let her hurt and anger overpower everything else.

Some Christian she was!

But the good news was that God was still there. Her heart swelled, knowing He still loved her, and He would forgive her if she only asked.

Haley bent her head and poured out her heart to God.

Half an hour later, tears of a different kind flowed down her cheeks. She felt clean and pure, now that her anger was gone. She blotted her eyes with a tissue.

Everything she had belonged to God. And if God wanted the Cowpoke Café to succeed, then He would see that it did. And if not, He would take her in a different direction.

Now what should she do about Scott?

The phone rang before she could formulate an answer. She jumped up and dashed back inside and found the cordless phone lying on the couch.

"Hello?" Her heart pounded like a chef pounding a piece of meat. What if it was Scott?

"Haley, this is Margo Hutchins from church. I was wondering if you'd given any more thought to doing something to help with the teens."

She flopped onto the couch, her mind racing, trying to remember who this woman was. She'd met so many people since starting back to church.

"I know you're really busy with your restaurant and all, but if we could get some solid young people your age to help the teens, I feel it would make a huge difference."

Ahh. . .now she remembered the forty-something woman with bright red hair. "Yes, Mrs. Hutchins. I've been thinking but haven't come up with anything yet. The problem is that I'm tied up with the café so much that I don't have a lot of free time."

"Yes, I know that's true. Well, I'm calling everyone on my list. We'd like to maybe start a coffeehouse or something like that where the kids could go on the weekends so they don't join that wild group that congregates out at the mall or race their cars up and down the busy streets."

Gidget hopped onto her lap and licked Haley's hand with her scratchy tongue.

"I'll pray about what I can do. Okay?"

"That would be great. Let me give you my phone number in case you think of anything."

Haley wrote down the number, hung up the phone, and carried Gidget out onto the porch with her. In light of all she'd been going through, she'd completely forgotten that she'd told Mrs. Hutchins she'd help out with the teen group. As she patted her cat, her mind raced with ideas.

What *could* she do? She'd been such a little snob as a teenager, all wrapped up in herself and her feelings.

As if she'd been physically slapped on the face, she realized she'd been acting the same way this past week.

But wasn't that different? The man she loved had betrayed

her. And the physical ache it caused was almost unbearable.

Haley sighed and closed her eyes. She couldn't walk with God and hang on to her hurt and pain. Darkness and light couldn't cohabit in the same place.

"Please, Lord, take this pain and anger away. Help me to forgive Scott. I understand why he did what he did, but it still hurts. I feel like he deceived me. And yet at the same time, I know he's not capable of being deceitful. Show me how to forgive him and myself. Also, if You want me to help the teens at church, show me how. Amen."

Haley stretched, feeling her anger wash away like a spring rain. She returned Gidget to the house and made a cup of coffee, then went back out to the porch swing. Why was it that she felt so much closer to God outside among His creation?

As she thought about her past and all she'd learned, she realized she had a lot to give. She could help teenage girls who were struggling and feeling the same way she'd felt in high school. She knew behind their giggles and smiles, many of the girls were hurting and needed someone older who cared and could show them how to walk with the Lord. She didn't have that much experience herself, but she could share what she had and maybe it would help some. But where? And how?

Suddenly an idea blossomed in her mind, just like a rose she'd seen quickly opening up with fast-action photography. It would mean a serious commitment of her time and resources, but if this idea was from God, she was willing.

Haley clapped her hands together, sending two nearby

sparrows to flight. Yes! It could work! She raced inside to find some paper and write down her ideas before they flittered away. Maybe this was the reason why God had blessed her with the Cowpoke Café.

Chapter 8

Haley couldn't wipe the grin off her face as she watched the youth pastor doing a country line dance with a group of teens in the middle of her restaurant. This was the second week she'd opened on Friday and Saturday evenings, and business was booming.

She placed cups of soda pop on the table for a group of parents who had come to check out her place to see if it was appropriate for their teens. "I'll be right back with your onion rings," she told them.

"Oh, miss," one lady said. "We want to try some of that pink stuff my daughter Ashley raves about."

Haley smiled. Her aunt's icebox cake was quickly growing in popularity. "I'd be happy to bring you some. Who all would like a bowl?"

All four parents raised their hands, and Haley nodded. She skirted around the dancers and moved into the quieter kitchen. Mario flipped burgers, while Stacy prepared the buns and made up plates of nachos. Haley grabbed a plate of chips and added some warm cheese sauce and a pile of jalapeños.

"Business sure is good," Mario said as he glanced over his shoulder. "I have to admit I was skeptical. I'm glad it's worked out though. I can use the extra hours."

"Yeah, me, too," Stacy said as she placed sliced pickles on a bun.

"God has blessed us, for sure." Haley washed her hands and picked up the nachos and the onion rings Mario had just placed on a large plate; then she headed back into the noisy dining room.

Normally she didn't wait tables, but one of her girls had called in sick. She delivered the rings and nachos and refilled drinks for three teen girls who sat at a booth, totally engrossed in their board game.

Margo Hutchins waved as she entered with her husband, and Haley hurried to greet her.

"This was such a great idea, Haley. It's just what the kids needed." Margo laid her hand on Haley's arm. "Are we too late to eat?"

"No." Haley shook her head. "The kitchen's open until nine. Then we close so the worship team can play a few songs and the youth pastor can do a short devotional with the kids."

She escorted them to a booth just as one of the older teens put on a CD of a popular Christian singer. The kids who had been line dancing returned to their tables. Haley knew there'd be no rest for the next half hour as many of the teens would order something before the kitchen shut down.

Forty-five minutes later, Haley leaned against the wall near the front door and listened to the smooth music of the worship team from church. She closed her eyes, enjoying a moment's rest, and breathed a prayer of thanks to God for giving her this dream and helping her to realize it.

Last Friday night, she'd had the opportunity to talk to a fourteen-year-old girl who was considering suicide because she thought nobody understood what she was going through. Haley smiled, knowing the girl had rededicated her heart to God on Saturday and now was across the room, singing and worshipping Him.

She felt a warm hand on her arm and opened her eyes. Her heart stampeded like a herd of cattle. Scott stood beside her, looking more wonderful than she'd ever seen. His black hair had grown out, and his beautiful dark blue eyes gleamed. Oh, how she'd missed him.

❧❦❧

Scott's pulse raced as fast as a jackhammer. Smooth Christian music resonated in the Cowpoke Café. He'd driven by on a whim, never expecting to find the place open and bustling with teenagers. He wanted to take in all that was happening but could only stare at Haley. She looked happy to see him, and there was no animosity in her gaze. He nudged his head toward the door behind him, and she nodded.

They stepped outside, and the door shut, drowning out much of the music and singing. Scott looked at the woman he loved. She'd cut her honey blond hair short, and it gave her a cute, Meg Ryan look, except for her lovely brown eyes.

"So"—he waved his hand toward the café—"what's all that about?"

Haley was all smiles. "I decided to open on Friday and Saturday nights, so Christian teens would have a place to go. God has blessed us. It's been a big success. We had four kids give their hearts to God last weekend and hope for more tonight."

Joy surged through Scott's heart. Here he'd thought Haley was sulking and still mad at him, and she'd been out working for God. It shamed him to think he'd thought less of her. "That's awesome! I'm so glad things are going well."

Almost too well. Did she even miss him?

"Yeah, it's amazed me what God has done so quickly. But I'm glad. The teens really seem to enjoy it. By the way, you missed the country line dancing." She nudged him in the arm.

"Did you dance? I'd like to see that."

She shook her head and laughed. "No, not tonight. Marissa called in sick, so I had to wait tables."

"Well, maybe next week." He shoved his hands in his pockets to keep from touching her. She was so pretty. So bubbly and full of energy.

She glanced up at him, looked away and then back, one side of her bottom lip tucked between her teeth. "I missed you."

Behind her the cars on Peoria whizzed by. Off to his right, a group of teens stood beside a Mustang convertible, talking. He reached out and grasped Haley's hand and pulled her around the side of the building where it was quieter.

Insects danced around the faintly buzzing fluorescent light at the back of the café, so he stopped halfway to the alley. He faced Haley, knowing his heart was in his eyes, and he studied her. "I missed you *so* much."

Her lips turned up in a shy smile.

With shaking hands, he cupped her cheeks and leaned his forehead against hers. "I'm so sorry, Haley. I should have told you about Dad's restaurant as soon as I learned about it, but I was afraid you wouldn't want to have anything more to do with me."

She stiffened but quickly relaxed again. "I'm sorry for storming out of your dad's place and not giving you a chance to explain. One thing you have to learn about me is that I'm like a geyser. I blow up, make a big show, but then I get over it. But God is helping me with that."

He slid his hands down to her shoulders, glad to finally be touching her after dreaming about her for weeks. "All right. I'll remember that."

Haley's sigh smelled sweet like soda pop. "Scott, God used this time apart to show me so much. I had to turn loose my anger and forgive you. I've been planning on calling you but hadn't felt God give me the go-ahead yet. I also realized that I was leaning too heavily on you and not enough on Him. It was hard to be apart, but it was good, too. I know now that God is the only One I can trust totally."

"I'm sorry I hurt you. I never meant to."

Haley brushed at something on his shirt. "I know."

A loud cheer rang out from inside the café, and Haley grinned. "Someone just gave their heart to God."

Scott's heart was so full he thought it might explode. All his prayers for Haley hadn't been in vain. She *had* forgiven him, and

God had done a great work in her during their time apart.

She looked up at him with a twinkle in her eyes. "So, are you going to stand there all night, or are you going to kiss me?"

His stomach did a flip-flop, and he leaned forward, his lips touching hers. When he started to pull back, she grabbed his shirt, then wrapped her arms around his neck and held him in place. Scott realized his dreams were coming to life, and he kissed her back. Finally, he pulled away, his breath coming fast.

"You're some kisser, Miss Tannehill."

"It's about time you found out." Haley grinned and gave him a playful punch. "So where do we go from here?"

He smoothed a strand of hair from her face, reveling in its softness. "I'm thinking church. . .flowers. . .friends and family. . . cake."

Haley stepped back, her mouth open wide. She blinked several times. "Are you asking me to marry you?"

"Yes, but not right away. We haven't known each other all that long, and I'd like to finish college first." Scott rubbed the back of his neck. "Haley, maybe it's too soon for you, but I have cared for you for years."

"Why didn't you ever say anything before?" She took his hands and swung them slowly back and forth.

"I tried once in high school, but you snubbed me. And I never got the nerve up again. I was a bit of a chicken back then."

"So the Army made a man of you." Her pretty brown eyes gleamed with an ornery twinkle.

"I guess. I think I needed to grow up. There's just one thing though. . . ."

Haley's eyes widened and her brows lifted. "What?"

"My sister wants the recipe for your pink stuff."

"It's an old family recipe."

He shrugged and tugged her closer. "So marry me, and we'll keep it in the family."

"Okay."

"Okay?" Scott's heart raced.

"Yeah. Okay. I'll marry you."

"Yahooo!!" He wrapped his arms around her and kissed her long and hard. When they came up for air, he kissed her cheeks and her eyes and the end of her nose. "I love you so much, I can hardly stand it. Maybe I'll take some interim classes, so I can graduate sooner."

Haley laughed. "I'll give you a recipe now if you want."

His mind raced, wondering what she meant. "Okay, sure."

She pressed her lips together, as if she was trying not to smile. "Take a cup of attraction, a pinch of kindness, a handful of patience, a bushel of faith, and an armload of love, and you have a recipe for romance."

Scott chuckled at her cleverness. "Yes, ma'am. Sounds good. Maybe we can put that on our wedding invitations."

Scott wrapped his arm around his beloved and steered her back inside. Teens of all ages mixed with several adults singing praises to God with their eyes closed and hands lifted. He shook his head. Who would have dreamed this could have happened at the Cowpoke Café?

He smiled, knowing the answer to his own question. God knew.

A RECIPE FOR ROMANCE

AUNT MILDRED'S ICEBOX CAKE (pink stuff)

1 small package strawberry Jell-O
3/4 cup boiling water
Scant 1/2 cup sugar
1 small can crushed pineapple with juice
1 cup miniature marshmallows
Scant 1/2 cup chopped pecans (optional)
1 container (12 ounce) frozen whipped topping, thawed
Vanilla wafers
3–4 medium bananas

Mix together Jell-O, water, and sugar. Cool a little. Add pineapple, marshmallows, and pecans. Fold in 3/4 of whipped topping. Set aside. Line an oblong cake pan with vanilla wafers. Top with a layer of thinly sliced bananas. Spoon on Jell-O mixture and even out across the top. Spread on remaining whipped topping. Cover with plastic wrap and keep refrigerated. Serves 12–16.

VICKIE MCDONOUGH

Award-winning author Vickie McDonough believes God is the ultimate designer of romance. Vickie loves writing stories where the characters find their true love and grow in their faith. Her first novel, *Sooner or Later* was released in 2004, and she has several more Heartsong Presents novels coming out in the next few years. She has also authored four novellas, which are included in *A Stitch in Time, Brides O' the Emerald Isle, Lone Star Christmas,* and *Kiss the Bride.* She is a member of numerous writing and critique groups and has been a book reviewer for four years. Vickie is a wife of thirty years and a mother to four sons, three of which still live at home. When she's not writing, she enjoys reading, watching movies, and traveling. Learn more about Vickie and her books at www.vickiemcdonough.com.

Tea for Two

by Carrie Turansky

Dedication

To my daughters Melissa, Elizabeth, Megan, and Melinda.
You're each a joy and blessing beyond compare. . .
so beautiful and special to me. I love you!

*[Love] keeps no record of wrongs. . . . It always protects,
always trusts, always hopes, always perseveres.*
1 CORINTHIANS 13:5, 7

Chapter 1

The bell over the front door of Sweet Something Tea Shop jingled. The mailman stepped inside and pushed the heavy oak and glass door closed behind him, making the bell jingle a second time. A brisk March breeze swept through the shop, ruffling the white lace curtains at the front windows.

Allison Bennett walked into the gift shop area. "Afternoon, Howard."

He nodded and handed her the small stack of mail. "Here you go."

She smiled and thanked him. "Can I get you a hot cup of coffee or tea?"

"Thanks, but this weather has me behind schedule." He adjusted the plaid wool scarf around his neck. "I gotta get moving. You have a good day."

"Okay." She waved and watched him duck out the door, trudge past deep piles of slushy snow, and step into Princeton Interiors next door.

Leaning closer to the front door's cool glass, she glanced at the gray, brooding sky overhead and then down the empty sidewalk toward Princeton University. This morning she'd read an article in the *Princeton Packet* calling this the worst winter in thirty years. No one had to tell her twice. She knew it was true. Foot traffic along Princeton's historic Nassau Street had almost disappeared, taking most of her customers with it.

A dizzy, sick feeling washed over her as she thought of all she'd invested in her business over the last year and a half. If the weather didn't warm up soon, she'd be forced to close Sweet Something permanently.

She sighed and closed her eyes. *Please, Lord, help us get through these next few weeks. Send us an early spring.* She looked out the window again, imagining all the shoppers and business people who would stroll down the street and in the door for lunch or afternoon tea once the temperature rose and the sun came out. They'd come again. She had to believe it. Not just for herself, but for her sister's sake.

"Was that the mailman?" Tessa Malone, Allison's older sister, wiped her hands on her crisp white apron and glanced toward the front door. Short dark hair framed her pleasant face with a wispy fringe. Her cheeks glowed from working in the warm kitchen. Beaded earrings dangled from her ears. She crossed from the antique desk that served as a hostess podium and stepped down into the gift shop area to meet Allison.

"Yes." Allison shifted her gaze to the mail in her hand. "Hopefully he didn't bring us any more bills."

Tessa sent her a serious look. "Better check and see."

Allison leafed through the pile, flipping past a colorful grocery circular from McCaffery's Market and a coupon for a free session at Princeton Biofeedback Center. On the bottom of the pile, a plain white envelope with a neatly typed address caught her attention.

"I hope it's not one of those fund-raising letters from the hospital." Tessa lifted her dark brows. "Don't even think about giving them any money right now."

Allison let Tessa's words pass without comment. She knew her sister's tendency to mother her came from their twelve-year age difference and close sister-bond. They shared management of the tea shop, and though most of the financial investment came from Allison, Tessa faithfully oversaw the baking and food preparation.

Allison slid her finger under the edge of the envelope and tore it open. Peeking in, she caught a glimpse of a cashier's check. "Oh my goodness. Look!" She pulled out the check with a trembling hand.

Tessa leaned closer and scanned the check's inscription. Her dark eyes bulged, and she snatched the check from Allison. "Three thousand five hundred dollars! Look at the memo line: *FOR ALLISON AND SWEET SOMETHING.*" She stared at Allison. "It's just like the other one."

Allison nodded, recalling the cashier's check for five thousand dollars she had received shortly before she opened the tea shop on Valentine's Day a little over a year ago. "I can't believe this. Who would send me this much money?"

"I don't know. Maybe someone heard we're having financial problems."

"I haven't told anyone. Have you?"

Tessa shook her head. "I'm sure Matt wouldn't say anything. He's a stickler about ethical things like that."

Allison nodded. She trusted her brother-in-law completely. He was an experienced CPA and handled all the finances for Sweet Something. "I know we really need this, but it's a little spooky. How would someone know how much we need to cover the rest of this week's payroll and the increase in our rent?"

"They must have a direct line to You Know Who upstairs." Tessa lifted her gaze toward the ceiling.

Allison knew she wasn't talking about the architect who rented the office above the tea shop. Goose bumps raced down her arms. "Right. But I'd still like to know who He used to send it."

Tessa's eyes lit up and she grinned. "I bet it's Peter."

Allison pulled back and wrinkled her nose. "It couldn't be."

"Why not? He has the money, and you know he's interested in you. He's here practically every day."

Allison couldn't imagine Peter Hillinger, the owner of Princeton Interiors, giving money to anyone anonymously. It wasn't his style. He wore perfectly tailored clothes from the best stores in Princeton and drove a new black BMW. He never missed an opportunity to mention his successful business, even though he'd inherited it from his father less than two years ago.

"It would be easy for him to see how slow things have been."

"I just don't think Peter would do something like this."

"Well, he certainly could if he wanted to." Tessa pursed her lips and seemed offended that Allison didn't agree with her.

Allison glanced at the check again, remembering Peter's thoughtful comments about the tea shop, his interest in her artwork, and his new habit of attending church with her. He seemed sincere. Maybe she was being too judgmental. Whoever had sent the check was very generous and most likely listening to the Lord. How else could he know their need?

"I suppose it could be Peter." Allison chewed her lower lip as she turned over the idea in her mind. "But I got the first check over a year ago at church through Pastor Tom, and Peter didn't start coming to church with us until we invited him last fall."

"Okay, so Peter might not have given you the first check, but this one has to be from him. Who else could it be?"

"I don't know."

Tessa grinned. "I think you should say yes next time he asks for a date."

Allison's stomach tightened. She turned away and tucked the check back in the envelope. "He hasn't asked me out since I turned him down for Valentine's Day."

"I'm sure all he needs is a little encouragement."

"But it doesn't seem fair to encourage him. We're just friends. That's all I—"

"Friendship is a great place to start. Spend more time with him. Give it a chance." Tessa touched Allison's cheek, a look of concern in her eyes. "There's someone special out there for you.

I know it. But you have to be willing to let go of the past, open up your heart, and try again."

Tears misted Allison's eyes. Of course her sister was right. She needed to bury those painful memories once and for all. Six years was long enough to wait for someone who was never coming back.

<hr/>

The tantalizing scent of freshly baked blackberry pie drifted toward Tyler Lawrence as he stepped into the warmth of Sweet Something Tea Shop. Rubbing his hands together to warm them, he glanced around the cozy shop.

Antique sideboards and small tables displayed interesting collections of china teapots, cups, and saucers. Whimsical birdhouses and small table lamps with painted shades sat on the shelves between the front windows. Little packages of specialty teas in cellophane bags tied with pink ribbons sat in neat rows ready for purchase. He hadn't expected Sweet Something to have a gift shop as well as a tearoom. But, knowing Allie's love for art and her romantic, creative style, it made sense.

The shop's feminine ambiance announced its owner as clearly as if her name had been painted on the WELCOME sign. He glanced into the quiet tearoom and saw only two tables occupied.

Allie stepped down into the gift shop and past a large armoire filled with round hatboxes, dried flowers, and antique crystal dishes. Her gaze connected with his, and recognition flashed in her eyes.

Tyler smiled. "Hi, Allie." She looked just as beautiful as she had the day he'd left Princeton six years ago. She'd cut her rich caramel-colored hair in a new style that brushed her shoulders. A few soft lines at the corners of her eyes testified to the passing years, but those were the only hints of change he noticed.

She stared at him, questions shimmering in her dark blue eyes.

"I heard about your shop. I thought I'd stop in and say hello."

She darted a glance over her shoulder and then back at him. "I'll get you a menu." She turned and walked toward the tearoom, leaving a faint flowery fragrance in her wake. She wore a mocha-colored blouse with soft flowing ruffles at her neck and wrists, and a long, slim black skirt. He spotted-brown leather boots through the slit in her skirt as she stepped up into the tearoom.

He followed, sending off a prayer for grace. He didn't deserve it, but over the past two years, he'd learned God's grace and forgiveness could cover a multitude of sins. He needed both from Allie.

In all those years he'd seen her only once—a little over year ago on Christmas Eve at church. The scene flashed through his mind as he crossed the tearoom. He'd returned to Princeton to spend the holidays with his mother for the first time in five years. After the service, he'd unexpectedly bumped into Allie and fumbled a lame apology, saying something about being sorry he hadn't kept in touch. Of course that was true, but it didn't even begin to address the real issues between them. It certainly didn't ease his guilt or erase the pain in her eyes.

Allie led him to a small table for two in the corner.

He sat down and smiled up at her.

She averted her eyes and handed him a menu printed on light pink paper. "We have several choices for lunch, or our tea and dessert menu is on the back. Can I get you something to drink?"

Her cool formality cut him to the heart. "Can you sit down for a few minutes?"

"No, I'm busy," she said, without missing a beat.

"It doesn't look like you have too many customers right now. Couldn't you take a break? I'd like to hear more about Sweet Something. How long have you been open?" Of course he knew the answer to that question, but he hoped it would draw her into a conversation.

Her gaze dropped to the menu in his hand. "All right, but let me take your order first."

"I'd like tea and something sweet. What do you recommend?"

She hesitated a moment. "The apple cinnamon scones are popular, or if you'd like something more substantial, you could try the blackberry cobbler or lemon lush. They're in the glass case over there if you'd like to take a look." Allie seemed to relax a little as she described the dessert choices.

"What's your favorite?" he asked, keeping his tone light.

"They're all good. Tessa does our baking."

"Your sister works here with you?"

"Yes." Allie smoothed an unseen wrinkle on her skirt.

"That's great. How's she doing?" He hoped this question

might transition the conversation to a more personal level.

"Her husband's business failed a couple years ago. They lost their house and most of their savings." She spoke in an even tone, but her eyes revealed her concern.

"I'm sorry. That sounds like a tough situation."

"Matt and Tessa are trying to get back on their feet. That's why we opened Sweet Something." Allie's face flushed and she bit her lip.

Tyler realized he'd better shift the direction of the conversation. "I like the way you've decorated the shop." He hesitated, glancing around the almost empty room again. "How's business?"

"We're doing all right."

"Really?"

Her bravado melted. She lowered her gaze, frowning slightly. "Actually, the weather's hurt us. There's not much parking on the street, and the closest public lot is four blocks away. Most people don't want to hike that far on slushy sidewalks when it's freezing." A look of tired resignation filled her face.

"Maybe I can help."

She cocked her head, looking doubtful. "What do you mean?"

"Please, sit down. Let's talk."

She stood a moment more, then finally took the seat on the opposite side of the table. "Okay. I'm listening."

"I have a new job with an ad agency here in Princeton. Maybe I could do a little promotional work for you. You know, raise your visibility and get some more customers coming in the door."

Her face flushed. "We've already used all our advertising budget for this year."

"Oh, I wouldn't charge you. I'd do it on my own time."

She sat back, shaking her head slightly. "I couldn't let you do that."

"Come on, Allie." He leaned toward her, his excitement growing. "I could create a logo, a new sign, and menu. I could check out your local advertising options and see what's available. It won't cost you a penny, I promise." Confidence flowed through him. With his help, her business could flourish no matter what the weather sent her way.

Suspicion clouded her eyes. "Why would you do that for me?"

A painful realization twisted through him. She didn't trust him or his motives. Why should she? She only knew him as the man he'd been six years ago, when he'd left town with no explanation and broken every promise he'd made to her.

"I just want to help you." He pulled in a ragged breath, struggling to remember the apology he had so carefully crafted back at his office. But it evaporated like a frosty breath on a winter day.

She stared at him, her expression unreadable, as though she'd constructed a wall around herself.

"Look, I know I messed up before, and you have no reason to trust me. But honestly, all I want to do is make up for what happened. We had something special, Allie. I'm sorry I let you go."

Her deep blue eyes flashed a warning, and her mouth firmed

into a straight line. She rose from her chair and turned away.

Tyler stood. "Allie, wait. That's not what I wanted to say."

She spun around, and her piercing gaze nailed him to the spot. "I don't want your help with my business, and I'm not interested in discussing the past."

Regret swamped him. If he could only go back and change his foolish choices. But that was impossible. He'd already reaped a harvest of pain from those mistakes, but it looked like harvest season wasn't over yet.

He turned to go, but something made him look over his shoulder. Allie stood in the same spot, watching him, a sorrowful expression filling her face. That gave him the courage to turn around and walk back toward her. "If you change your mind, I'd still like to help you get the word out about Sweet Something." He took his business card from his pocket and held it out to her.

A spark of some indefinable emotion flickered in her eyes. She reached out and accepted his card.

Chapter 2

Allison wiped the stainless-steel counter while visions of yesterday's confrontation with Tyler clouded her mind. The warmth of the tea-shop kitchen and slow pace of the afternoon lulled her into a dreamy fog.

Or had the air suddenly become strangely hazy?

She stopped to sniff. *Smoke!* She spun toward the oven. Little curls of blue gray smoke leaked out around the edges of the oven door. She gasped and lunged for a heavy-quilted oven mitt.

Tessa rushed in from the tearoom. "Something's burning!"

"I know!"

"Hurry, we don't want the smoke alarms to go off again." Tessa flipped on the overhead fan and unlocked the back window.

Allison jerked open the oven door. Clouds of smoke puffed into the room. Coughing, she grabbed the cookie sheet of scorched scones and crossed to the open window. In one swift motion, she flipped the cookie sheet and dumped the smoking triangles onto the brick walk out back. They looked more like smoking volcanic rocks than anything edible. Even the poor birds wouldn't be interested in that mess.

Allison moaned and tossed the cookie sheet into the deep stainless steel sink. "I can't believe I did that twice in one day!"

"Me neither." Tessa flapped a blue-striped kitchen towel back and forth.

"I'm sorry. I should have set the timer."

The air began to clear, and Tessa hung the towel on a hook by the sink. "You've been distracted all morning. Does this have anything to do with Tyler stopping in yesterday?"

Allison scowled. "No!"

Tessa crossed her arms. "Come on. Admit it. You were thinking about him instead of keeping your eyes on those scones."

Allison pushed her hair back from her warm face. "Okay, I was. But you'd be distracted, too, if you'd heard what he said. I can't believe he thinks he can just walk back in here and have a friendly conversation after six years with no communication."

"You never heard from him that whole time?"

"No!" She faltered, remembering that wasn't exactly true. "Well, I did see him once, on Christmas Eve a year ago." She fiddled with her watch clasp. Confusion swirled through her as she recalled his tender look and halting apology. She forced those thoughts away and focused on the painful end of their relationship six years ago. He'd made her believe he loved her. They'd even talked about getting married, but then he'd left without even saying good-bye. She still didn't know why. She sighed and rubbed her stinging eyes.

"I'm sorry." Tessa laid her hand on Allison's arm. "I didn't know it still bothered you."

"Neither did I, until yesterday." She steeled herself against those painful memories. "He has a lot of nerve, waltzing in here and offering to do promotional work for Sweet Something."

"Wait a minute. He wants to do promotional work for us?"

"Yes. Can you believe it?" Allison tossed the oven mitt onto the counter. "He works for some ad agency and thought we might like some free advertising advice."

Tessa gasped. "He wouldn't charge us?" She grabbed Allison's arm. "Please tell me you said yes."

"Nooo!" Allison vigorously shook her head.

"And why not?"

"You remember what happened! Not only did he walk out on me, he dropped out of grad school, got arrested for DUI, and our friends said he was just a. . .player."

"A player?" Tessa leaned back against the counter.

"You know—a guy who goes from girl to girl, playing with their emotions, just looking for. . ." She sent her sister a meaningful glance.

"Oh. . .well, that was a long time ago."

Allison touched her heart. "It doesn't feel like it to me."

Tessa frowned, but only for a moment. Then her face brightened. "That was personal. This is business." She crossed her arms. "I hope you weren't rude to him. What did you say?"

"Well. . .I think I said I didn't want his help." She'd practically kicked him out of the shop, and his calm response totally stumped her. Where was the cocky, self-assured man who always had a quick comeback or persuasive excuse for everything?

Tessa groaned. "Allison, how could you? Call him right now, and tell him you've changed your mind."

"I can't do that!"

"Oh, yes you can. We need his help. And if you're worried about things getting uncomfortable, just insist on keeping it strictly business."

Conflicting thoughts tumbled through her mind. Spending time with Tyler would be awkward. But keeping her business afloat was worth dealing with a little emotional upheaval. Certainly she could set aside her personal feelings and deal with him on a professional level. After all, she was an experienced businesswoman now.

She looked up at Tessa and nodded. "You're right. I can do this." She reached into her apron pocket and pulled out his business card.

Tessa leaned closer. She read it and sucked in a quick breath. "He works for Kent & Sheldon?"

"Yes. What about it?"

"That's one of the most prestigious ad agencies in Princeton. I heard the CEO is a Christian. He gives a lot to charity, and his agency only works with companies who are very ethical."

Allison studied the card again. Why would Tyler choose to work for a company like Kent & Sheldon?

Tyler raised the collar of his navy wool overcoat and tucked his small portfolio under his arm. He hopped a slushy puddle and crossed Nassau Street with the WALK signal. A bone-chilling breeze whistled around the edge of his collar and cuffs, but the sun had come out. The sidewalks were dry, making it a little less intimidating to walk around town.

The last forty-eight hours had been a mad dash of creativity as he'd followed up on Allie's surprise phone call. With permission from Ronald Sheldon, he'd taken time off to research tea shops and come up with several creative ideas for Sweet Something.

He smiled remembering Allie's call. "I'm sorry I was so quick to dismiss your offer. I've talked it over with Tessa, and we'd appreciate any advertising advice you could give us."

In a businesslike tone, she reminded him that their budget might not allow them to implement his ideas right away, but she'd like to see what he had in mind. He assured her he could come up with several options for free or low-cost advertising, and he'd do the graphic design at no charge.

"Let me work on this for a couple of days," he told her. "I'll get back to you. Shall I call you at home?"

"Call me at the shop," she said quickly. "I appreciate your help, but this is strictly business. I'm not interested in anything else."

That had deflated him a little, but his goals were to help Allie's business become successful and try to make up for the past. Anything else between them was up to the Lord. He didn't intend to push or manipulate the situation, no matter how strongly the old attraction pulled him. Pure motives. Pure actions. That had to be his focus now.

Tyler slowed as he passed Princeton Interiors, the shop next door to Sweet Something. Warm light glowed on a dazzling array of expensive antique furniture, chandeliers, and unique home furnishings. One glance at the busy shop, and he could tell the owner did a brisk business.

He continued on and pulled open the door of Sweet Something. As he stepped inside, he looked past the gift shop into the tearoom. Customers filled more than half the tables. Tyler smiled. That ought to raise Allie's spirits and give her business a boost.

Allie hurried down the steps, her gaze fixed on the group of three middle-aged women who had come in before him. He stepped back and watched her welcome and seat the women at a round table in the center of the room.

Today Allie wore a royal blue blouse, the same color as her eyes, and a dark print skirt with swirls of sable brown, olive green, and deep blue. A white apron edged with lace topped her outfit.

He looked for other servers, but saw only one young woman weaving between the tables, carrying a tray of dirty dishes toward the back of the shop. Two other tables nearby still needed to be cleared.

He stepped into Allie's line of vision. When their gazes connected, her smile faltered for a moment but then returned. She nodded and walked toward him.

He smiled. "Looks like business is improving."

"Yes, this is the best day we've had in quite a while." Her

cheeks flushed a pretty pink, and she sent him a cautious glance. "I know I asked you to come at three thirty, but I don't think I can meet with you today. Tessa had to leave early to take her daughter to the orthodontist, and two of my servers called in sick."

"Sounds like you're in a bind."

"Kayla and I will be tired by six, but we'll make it." She glanced at the clock and pulled in a sharp breath. "I have a group of ten from the Princeton Historical Society coming at four, and I haven't rearranged the tables in the other room."

The bell jingled, and two young college-age girls in faded jeans, heavy jackets, and knitted caps came in the door.

Allie hesitated, looking torn. "I'm sorry. I have to take care of them." She excused herself and seated the girls. The other server hurried past with a tray of three small teapots, cups, and saucers.

Tyler surveyed the scene a moment longer and made his decision. Slipping off his coat, he followed Allie across the room. "Where can I stash this?"

She turned and looked at him quizzically. "I'm sorry. I really can't meet with you today."

"I know. That's why I'm going to help you."

"What?" Her blue eyes widened.

"I've never actually served tea before, but I can rearrange tables, seat people, or do whatever else you need."

She stared at him as though she couldn't quite believe he was serious.

"Allie, you're shorthanded, and I have the rest of the afternoon off. This sounds like the perfect solution."

"But you can't do that," she sputtered. "You're a. . .professional, not a waiter."

"True, but I'm also a friend who wants to see your business succeed."

Her expression softened. "You're serious?"

"Sure. Where do I get one of those aprons?" He gestured toward the lacey one she wore.

She laughed, and it sounded like the tinkling of delicate wind chimes. "All right. You're hired. Come with me, and I'll show you where you can hang your coat." She led the way into the kitchen.

A few minutes later he had taken off his suit jacket, rolled up his sleeves, and tied a more masculine version of Allie's apron around his waist. She led the way to a side room and quickly mapped out the new table arrangement. Then she laid out one place setting on a side table as an example and showed him where the dishes were kept.

"I'll be back in a few minutes." She smiled at him over her shoulder, then returned to the tearoom and left him to his work.

Kayla, Allie's only other server, swept in and dropped off a pile of fresh table linens. The young blond didn't look more than eighteen. She hung around and asked him several questions. He gave brief answers as he moved tables and covered them with tablecloths. She finally turned to leave the room, sending him a seductive smile. He turned away from her obvious invitation, thankful those old temptations didn't have as much pull as they used to. A few years ago it might have been more of a struggle, but he was committed to a new path now.

Setting the table took a little longer than he'd expected. He finally stood back and surveyed his work with a satisfied smile.

Allie walked in carrying two small teapots holding arrangements of fresh flowers. She stepped up beside him, her gaze searching the table. "This looks perfect." She set the flowers on the table and beamed him a dazzling smile. "Thank you, Tyler."

He pulled in a deep breath and felt like he could walk a mile in the cold with the memory of that smile to warm him. "What's next?"

"Oh, you don't have to do anything else. This was a huge help."

"Hey, I'm not leaving now. I signed on for the whole afternoon." He straightened a knife and spoon at one place setting. "When this group shows up, you're going to have your hands full. I can greet and seat your other customers. And if that doesn't keep me busy, I can clear tables."

Allie protested, but he insisted. Soon he was doing double duty as host and busboy, while Allie and Kayla took orders and delivered food and drinks. The afternoon passed swiftly, and before he knew it, the clock by the front door struck six, and Allison flipped the OPEN sign to CLOSED.

With a relieved sigh, she smiled and gestured toward the closest table. "Why don't we sit down and take a look at your designs?"

He reached to untie his apron. "I'm sorry. I'd love to show them to you, but I'm supposed to meet a client at the Nassau Inn for dinner." He glanced at his watch and knew he needed to hurry or he'd be late.

She bit her lip a moment, then lifted her gaze to meet his. "Are you busy after that?"

He could hardly hold back his smile. "No. I don't have anything else planned tonight."

Allie took a business card from the basket and wrote something on the back. "I live just a few blocks from Nassau Inn. Here's the address. Could you stop by after dinner?" Her hand trembled slightly as she passed him the card.

Suddenly, he realized how much it had cost her to give the invitation. He smiled and nodded. "This dinner won't take long." He'd make sure it didn't.

"All right. I'll see you later then."

His hopes soared at her smile.

Chapter 3

Allison hurried up the steps and unlocked her front door. Her Persian cat, Miss Priss, jumped down from the back of the couch to greet her.

"Hello, sweetie." She gave Miss Priss a quick pat on the head and kissed her cold nose; then she hurried into the bathroom to brush her hair upside down, wash her face, and dab on some makeup. She changed twice before she finally settled on dark brown slacks, a white turtleneck, and a dark brown sweater with a snowflake pattern across the front.

Glancing in the mirror, Allison plastered on a smile and tried to think positive. But those last fifteen pounds she always intended to lose remained firmly attached in all the wrong places. She tugged at the bottom edge of her sweater, wishing it were a little longer. Why hadn't she kept up her exercise routine this winter, or at least said no to all those desserts Tessa asked her to try?

Blowing out a resigned sigh, she turned and walked away from the mirror. It didn't matter. This was not a date. They were simply going to look over his designs and discuss promotional ideas for Sweet Something.

R–i–i–ight. She rolled her eyes and knew she hadn't even fooled herself. She hurried into the kitchen and fixed a pot of coffee.

The doorbell rang. Her heart jumped. She hurried across the living room but then slowed and pulled in a deep breath. *Lord, help me calm down and not act like a complete idiot.* They were going to discuss business and that's all. Relaxing a little, she pulled open the front door and greeted Tyler.

He smiled, looking as handsome as ever, his face flushed from the cold and his brown eyes glowing. A few snowflakes melted in his light brown hair and dusted the shoulders of his charcoal gray coat. She invited him in. He took off his coat, suit jacket, and scarf, and she hung them in the closet.

"This is very nice." He looked around her living room with an appreciative glance. Tyler had always noticed color, texture, and style. She guessed it was part of his artistic nature. Allison liked that about him. He understood her need to use her creativity and be surrounded by beauty.

"How about some coffee?" she offered. "I just made a pot. Or I have tea or cocoa."

"Coffee sounds great. Thanks. It's freezing outside." He rubbed his hands together and followed her into the kitchen. He slowed and slipped his hands into his pockets as he studied the painting on the wall near her kitchen table.

The painting featured a cozy living-room setting, with two red wingback chairs pulled up by a stone fireplace where a welcoming fire glowed. A round table set for dessert stood between the chairs. A sleepy gray cat sat curled up in one of the chairs, and an open Bible lay on the footstool by the other.

He leaned closer, looking as though he wanted to take in every detail of the painting. "This is an original, isn't it?"

"Yes, it is." She pulled two mugs from the cabinet.

"Who's the artist?"

Allison looked up and met Tyler's gaze. "I am."

"I thought so." He smiled at her for a brief moment then turned back to the painting. "Why no signature?"

"It's there, but when I had it framed, the mat covered it." She filled the mugs with steaming coffee and carried them over to the kitchen table.

He spun and looked at her with a glint of excitement in his eyes. "Do you have other paintings?"

She nodded, wondering why he was so interested. "I have two upstairs in my bedroom and probably a dozen or so stored in the hall closet."

He sent her a baffled look. "In the closet?"

"Yes. It's too expensive to have them all framed."

"You know, there's a huge market for paintings like this. I saw several artists advertising their limited-edition prints when I scanned some home-decorating magazines, looking for logo ideas for Sweet Something. None of those paintings were as good as yours. You should have prints made."

A warm glow spread through her. Tyler was also an artist, making his compliment even more meaningful. They'd met in an art class in college. He had chosen to focus on graphic design and advertising, while she had decided on fine art and teaching, but their love of art had been a common thread woven through their three-year relationship.

She glanced at her painting, considering his idea. "That would probably take a big investment of time and money, and I need to focus on the shop right now." She set the mugs on the table and offered him sugar and cream.

"Why don't I look into it for you?" Tyler stirred a spoonful of sugar into his coffee. "It might not cost as much as you think."

She started to shake her head, but the hopeful look in his eyes stopped her. "I guess it wouldn't hurt."

"Great!" His smile spread wider. "I can see it now—original paintings and prints by Allison Bennett hanging in galleries all across the country. You'll become famous, and before we know it, that'll draw huge crowds to your tea shop. That's probably the best promotional idea we could ever come up with."

She laughed. "Tyler, you always were a dreamer."

He took a sip and gazed at her over the rim of his mug. "I've always known you had a special gift." He nodded toward her artwork. "That painting proves it. It draws you in, makes you feel like you could step right into that room." He focused on the cozy scene. "You've invited a good friend over for the evening. You light the fire, put on the coffee, slice the pie, and get out your Bible so you can sit down and talk about what you've been learning."

She sent him a curious glance. "That's exactly what I had in mind." Most people who'd looked at the painting didn't even realize the open book on the footstool was a Bible. But Tyler had.

He nodded, looking pleased, and took another sip of coffee. "So, are you ready to take a look at my designs for Sweet Something?"

She agreed, picked up her cup, and led the way to the living room.

Tyler opened his portfolio and spread out his designs on the coffee table, then took a seat beside her on the couch. "I worked with several different concepts, but these three are the strongest. Of course we can always combine ideas and change things around."

Allison was suddenly very conscious of Tyler's nearness. His shoulder brushed against hers as he reached to pick up the first design, and the warm spicy scent of his aftershave tickled her nose. She clasped her hands and forced herself to focus.

Tyler explained how he came up with the logos. Then he showed her each one on menus, business cards, a new outdoor sign, a Yellow Pages ad, a newspaper ad, even gift certificates and discounts coupons. "So what do you think? Which do you like best?" Confidence and expectation glowed in his eyes. He seemed to have no doubt she'd like his work.

"They're all beautiful. I'm not sure how to choose one."

"Go with your feelings. Which one stands out to you?"

"Well. . .I guess I'd say this one." She pointed to the logo featuring a delicate teacup and a soft pink rose in full bloom. The swirling green type and soft pastel colors in the rose and cup looked sophisticated yet fresh and inviting—just the image she wanted to project.

"That's actually my favorite, too." He turned to her and

smiled. His expression softened, and tenderness filled his eyes as his gaze traveled over her face and hair.

Allison felt certain he wasn't thinking about logo designs anymore. Her heartbeat sped up, and she held her breath, waiting to hear what he would say next.

The doorbell rang. Allison jumped as if someone had poked her with a sharp stick. "Sorry. Excuse me a minute. I'll see who that is." She crossed the living room, pulled opened the door, and stared in stunned silence.

"Hello, Allison." Peter Hillinger leaned forward and kissed her cheek.

How could she have forgotten she had a dinner date with Peter? Her mind whirled back to the day she had received the anonymous check. Right after Tyler had walked out the door of her shop, Peter had come in. When he'd invited her out to dinner, she'd been so flustered she'd said yes without thinking it through or writing it down.

"May I come in?"

"Yes, of course. . .I'm sorry." She stepped back and darted a glance at Tyler. He stood and looked Peter over warily.

A slight frown creased Peter's high forehead when he saw Tyler. He sent Allison a questioning glance.

She forced a tight smile. "Peter, this is Tyler Lawrence. He's. . .an old friend, and he's offered to do some promotional work for the tea shop." She turned to Tyler, her mind spinning as she tried to come up with an explanation. "This is Peter Hillinger. He owns Princeton Interiors, the shop next to ours."

The two men shook hands, a challenge obvious in both their eyes.

Peter turned back to Allison. "Our dinner reservations are for eight o'clock. But I think they'll hold them for a few minutes if you'd like to change."

She glanced down at her outfit. "Oh. . .yes, I guess I should." She turned to Tyler, wishing she could explain. "I'm sorry. It looks like we'll have to finish this another time."

"No problem. I'll call you." He smiled, but disappointment clouded his eyes. At least she hoped it was disappointment and not irritation because she'd cut their evening short.

⟡

Tyler watched Allie walk down the hall and slip into the first room on the right. Regret burned in his throat. There would be no more opportunity to talk to her tonight.

He felt Peter's haughty glare even before he turned to face him. He wore an expensive-looking black wool overcoat, white silk scarf, and leather gloves. Tyler had spent less than two minutes with the man, but that was long enough to know he didn't like him. His puffed-up attitude was bad enough, but the way he'd kissed Allie and walked into her house like he owned it, bothered him even more.

"So you're an old friend of Allison's?" Peter pulled off his gloves.

"Yes, we've known each other since college."

"That's funny." Peter sent him a smug smile. "I don't remember her ever mentioning you."

298

Those words cut deeply, and it took him a moment to recover. "Allie and I lost touch for a few years, but I'm back in Princeton now."

Peter glanced at the designs on the table. He lifted his brows for a brief moment, looking impressed, then glanced back at Tyler. "Interesting. But I'm not sure Allison needs any of this."

"I suppose that's up to her, isn't it?" Tyler gathered up his artwork, slid them back into his portfolio, and closed the flap.

"I appreciate your wanting to help Allison with her business, but I hope that's all you have in mind."

Tyler gripped the handles of the portfolio, wishing he could knock the pompous expression off Peter's face. A verse he had memorized flew to the front of his thoughts. *A foolish man gives full vent to his anger, but a wise man keeps himself under control.* He walked away from Peter and grabbed his jacket and coat from the closet.

Peter followed as though he were the host and intended to show Tyler out the door. "Allison has been through a lot over the past year, helping her sister through everything that's happened, and she's had a rather difficult time getting her business up and running. I've been there for her every step of the way." He narrowed his steel gray eyes, looking as though he wanted to make sure Tyler understood the message behind his words. "We've grown very close. I wouldn't want anyone to hurt her."

Tyler squared his shoulders and locked gazes with Peter. "Neither would I." He turned and walked out the door.

Chapter 4

Y ou invited him over to your house?" Tessa turned from brushing crumbs off one of the tearoom tables and stared at Allison.

"Well, he wanted to show me his design ideas." Allison straightened the stack of menus, trying to ignore the disapproval in her sister's eyes.

"Right, I'm sure he had all kinds of *designs* he wanted to show you."

"Tessa, nothing happened! We had coffee and looked at his promotional ideas for about twenty minutes. Then Peter came to pick me up for dinner." That thought left her feeling like a deflated balloon. After she'd changed for her dinner date and walked back into the living room, Peter was the only one waiting for her.

"So how was your date with Peter?"

"We went to Lambertville Station. The food was good. There was a jazz trio playing."

"So things are progressing?"

"I suppose. Peter's just so. . ." She squinted, trying to come up with the right word.

"Mature, confident, and wealthy?"

Allison rolled her eyes. "Too bad you're already married. You could date him!"

"We're not talking about me. We're talking about you and Peter."

"I know." Confusion swirled through Allison. "I like him. He's thoughtful and interesting, but there's something missing. It's like I have to try too hard with him. And I just don't feel a connection with him like I do with Ty. . ." She swallowed the rest of her sentence and turned to push in the chairs at the nearest table.

"You're not thinking about dating Tyler again, are you?" Tessa tapped her nails on the oak desk they used as a hostess podium.

"I didn't say that."

"Good. Remember what happened last time. He left town and broke your heart."

She winced at her sister's words. "I know. You don't have to remind me."

"Sorry. I just don't want you to get hurt again."

"Don't worry. I won't let Tyler talk me into anything more than a business relationship." But as Allison turned and glanced across the quiet tea shop, she remembered how Tyler had spent the previous afternoon greeting customers and clearing tables for her. He seemed different somehow—still charming and persuasive as ever, but there was a softening, a gentleness about him that was new. . .and very attractive.

"Allison?" Tessa tapped her on the shoulder. "Did you hear what I said?"

"No. Sorry, guess I was daydreaming."

"About Peter or Tyler?"

"Tessa, stop! I am not interested in Tyler." Allison huffed out an irritated breath and strode toward the kitchen.

─━◦❦◦━─

Four days was long enough to wait. Allison slipped Tyler's business card from her apron pocket and picked up the phone. She glanced at the clock by the front door, hoping she could make the call and connect with Tyler before her sister returned from the bank. The shop didn't open until eleven, so she didn't need to worry about taking care of customers for at least another hour. She quickly punched in his number and whispered a prayer. On the third ring the receptionist answered. Allison willed her voice to sound confident as she asked to speak to Tyler.

"I'm sorry, Mr. Lawrence is out of the office this morning. May I take a message?"

"Yes. Mr. Lawrence showed me some designs last Tuesday, but our meeting was interrupted. I've been expecting him to call so we could set up another meeting."

"I'm sure he meant to get back to you, but he's been sick for a few days."

Her heart jerked. "I hope it's nothing serious."

"I really couldn't say, but if you'd like to leave your name and number, I'll let him know you called."

Allison left the information and hung up the phone. She glanced out the tea shop's front windows. Gray storm clouds gathered overhead. Wind whistled in the eaves. Where was the promise of spring? She shivered and rubbed her arms. Over the past week her financial troubles had become increasingly clear. The anonymous check had been a wonderful gift that carried them through early March, but unless she could bring in more customers soon, her business was doomed.

She closed her eyes. *Father, I can't live off my savings forever, and You know how much Tessa and Matt need the extra income. We have to start making a profit. I need Tyler's help for that, but I'm afraid I've botched things with him, and now he's sick.*

Little vines of worry wrapped around her heart as she considered the possibilities. How sick was he? Had he seen a doctor? Was anyone checking on him?

Chapter 5

Allison slipped the heavy basket over her arm and rang Tyler's doorbell. Her heartbeat surged in her ears as she strained to hear any sounds inside his apartment. Nothing. She bit her lip and rang again. This plan had to work. Her only hope was to make amends with Tyler and convince him to follow through on his offer to do free promotional work for Sweet Something.

Finally, she heard a soft shuffle and the door swung open.

Tyler looked out at her through red-rimmed, watery eyes. His baggy gray sweatpants and a wrinkled navy blue T-shirt made it look as though he had just crawled out of bed. He blinked at her. "Allie, what are you doing here?"

Heat rose in her cheeks and she forced a smile. "I called your office, and they told me you were sick, so I thought I'd bring you some lunch."

"Wow, that's nice. Would you like to come in?" He stepped back and glanced over his shoulder. "Sorry, things are kind of a mess."

"You don't have to apologize. I can tell you've been sick."

He ran a hand over his bristly chin and sent her a sheepish grin. "I probably look worse than my apartment."

He looked adorable, but she quickly squelched that thought. "You look like a guy who needs to sit down and put his feet up." She pointed toward the dark brown leather couch. "Go on."

Tyler obediently headed for the couch. He tossed his pillow to one end and straightened the blanket and sheet before he sat down. "So what's in the basket?"

She set it on the coffee table next to a worn, brown leather Bible. That surprised her. Of course she knew Tyler had prayed and asked Christ into his heart when he was twenty-one. She'd been with him that night. But everything she'd heard about him since he'd left Princeton made her doubt his sincerity. If he was serious about his faith, how could he have been arrested for drinking and driving? And worse yet, how could he have a reputation for being involved in a string of broken relationships? Her stomach clenched at that thought.

Focusing on her basket, she folded back the blue tea towel. "I brought you some homemade chicken-noodle soup, blueberry muffins, applesauce, bottled water, tissues, and some cold and flu medication." She felt a little embarrassed by the overflowing collection she'd put together for him. But she needed him to get well as soon as possible.

He sent her an appreciative smile. "I haven't been able to eat much for a few days, but soup sounds great."

"Good. Why don't I warm some up for you?"

He glanced toward the kitchen. "I haven't cleaned up in

there for a couple days."

"It's okay. You lie down and rest, and I'll be back with some hot soup in a couple minutes."

"Okay, thanks."

She picked up the basket and headed for the adjoining kitchen. Her steps slowed as she scanned the room. Dirty dishes and sticky pots and pans cluttered the counter and sink. Newspapers lay scattered on the small kitchen table, as well as a stack of unopened mail, two empty coffee cups, and a take-out bag from Mrs. Chow's Chinese Restaurant.

She looked for a microwave, but didn't see one. So she checked the cabinet and found a pan, poured in the soup, and turned on the burner. She decided to rinse the dishes and load the dishwasher while she waited for the soup to warm. Glancing at the windowsill, she noticed a stack of 3 x 5 cards. Leaning closer, she saw a Bible reference written on the top card in Tyler's neat, all-cap handwriting. Surprise rippled through her.

"Are you finding everything you need?" Tyler called.

Allison jumped. "Yes, no problem."

"Sounds like more is happening in there than warming up the soup."

"I'm just loading the dishwasher." She leaned forward again and read the card. *FLEE THE EVIL DESIRES OF YOUTH, AND PURSUE RIGHTEOUSNESS, FAITH, LOVE AND PEACE, ALONG WITH THOSE WHO CALL ON THE LORD OUT OF A PURE HEART. 2 TIMOTHY 2:22.*

The power of those words warmed her heart. With damp fingers, she reached up and flipped to the next card. *YOU HAVE*

MADE KNOWN TO ME THE PATHS OF LIFE; YOU WILL FILL ME WITH
JOY IN YOUR PRESENCE—

"Allie, you don't have to wash dishes for me." Tyler's gentle rebuke startled her.

She glanced over her shoulder and saw him standing in the kitchen doorway. Plunging her hands in the soapy water, she began vigorously scrubbing a small frying pan. "I don't mind. Might as well make myself useful."

Tyler leaned against the doorjamb, his hands in his pockets. A small smile lifted the corners of his mouth. "Thanks, I appreciate it. I'm not usually such a slob, but the last few days have really wiped me out."

She blew out a deep breath. My, oh my, *slob* was *not* the word that came to mind when she looked at him. She silently chided herself and focused on the pan in her hands. What was the matter with her? She couldn't deny her attraction to Tyler, but starting something with him would be foolish. She'd made the mistake of following her feelings and trusting him before, and she didn't intend to get hurt like that again. Just because he memorized a few Bible verses, that didn't mean he had truly changed, did it?

"I think the soup is boiling." He pointed toward the stove.

"Oh, right." She dropped the pan back in the dishwater and dried her hands on a towel.

Tyler suggested they sit at the kitchen table. He gathered up the newspapers and tossed them in a box by the back door. Allison placed his steamy bowl of soup on the table.

"Looks like there's plenty," he said. "Would you like some?"

"No, that's okay. I need to get back to the shop soon."

"Can you sit down for a few minutes?" He looked reluctant to eat without her, so she pulled out a chair and sat down.

He extended his hand across the table toward her. "Would you pray with me?"

Stunned, she slowly nodded and took his hand. His grasp was warm and strong.

"Father, thanks for answering my prayers for strength and healing." Tyler's voice took on a gentle tone. "And thanks for sending Allie here today to encourage me and bring me this meal. I'm grateful. You've poured out Your grace and love in my life, and I pray You'll give me a chance to do that for Allie. Please help us spread the word about Sweet Something, and we ask You to bless and increase her business."

Warmth and sweetness wrapped around her heart. She'd never expected Tyler to pray for her. Relief washed over her as she listened to the rest of his prayer. He certainly didn't sound upset with her. He probably didn't care that she'd cut their meeting short or that she'd gone out with Peter. Why had she even worried about that?

"Amen." Tyler squeezed her hand.

She squeezed back and opened her eyes.

He grinned. "This soup is making my mouth water."

She laughed softly and enjoyed watching his expression as he savored the first spoonful.

"This is delicious. Did you make it?"

"It's Tessa's recipe, but I put it together this time." She got up, intending to finish the dishes.

"Where are you going?" He reached out and stopped her.

She felt a tremor at his touch. "I thought I'd finish cleaning up while you eat."

She hoped scrubbing pots and pans would take her focus off Tyler. Because sitting across from him in this cozy little kitchen was making it very hard for her to keep her mind on the reason for her visit.

They carried on an easy conversation as she finished the dishes, wiped the counters, and put the extra soup in the refrigerator. His gaze followed her as she moved around the room. Was he comparing the way she looked now to their college days? She groaned inwardly at that thought. She might have more style and confidence now, but she was also a little heavier.

After Tyler finished his soup, he stood up and stretched. The muscles of his broad chest expanded and filled out his wrinkly T-shirt. He certainly didn't carry any extra weight in the wrong places. She pulled her gaze away and searched for somewhere else to focus her attention. The photos on the refrigerator caught her eye, and she stepped closer.

"That's my niece, Emma. She's four. She always begs me to give her airplane rides or read her a story." Smiling, he pointed to the other photo. "And that's her little brother, Thomas. He's nine months and just learning how to pull himself up. He's big for his age, and he's got a killer grip. I bet he'll play football some day." He chuckled. "Sorry, don't get me started talking about them."

Allison smiled, touched by his description. "They're cute."

Tyler's eyes glowed. "Yeah, I can't get enough of that little

Emma. She's a real heartbreaker. Hope I have one just like her some day."

Allison stared at the photo. Had she heard him correctly? When they were dating, he'd said he never wanted children. It had been a nagging difference between them that had never been resolved. What had changed his mind? She told herself it didn't matter and shifted her thoughts to her reason for coming.

She turned to him. "I'm sorry about cutting our meeting short the other night. I totally forgot Peter was coming over."

His smile melted away. "Have you known him long?"

"A little over a year."

Tyler nodded. "He owns that antique shop next to Sweet Something, right?"

"It's an interior design company, but he does carry a lot of antiques. His father started the business. He passed it on to Peter two years ago."

"Old Princeton money." Tyler crossed his arms and leaned back against the counter, looking grim.

She smiled, hoping to lighten the moment. "Yes, and he likes everyone to know it."

Tyler's expression remained serious. "Is he a believer?"

Suddenly the room seemed too warm. "He attends Harvest Chapel with me."

Tyler studied her a moment, unspoken questions reflected in his eyes. "I haven't seen you at Harvest except for Christmas Eve a year ago."

"Oh. . .well, I usually go to second service." A little cloud of guilt settled over her as she spoke. That wasn't completely true. Since she'd opened her tea shop, she only attended church one or two times a month.

"So, are you and Peter serious?"

Allison's stomach fluttered nervously. "Well, we're dating. . . and we—"

Tyler held up his hand to stop her. "Sorry, that's none of my business."

Now she felt awful. "No, it's okay. I don't mind your asking. If you were dating someone, I'd probably ask you the same question." She chewed her lip a moment. "You're not dating anyone, are you?"

Tyler's gaze held steady. "No, I'm not."

Relief washed over her, then embarrassment. "Well. . .I'm sure there's someone very special out there for you."

Tyler nodded, a small smile lifting the corners of his mouth. "I'm praying for her."

Confusion swirled through her. What did he mean? Was he talking about her? But she'd just told him she was dating Peter. She didn't want to give him the wrong idea about them, but if he knew how uncertain she felt about Peter, it might encourage him to pursue her again and that would be—

"I'm sorry I haven't gotten back to you about the designs for your tea shop. I still want to do that work for you."

"Oh, that would be great!" Relief washed over her. "I love that rose and teacup design."

His smile returned. "Good. I'll start working on it today."

"But you're sick. You need to rest."

KISS THE ~~COOK~~ *Bride*

"It's okay. I have my computer with my design programs here at home."

"If you're sure it wouldn't be too much trouble." She glanced at her watch and took the empty basket from the counter. "I better go. I don't want to leave Tessa shorthanded for too long." She walked into the living room and picked up her jacket.

Tyler followed and helped her slip it on. "Thanks for coming."

She turned back toward him, suddenly wishing she didn't have to leave, or that she could do something else for him. "Would you like me to pick up some DVDs for you? I could bring them by after work tonight."

"Thanks, I appreciate the offer, but I don't have a TV."

She glanced around the living room. His apartment was nicely furnished with a leather couch and chairs, full book-shelves, a computer desk in the corner, and original art on the walls. Money didn't seem to be a problem.

He grinned. "I know, that sounds weird doesn't it?"

"I have a small TV at home you could borrow."

"Thanks, but I don't really want one."

She lifted her brows. "How come?"

"I used to complain my life was too busy, so one of my friends challenged me to get rid of it for six months. It was hard at first." He chuckled. "Guess I was addicted. But I like it now. And I have more time for important things like studying my Bible and reading."

"Oh." Allie didn't know what else to say.

"I've started running and playing racquetball again," he

added. "And I've set aside a couple evenings a week to spend time with my mom and my brother Jeff and his family. My dad's remarried and lives down in Florida now, so I try to keep in touch with him by phone."

She stared at him. How could that be true? During the last few months of their relationship, Tyler's parents had finalized a messy divorce. Tyler blamed his father for his unfaithfulness, but he also scorned his mother for her vengeful response. Then he cut himself off from his family, and a few weeks later he'd left her, as well. She could understand the pain and disappointment he felt toward his parents, but why had he turned his back on her when she truly loved him and had tried to be there for him through the whole terrible ordeal? Now he spoke to both his parents each week?

"Thanks for coming by. I'll call you when I have those designs ready."

"Okay." She walked out the door, feeling more confused than she'd been before their visit.

Chapter 6

Tyler rolled over, opened one eye, and squinted at his bedside clock. Surprise jolted through him, bringing him fully awake. How could it be ten fifteen? He'd already missed first service, and he'd have to hustle to make second.

Memories of his late-night design marathon resurfaced as he threw back the covers and climbed out of bed. That must be why he'd slept past his alarm—that and the fact he was still recovering from the worst case of the flu he'd had in years. But it didn't matter. At least all the designs for Allie's tea shop were finished. He just needed to show them to her one more time, and then he'd send them off to the printer and sign company.

Rubbing his hand down his face, he headed for the bathroom. Maybe he could catch her at church and invite her out to lunch, or better yet, they could come back here and cook lunch together. He smiled. Sleeping in and going to second service might work out for the best after all.

His smile faded as he recalled the uncomfortable look on

Allie's face when she'd tried to explain why he never saw her at church. They did attend different Sunday morning services, but why hadn't he seen her on Sunday evenings or at the singles' Bible study? What was going on with Allie spiritually?

During college she'd always been so certain about her faith. She was the one who'd patiently explained the importance of making a personal commitment to the Lord. It had taken him two years before he'd finally surrendered his life. Allie had been with him that night. But after his parents' divorce, he'd turned away from his faith and everyone associated with it. Thankfully, God hadn't given up on him. He sighed and looked in the bathroom mirror. Fine lines creased his forehead and surrounded his eyes, lingering evidence of the wild life he'd left behind.

But what about Allie?

The thought that she might have drifted away from her faith weighed him down like someone had just placed a thirty-pound pack on his shoulders. It couldn't be true. She'd never turn her back on God, would she?

Forty-five minutes later, Tyler walked into the second service at Harvest Chapel just as the first song began. He scanned the large sanctuary, searching for Allie, but he didn't see her.

Another wave of apprehension settled over him. Where was she? He purposefully shifted his thoughts to the words of the song. The music lifted his spirit, and he turned his concern for Allie into a prayer and released her back to the Lord's care, firmly reminding himself that's where she needed to stay.

His motives needed to remain pure. Build a bridge, ask

forgiveness, help her business succeed. That's all. But as he remembered her visit to his apartment, her sweet caring expression, and the way she'd prepared that hot soup for him, he couldn't keep from hoping there might be more.

The final notes of the song faded. Tyler glanced to the right. A couple moved into the row in front of him. His stomach clenched into a hard knot as Allie and Peter sat down in front of him. Peter helped Allie slip off her coat; then he placed his arm around her shoulder.

Allison shifted and tried to scoot a few more inches to the left, away from Peter. But he kept his arm around her and settled in a little closer. She sank a bit lower in the pew, wishing she could vanish.

They didn't usually sit this close to the front, but coming in late hadn't left too many choices. She hadn't realized Tyler was sitting behind them until greeting time when she'd stood and turned to face him. He'd said hello and reached to shake her hand. Her knees felt like noodles as she realized he must have seen every whisper and possessive movement Peter had made. She'd managed to mumble some sort of greeting before she sank back into her seat.

Allison silently chided herself and corralled her runaway thoughts. She was here to worship the Lord. Lifting her gaze, she focused on Pastor Tom's face.

"God wants more than just a piece of our heart. He wants all of it. Nothing should take His place. That's why Jesus says in Mathew 6:33, 'Seek first his kingdom and his righteousness, and all these things will be given to you.' " Pastor Tom's voice rang with passion and sent a shiver up her back.

"If you're struggling today, ask yourself this question: 'Am I honoring God and giving Him first place in my life?' If the answer is no, then I suggest you spend some time with Him, straighten out your priorities, and get your life back on track.

"I know some of you may say, 'Oh, Pastor, you don't know all the trouble I'm facing in my life.' You're right. I don't. But God does, and He is able to meet you right where you are and help you bring your life back in line with His Word and His purpose for you." Pastor Tom scanned the sanctuary.

Allison felt his gaze settle on her.

"You may have some painful choices and decisions to make. Trust God. He has a plan, and He is able to carry you through, if you will humble yourself and give Him first place."

His words pierced Allison's heart. She hadn't put God first or trusted Him to work out the problems with her business. She hadn't prayed more than five minutes about it. Instead, she'd worried and spent her time scheming, trying to use Tyler's friendship and free promotional help to get what she thought she needed.

Tears gathered in her eyes, and she bowed her head. *Forgive me, Father. I've been so wrapped up in my problems that I haven't even asked what You want me to do. I'm asking now. Please lead me and show me Your plans for Sweet Something. And what should I do about Peter? Am I dating him because Tessa says I should, or because he's rich and he knows everyone who's anyone in Princeton?*

Am I using him, too, hoping his money and position will somehow improve my business? Those thoughts turned her stomach. What had happened to her? How had she gotten so far off track?

Peter leaned closer. "Everything all right?"

Allison slowly lifted her head and nodded. He patted her shoulder in a caring way, but it only made her feel worse. She closed her eyes and blew out a slow, deep breath. It was time she had an honest talk with Peter.

Two hours later, after an unbearably long lunch with Peter's parents and sister, Allison felt even more certain about her decision. She led the way up her front steps and stopped to retrieve her keys from her purse. Peter held out his hand and offered to unlock the door for her. But she clutched the key tightly. "We need to talk."

"I can come in for a few minutes, but I have to be back at the shop by three to meet a client."

"What I have to say won't take long." She bit her lip, then looked up at him. "I'm sorry, Peter. I don't want to lead you on. This just isn't working."

He frowned slightly. "What do you mean?"

"I can't date you anymore. It's not fair to you. We're worlds apart, and you deserve someone who appreciates you for all the fine things about you and your life. . .but I'm not that person."

"I don't understand. How can you say we're worlds apart? We've both lived in Princeton all our lives. We both own businesses. We like theater, jazz, art museums, spending time with our families. What's the problem?"

"We do have a lot in common, but there's one important

area of my life that I've been neglecting—and that's my faith."

His frown deepened. "But I've been attending your church for over six months, sitting through those long sermons, learning all those songs, and meeting all kinds of people I might never associate with." He wrinkled his nose slightly. "Doesn't that count? Isn't that enough to show you I'm interested in religion?"

Her heart twisted. "If I've given you the impression that an interest in religion is what's important to me, then I'm very sorry. My faith is based on a personal relationship with Jesus and a commitment to love Him and give Him first place in my life. Pastor Tom reminded me of that this morning in his sermon."

She waited expectantly, hoping it would all click with Peter. But he looked more puzzled than ever. Regret weakened her resolve. She'd done more damage than she realized. No wonder he was confused.

She reached for his hand. "I owe you a big apology. I haven't been a very good friend or example of what it means to live the Christian life. I've been self-centered about everything. I'm sorry, Peter. Will you forgive me?"

He looked down at their clasped hands. "I care a great deal about you, Allison. I thought we had a chance to build a future together. Maybe if we just took a break—"

"No, I care about you, too. And that's why I'd like us to stay friends if possible, but no more dates."

His gray eyes softened. He lifted his finger and traced the side of her face. "Are you sure?"

She swallowed and nodded. "Yes, I'm sorry." She had no idea what the future held, but dating Peter wasn't the right choice for her.

He pulled her closer and pressed his lips against hers. The only thing she felt was a powerful wave of sadness, but she stayed in his arms for several seconds. At least she owed him that much.

Tyler pulled into a parking place across the street and one house down from Allie's. Hopefully, he could catch her at home and show her these final designs. Reaching across to the passenger seat, he grabbed his computer case. As he turned and glanced toward Allie's house, he noticed a black BMW parked in her driveway and two people standing on the porch. His stomach clenched as he recognized Allie and Peter. Leaning to the left for a better view, he saw Peter trace his finger down the side of Allie's face. She looked intently at Peter, mouthing words Tyler didn't even want to imagine.

His heart hammered as he watched them. Should he get out of the car and interrupt their little tryst on the porch? He reached for the car-door handle, but froze as he watched Peter take Allie in his arms and kiss her. This was no friendly I'll-see-you-later kind of kiss, but one full of passion and deep emotion.

Tyler felt like a knife had slit his heart. What a fool he'd been. Sure, he could say his motives were pure and all he wanted to do was help Allie's business grow, but underneath it all, he wanted her back.

Oh, Father, I haven't been honest about my feelings for Allie. But You've known what's been in my heart all along. I still love her. But she obviously doesn't feel the same way about me. Give me strength to deal with this, and help me let go of any claim I have on her... even if it's only been in my heart.

Chapter 7

Allison shifted her purse strap on her shoulder as she rounded the corner of Nassau Street. The bright April morning sun winked at her through the bare branches of an oak tree. She smiled at Tessa. "Looks like a beautiful day."

Her sister shaded her eyes and scanned the sidewalk ahead. "It's still a little cool for this time of year."

"It'll warm up later. I bet we'll be busy." Allison's voice lifted, optimism flowing through her. She could hardly believe the way her new commitment to put the Lord first had lightened her load—that and no longer feeling the pressure to try and make things work with Peter. What a relief! She hadn't realized how her anxious thoughts and gloomy outlook had weighed her down. Well, she was through with all of that now.

Tessa gasped. "Look, they put up the new sign!"

Allison lifted her gaze to the beautifully carved wooden sign hanging over the front door of the tea shop. Sunlight reflected off the words SWEET SOMETHING, making the gold paint glow.

"Wow, it looks great!"

Tessa grabbed her arm. "You didn't tell me they were putting in window boxes and planters. Oh, I love it! Tyler's a genius!"

Allison lowered her gaze and stared at the three large, wooden flower boxes hanging below the front windows, each filled with bright yellow daffodils, pink tulips, little blue grape hyacinths, and dark green trailing ivy. Four round cement planters holding the same colorful flowers lined the walk leading to the front door, giving their shop a fresh, inviting look.

Tessa gave Allison a hug. "Spring has arrived!"

Laughing, Allison squeezed her sister back. "I have to call Tyler. I can't believe he arranged for all of these flowers without even telling me."

"You didn't know?" Tessa stepped back, concern filling her eyes. "Those had to cost a fortune. Are you sure he isn't sending us a bill?"

"His assistant said there was no charge for the menus and business cards when she dropped them off last Friday, but she didn't say anything about the sign or planters."

Old fears sent a wave of uncertainty through Allison. What was going on with Tyler? She hadn't seen or heard from him in over a week—not since she and Peter sat in front of him at church. She'd called his office last week to thank him for the menus and business cards, but his assistant said he was in a meeting. He'd never called back.

"You better get in touch with him." Her sister bent and sniffed the flowers. "I suppose we might be able to keep these if they'd let us pay over several months."

Allison nodded. "I hope so. They're beautiful." As she climbed the steps and unlocked the tea shop's front door, an idea formed in her mind. She turned to her sister. "Hold down the shop. I'll be back in a little while."

"Hey, where are you going?"

Allison smiled over her shoulder. "I'll explain later."

⊱⋅⊱⋅⊰⋅⊰

Tyler stepped back from his desk and crossed his arms as he studied the enlarged newspaper ad he had created for the Grounds for Sculpture anniversary celebration. Hopefully, it would draw a large crowd and help provide the funding they needed to continue their unique work for another year.

His intercom buzzed. "Tyler, there's a delivery for you. I think you should come sign for it."

"Okay." The smile in his assistant Jolene's voice made him curious. He strode out of his office and into the reception area. Jolene stood in front of her desk with Mr. Sheldon's secretary Linda.

A deliveryman in neat khaki pants and green polo shirt stepped forward, holding a basket of plants and flowers. "Tyler Lawrence?"

He nodded and glanced at the basket brimming with shiny ivy, little daffodils, and tiny pink tulips. A miniature teacup and saucer sat on a mound of soft, green moss. His heartbeat kicked up a notch. It had to be from Allie.

"Please sign here." The deliveryman held out a clipboard.

Tyler quickly jotted his signature on the line and accepted the basket.

Jolene leaned toward Linda. "He must have a secret admirer."

Tyler cleared his throat. "Very funny. It's from a client."

The women laughed softly and exchanged knowing looks.

He returned to his office and set the basket on the corner of his desk, then searched through the greenery and found a card tucked in next to the tulips. When he recognized Allie's feminine handwriting, his heart clenched. It had been a long time since he'd seen her write his name. He quickly tore it open and read the note.

Dear Tyler,

Thanks for giving Sweet Something a beautiful new image. I love the menus, business cards, and sign. The planters are gorgeous. What a fun surprise! Tessa and I would love to keep them, but we're not sure about the price. Please let me know. Thanks so much for using your time, talents, and resources to bless my business and me. I'd like to make you dinner. Can you come over tonight at seven?

Allie

Tyler quickly scanned the message again. She wanted to make him dinner tonight? His hopes rose, but he quickly reined them in. She probably just wanted to thank him for the free work he'd done for Sweet Something. But as he grabbed the phone and dialed her number, he couldn't keep his hopes from rising.

⁂

Tyler hustled up Allie's front steps. He hesitated as he crossed the porch, recalling how Peter had stood in that very spot and kissed Allie. His anger flared for a moment, but he shook it off. Tonight he was the invited guest. Not Peter. Hopefully, that meant there was still a chance—at least a chance to ask forgiveness and straighten out the past.

He knocked on Allie's door, then jammed his hands in his jacket pockets and blew out a deep breath. *Father, please help me keep my focus on You tonight. That's not going to be easy. You know how I feel about Allie. Help me want what's best for her even if things don't work out the way I hope.*

The door opened. Allie smiled and pushed back the screen. "Hi, come on in."

"Thanks." She looked great in a red blouse and slim, black pants. Soft rose color flushed her cheeks, and her blue eyes sparkled. He realized he was staring, but she was beautiful. Not like a fashion model or TV star. Allie's beauty came from her heart and showed in her smile and caring ways.

As they walked into the living room, he noticed she had moved the two red wingback chairs closer to the fireplace and positioned a small round table between them. The table was set for dinner, complete with sparkling silverware and crystal water glasses. Three large white candles flickered on the mantle and a small fire crackled behind the hearth screen. Wow. She had gone to a lot of work to create a nice atmosphere.

He pulled in a deep breath. "Something smells great."

"Do you mean the candles or the beef stroganoff?"

He returned her smile. "Both."

Allie laughed softly. "Dinner's all ready. I just need to bring it in."

He laid his coat over the end of the couch, then followed her into the kitchen and offered to help. She handed him a basket of rolls. Then she took two dinner plates filled with beef stroganoff, mashed potatoes, and green beans from the oven, and they headed back into the living room.

As Tyler set the basket on the round table, he noticed a Bible lying on the footstool next to one of the chairs. Stepping back, he took in the scene, and smiled. "This looks just like your painting." He motioned toward the chairs and table.

She set down their dinner plates, her eyes glowing. "I wondered if you'd notice."

Tyler fingered the white linen tablecloth. "This is really special, Allie. Thanks."

"You're welcome. It's the least I could do."

"And thanks for the basket you sent to the office."

She glanced at him as she sat down. "I wanted you to know how much I appreciate everything you've done. I hope that was okay."

He took a seat. "Well, I've never received flowers from a woman before."

Her cheeks flamed. "I told them to make it mostly plants and not to put on a bow. I hope it didn't embarrass you."

"No. It was really thoughtful. I put it on my desk, and every time I see it, I remember to pray for you and Sweet Something."

"Thanks." She stared at him and slowly shook her head. "I don't understand. What happened to you, Tyler? You're so . . . different."

His stomach tensed. This was the opportunity he had been praying for. "I'm glad you see a difference in me. I want to leave the past behind and build a new life with the Lord at the center."

"I'm happy for you. I really am. But sometimes I still feel tied to the past." She lifted her gaze to meet his. "I don't understand what happened to us."

The hurt in her eyes hit him hard. This was going to be more difficult than he'd imagined. He sent off an urgent prayer.

Tell her the truth. Don't hold back.

New strength filled him, and the words became clear. "For a long time, I didn't understand it either. But over the last couple years, I've learned a lot, and I think I can explain it now." He reached for her hand. "But there's something more important than an explanation, and that's an apology. Whatever my reasons were for leaving, I know I hurt you, and I'm truly sorry for that. Will you forgive me?"

Tears glistened in her eyes. "Yes," she whispered.

He looked down at his plate, fighting the emotion tightening his throat. "I don't want our dinner to get cold. Maybe we should eat first, and I can explain more later."

She shook her head. "I've been waiting six years to hear this."

"Okay." He took a deep breath and blew it out slowly. "When I found out my dad was having an affair, I didn't know how to handle it. I couldn't get past the anger to the hurt underneath, so I kept it inside and pushed you and everyone else away.

"While my mom and dad were going through the divorce, I was fighting my own battle, telling myself I never wanted to be like my dad, but I was afraid that's exactly what would happen. All kinds of doubts ran through my mind. Could I be faithful to one woman for the rest of my life? Or would I crash and burn in the relationship department like my dad? Did I have what it takes to be a good husband and father? Or would I end up hurting the people I loved the most?

"Then seeing the way my mom tried to destroy my dad totally blew me away. They betrayed each other, and I never wanted to be in a relationship where that much pain was possible.

"So I could see only two choices—stay together, get married, and eventually end up divorced like my parents, or break up and avoid that possibility. I know that sounds crazy now, but that's what was going through my head."

She nodded slowly, questions still lingering in her eyes.

"I took a job in New York and made a whole series of bad choices that led me farther away from everyone I loved. Then about three years ago, I met a guy at work who really lives his faith. We became friends, and I started attending a Bible study he was leading. He challenged me to recommit my life to the Lord, and go back and ask forgiveness of anyone that I'd hurt. That was tough, especially going to my friends in New York who aren't believers. Most of them didn't understand where I was coming from. But having a clear conscience was worth it to me."

"So that's why you came back and wanted to help me—so you could have a clear conscience?"

He swallowed, struggling to find the words. "Yes. . .and no. I owe you so much, Allie. If you hadn't told me about the Lord and loved me into His family, I don't know what would've happened to me. Even when I took off and was doing stupid things, I couldn't run away from God. I was part of His family, and He wouldn't let me go."

Her eyes glistened with unshed tears. "I'm glad. I prayed for you."

"Thanks, Allie." He took her hand again. "I have to be honest. There's another reason I came back." Looking into her eyes, he felt like he stood on a high cliff about to jump off into a choppy ocean. "I never forgot you, Allie. No matter where I went or what I was doing. You were always with me. I came back to ask your forgiveness, but I also wanted to see if there was a chance for us to be together again."

Her stunned expression made his heart take a dive.

"Oh, Tyler," she whispered.

Feeling like a fool, he dropped her hand. "Hey, it's okay. I should've known you'd be dating someone else by now, not sitting around waiting for me to get my life together."

Her blue eyes widened. "But I'm not dating anyone else."

"What about Peter?"

"We're just friends."

"Come on, Allie, I saw you kissing him right out there on your front porch."

Hurt clouded her eyes.

Immediately he regretted his tone. "I'm sorry. I wasn't spying on you. I stopped by last Sunday afternoon to show you the final designs for the sign and promo pieces."

Her face was flaming now. "That was just a good-bye kiss."

"Well, if that's good-bye, I'd like to see hello."

"No, I mean I'd just told him good-bye for good."

Tyler stared at her, hoping he'd heard her correctly. "You're not dating him any more?"

"No, it wasn't working out. We had a lot in common, but he's not serious about growing in his faith, and that's important to me."

"So you and Peter aren't together?"

She shook her head and sent him a soft, sweet smile. "No, we're not. I knew it wouldn't be right for me to keep dating Peter, especially when I still had feelings for you."

He leaned back and blew out a deep breath. "Wow, I'm so surprised, I don't know what to say. I mean I've been praying and hoping you'd forgive me, but I didn't think there was much hope that we. . ."

She raised her finger and pressed it gently against his lips to quiet him. "I've been praying, too. And I always wished things would've worked out differently for us, maybe now we have a chance to see if they will."

His heart soared. He lifted her hand and kissed her fingers. "You won't be sorry, Allie. I've really changed. I'm a different man."

Chapter 8

Tyler glanced out the passenger window at the spacious, green lawn of the Princeton Battlefield Park. He turned to Allie. "Why are we stopping here?"

She turned off the car. "Close your eyes. I want to show you something."

"How can I see it if my eyes are closed?"

"Very funny. Come on, I want it to be a surprise." She sent him an impish smile that got his heart pumping.

"Okay." He scrunched his eyes closed, sorry to lose sight of her. "I wouldn't do this for anyone else, you know."

She laughed softly. "Good."

He heard her car door open, and then a few seconds later, his opened.

"Keep your eyes shut," she said, a smile in her voice.

Grinning, he climbed out of the car. "I hope I won't regret this."

"You can trust me." She took his hand and led him across the soft lawn.

The early afternoon sun warmed his back, and the scent of freshly mowed grass filled the air. A light breeze carried the fragrance of some kind of flower he couldn't identify. "If I'd known we were going on a hike, I would've worn my boots and packed a snack."

Laughing, she squeezed his hand. "Don't worry. We're almost there." They walked another thirty seconds or so, and she pulled him to a stop. "Okay. You can open your eyes now."

Tyler obeyed, then blinked at a sea of yellow daffodils stretching across the grass in all directions. The bright, golden flowers bobbed in the breeze like dancers on stage, their slim, silvery leaves flickering beside them. Tall evergreens at the edge of the park swayed in the breeze, providing a peaceful, deep green background. "Wow, this is amazing." He glanced over at Allie as she took in the scene.

Her expression grew pensive. "The Princeton Garden Club planted seven thousand bulbs in memory of those who died on September 11. The flowers come back every spring." She turned to him. "It's beautiful, isn't it?"

"Very special." He lifted her hand and kissed it. "Thanks for showing me."

"I knew you'd like it." Her smile warmed his heart.

He slipped his arm around her shoulder, and contentment washed over him. It had been an amazing three weeks. He and Allie had seen each other almost every day and checked in by phone on days when other commitments kept them apart. Even in that short time they'd made some wonderful memories together—walks across Princeton University campus, an organ concert at the University Chapel, quiet dinners at her apartment, a visit to the Princeton University Art Museum, and discovering their favorite flavors at a unique little ice cream shop in Palmer's Square called the Bent Spoon.

These were some of the same types of things they'd enjoyed six years ago, but everything seemed different now that there was a spiritual dimension to their relationship. They often prayed together to end the evening, and enjoyed attending church together.

Tyler lifted his gaze to the field of daffodils again. Allie didn't know it yet, but he was working on some surprises of his own. In two weeks they'd celebrate her birthday, and he couldn't wait to see her reaction when he showed her the limited-edition prints he'd had made from one of her paintings. He felt certain it would launch her artistic career, especially since he'd already contacted art dealers in Princeton and New York who were interested in carrying Allie's prints.

"Thank you, Tyler," she said softly.

He looked into her eyes and read the message of love reflected there. Gratefulness washed over him. "Why are you thanking me? You're the one who brought me here."

She smiled at him sweetly. "Because sharing it with you is what makes it special."

He wrapped his arms around her and kissed her cheek. "You're the one who makes every day special."

Rain drummed on the front windows of Sweet Something.

Allison glanced at her watch, concern tightening her stomach. Six forty-seven. Where could Tyler be? He'd said he would meet her at the shop after work, then take her home to change before they went out to dinner to celebrate her birthday. She straightened the little packages of specialty teas and adjusted the row of teapots on the next shelf. She shouldn't worry. Tyler probably had a perfectly reasonable explanation for being late.

Then why hadn't he called?

Tessa stepped down into the gift shop. "Hey, I didn't know you were still here. I thought Tyler was picking you up at six."

"I'm sure he'll be here any minute. You can go. I'll lock up."

"Allie, it's almost seven. Are you sure he's coming? I don't want to leave you here without a ride."

"We have dinner reservations at The Ferry House. He'll be here soon." But little vines of doubt wrapped around her heart, squeezing out her confidence and replacing it with old fears she couldn't quite shake. Memories of another rainy night six years earlier flew into her mind and sent a chill up her spine.

Tessa frowned and crossed her arms. "Did you call him? Maybe he got held up at work."

"I tried. No one's there."

"How about his cell phone or home?"

"I called those, too. He didn't answer." She wrapped her arms around herself as she stared out the rain-spattered windows. The glow from streetlights glistened on the wet pavement. Cars splashed through the puddles, making their way down Nassau Street. "The weather's awful. I hope nothing's happened to him."

"Maybe his car broke down again." Tessa glanced out the window and back at Allison. "Did you tell him how worried you were when that happened last time and he didn't call?"

She averted her eyes. "No, I didn't want him to think I was one of those clingy women who can't let her boyfriend out of her sight for more than ten minutes."

Tessa sighed. "You need to be honest with him. He should call if he's going to be late, especially on your birthday! We wanted to have a family party tonight, but we had to change our plans because he said he was going to take you out."

"I know, I know." Allison rubbed her forehead. "This is probably just a mix-up or something."

Tessa leveled her gaze at Allison. "I don't know what's going on. But remember this, people put their best foot forward when they're dating. And if this is Tyler's best, then. . ."

"Tessa, please. That's not helpful. I'm sure there's an explanation."

"Okay. I hope you're right." Tessa walked over and stood by Allison. "Just don't give your heart away until you're sure Tyler respects and cherishes you." She gently touched Allison's arm. "Think about it, okay?"

The clock by the door struck seven. Allison looked into her sister's eyes. "Okay. I hear what you're saying."

Tyler pushed open the heavy glass door of his office building and dashed into the rain.

The limo driver of the Lincoln Town Car sprang into action

and opened the rear passenger door for him.

As Tyler bent to step in, his cell phone slipped from his hand and splashed into a puddle at his feet. Irritation coursed through him. Fishing through the cold water, he retrieved the phone. He wiped it on his pants' leg and gave it a good shake before he climbed in the car.

"Which airline are you flying with, Mr. Lawrence?"

"US Air." Tyler hooked his seat belt and flipped open his phone. Little drops of water fogged his screen and dripped from the buttons. He swiped his coat sleeve over the phone's screen and punched in speed dial for Allie at Sweet Something. Lifting it to his ear, he prayed it would work, but the silence buzzed back at him. A crazy mixture of fear and foreboding coursed through him. He had to explain things to Allie before he left town. He needed her prayers.

Sighing, he laid his head back and closed his eyes. Hopefully, he'd have time to call her from the airport.

Forty-five minutes later he hustled through the revolving door of the Newark International Airport and scanned the scene in Terminal A. Crowds of people, toting bulky suitcases, stood between him and the check-in counter. Tyler shot off an urgent prayer. He had less than thirty-five minutes to get through the line and onto that plane for Tampa. His step-mother's call left little doubt. His father's situation was serious. He had to come now.

He spotted a tall, blond agent, with a caring smile, helping passengers find the correct line. She listened to his story and took him directly to the ticket counter. In less than seven minutes he had paid for his ticket and had his boarding pass in hand. The same agent took him to the head of the security line. He thanked her and quickly made his way through the checkpoint.

Running down the concourse toward his gate, he spotted a pay phone. He hadn't used one in ages and soon realized he needed coins he didn't have. Dashing into a bookshop across the concourse, he tried to persuade the clerk to give him change for a five. But he refused to open the register unless Tyler made a purchase. He grabbed a bag of peanuts and tossed the five-dollar bill on the counter. The clerk passed back a handful of change.

Tyler glanced at his watch as he approached the phone. He had less than seventeen minutes before the plane took off. Frustration swelled in his chest. Allie must think he was a jerk for standing her up on her birthday. He wearily rubbed his eyes and pulled in a deep breath. He had to get a grip. She would understand. They'd been praying for his dad, asking the Lord to give Tyler an opportunity to speak to him about his faith. He just never expected their prayers to be answered like this.

He punched in her home number and waited for the call to go through. Gripping the receiver, he counted four rings, and then the answering machine clicked on.

Disappointment pulsed through him. He didn't want to talk to a machine. Emotion rose and clogged his throat, stealing his words for a few seconds. Finally he spoke. "Allie, it's me. My stepmom called from the hospital in Clearwater. My dad had a heart attack on the golf course this afternoon. She's pretty upset. She wants me to come right away. I'm at the airport now, catching a seven-ten flight. Please pray. I'm not ready to say good-bye to my dad." Tyler's voice choked off. He closed his eyes and swallowed. "I'm sorry about tonight." He stopped to listen as they made the final call for his flight. "I have to go. I love you."

He listened to the silence on the other end of the line, and his shoulders sagged.

Chapter 9

A jumble of fear and frustration swirled through Allison as she stooped and picked up the Saturday morning paper outside Tyler's front door. It was almost ten thirty. Could he be sleeping in? Maybe he'd never come home. That thought sent a sickening wave through her. *Please, Lord, don't let it be something like that.* She lifted her hand and knocked.

Last night she'd finally given up waiting for him at the shop and left with Tessa. Her sister threw together a last-minute birthday party complete with a cake she pulled from the freezer and an off-key round of "Happy Birthday." Allison sang along for her niece and nephews' sake, but her heart wasn't in it. When she finally arrived home around nine, she checked her answering machine. There was only one message. It began with a long pause. She knew it had to be a telemarketer and quickly pushed the DELETE button. She was *not* in the mood to listen to a sales spiel.

She called Tyler's home and cell phone once more, leaving

a second round of messages. Then she fell into bed and gave in to her tears. Lying there, staring at the ceiling, she tried to fight off the assault of accusing thoughts and painful memories. But the old fears of abandonment and betrayal rose to the surface, mocking her for believing Tyler had truly changed. She didn't fall asleep until well after midnight, and she spent the night wrestling through disturbing dreams. When morning arrived, she resolved to stop fretting and do something.

She knocked on Tyler's door again, but he didn't answer. Standing on tiptoes, she took down the spare key and unlocked the door. Tyler had shown her his hiding place above the door frame last week when he'd been locked out.

She slowly pushed open the door and slipped inside, feeling more like a burglar than a concerned friend. She called Tyler's name and listened to her voice echo off the walls. A quick glance around the quiet living room and dining room revealed nothing unusual. She walked into the kitchen and spotted two coffee cups and a sticky cereal bowl on the counter. Looking more closely, she saw the cereal was hard and stuck to the bottom of the bowl. Definitely yesterday's breakfast.

A shiver raced up her back as she left the kitchen and headed down the hall. Peeking in the bedroom, she saw his empty bed. The blankets and comforter had been pulled up and straightened. A pair of white socks and gray sweatpants lay on the floor near the closet. She tiptoed across the soft, beige carpet and slowly pushed open the bathroom door. A towel, comb, and shaving gear cluttered the counter, but there was no sign of Tyler.

KISS THE ~~COOK~~ *Bride*

Allison walked back into the living room, running through all the possible explanations for Tyler's disappearance for the hundredth time. Should she call his mom or brother? The local hospitals or the police? Maybe she could find his dad's number in Florida, but she wasn't sure where he lived. Her gaze moved to Tyler's desk in the corner of the room. His open laptop sat in the center of the desk. A tropical beach screensaver slowly fade to a second photo with palm trees and aqua water. Allison walked over and touched a computer key. The screensaver immediately disappeared and a desktop photo popped up, filling the screen.

Her eyebrows lifted. She and Tyler stood arm-in-arm in the center of the sea of brilliant daffodils. She sank into the desk chair and stared at her own image smiling back at her from the laptop. She'd looked directly at the camera lens, but he looked at her. The affection in his eyes was unmistakable. Warmth flooded through her, relaxing her tense muscles. Tears misted her vision. How could she doubt his love?

She sniffed and glanced at Tyler's open Bible lying on the desk next to the computer. Leaning closer, she focused on a section Tyler had carefully underlined in 1 Corinthians 13. *Love is patient, love is kind. . . . It is not easily angered, it keeps no record of wrongs. . . . It always protects, always trusts, always hopes, always perseveres.*

Allison tilted her head slightly to read Tyler's handwritten note in the margin. Surprise rippled through her when she saw her name and the date of February fourth, over a year ago written there. What did it mean? Had he been thinking of her?

Praying for her? It seemed strange since they hadn't even been in contact at that time.

She focused on the verses again, letting their message sink in. The unconditional love described there was built on choices and decisions, not just feelings.

Did she have that kind of love for Tyler? Her heart ached as she considered that question.

What should I do, Lord?

Monday morning Allison hurried in the back door of Sweet Something and hung up her coat.

Tessa glanced up from arranging hot scones on a delicate blue china plate. "Good morning."

The question in her sister's eyes sent a ripple of uneasiness through her. She knew Tessa wanted to ask if she'd heard from Tyler, but she didn't want to talk about it. Her calls to the hospitals had turned up nothing. On Sunday, she'd left messages with his brother and his mother, but neither of them had called back yet. She'd made up her mind. If she didn't hear from him by the end of the day, she would contact the police.

Kayla breezed into the kitchen carrying a tray of dishes. When she saw Allison, embarrassment flashed in her eyes. "I'm sorry, Allison, Tyler just called a couple minutes ago. I told him you weren't in yet."

Allison's heart leaped. "Did he leave a message?"

Kayla set the tray by the sink. "He asked you to call, and he left a number."

"You're sure he didn't say anything else?" Tessa asked, her brows in a skeptical arch. "Like where he's been for the past three days?"

"Tessa, please." Allison turned to Kayla. "Where's the number?"

"Out front by the phone." Kayla led the way back through the tea shop. When they reached the antique desk they used as a hostess podium, she pointed to the pad of paper next to the phone.

Allison's heart hammered. The number began with an area code she didn't recognize. She thanked Kayla as she grabbed the phone and quickly punched it in.

After two rings a mechanical voice answered. "I'm sorry, the number you have dialed is no longer in service. Please check the number and dial again."

She immediately tried a second time but got the same message. She blew out a frustrated breath and called Kayla over. "That number's not working. Are you sure he didn't say anything else?"

Kayla thought for a few seconds. "No, he sounded kind of stressed or something." She bit her lip and looked at Allison with an apologetic expression. "It was kind of noisy when he called. Maybe I got the number wrong. I'm sorry."

"It's all right." She sent Kayla back to work and stared out the front window. At least Tyler had finally tried to reach her. But what would he think when she didn't return his call? She closed her eyes, praying for guidance. The verses she'd read in Tyler's Bible ran through her mind again. *Love is patient, love is kind. . . . It is not easily angered, it keeps no record of wrongs. . . . It always protects, always trusts, always hopes, always perseveres.*

Conviction flooded her heart. She'd allowed doubt and fear to fill her thoughts. She'd held onto Tyler's record of wrongs even though he'd asked forgiveness and shown her in so many ways that he was walking on a new path of faith.

If she truly loved him, she needed to forgive him once and for all and believe the best about him, even though she was unsure of the future.

She would need a supernatural infusion of faith and courage to love Tyler like that, with no strings and no guarantees. Assurance washed over her. If she was willing, God would help her. He'd promised to pour out His love in and through her so she would have a never-ending supply.

If love was her goal, she couldn't go wrong. This was her answer.

⊰✦⊱

Later that afternoon, she noticed a stack of letters and a small package the mailman had left on the front desk. She sorted through the pile and pulled out the package. Reading the return address in the top corner, she smiled. It was from her friend, Haley Tannehill in Tulsa, Oklahoma.

Tearing off the tape, she recalled how she'd first met Haley and two other young, single friends, Monica and Angel, at the National Restaurateurs' Convention in Dallas almost two years ago. Thrown together that first night of the convention when they'd been stuck in the hotel elevator, they found they had a lot in common. Besides attending seminars and walking the convention floor together, they'd shared several meals and confided in each other about their nonexistent love lives. After all, being in the restaurant business didn't leave much time for dating. At least, that's the excuse they gave each other.

Allison reached in the package and pulled out the apron with the words KISS THE COOK emblazoned across the bib. Smiling, she shook her head. How had Haley ended up with the apron? They'd all laughed when Angel tied it on to show it to them that last night in Dallas. She remembered how they had joked about passing the apron around among the group, but she didn't think they'd actually follow through. Looking closer, she noticed her friends had signed the apron.

Allison pulled out a folded letter from the package.

Dear Allison,

Here's a little gift for you! Hope it will remind you of the fun time we shared in Dallas. This apron has made the rounds among our little group, and I understand you are the only one who hasn't had the pleasure of wearing it. Now don't you dare toss it out! It's had a wonderful effect on each of us.

Angel took it home and fell in love within just a few months of her return to Florida. Did you hear she got married last June? She sent it on to Monica who got back together with Gil, a great guy she'd known years ago. They were married in August! It arrived in my mailbox about a year ago, shortly after Scott Jantzen returned from Kuwait.

TEA FOR TWO

It worked like a charm! Scott and I got engaged last summer and were married May first! So I'm passing it on to you. I don't believe it's magic, but I do think when you open your heart to all the possibilities and let the Lord lead you, some wonderful things can happen. I want you to tie it on and send me a picture! Don't disappoint me. Give love a chance. . . and see where it leads.

With love from the Cowpoke Café,
Haley

P.S. You are coming to the convention again, aren't you? Please, please say yes! And be sure to bring the apron!!

Allison lifted the apron once more. She smiled at the thought of her friends wearing it and falling in love. Would it help in her situation? She laughed at herself for even forming the question in her mind. She believed in Providence—the wisdom, care, and guidance of God—not lucky aprons. Still, what harm could it do to wear the apron and take a picture for Haley? It would remind her of her three special friends who cared about her and prayed for her. She slipped it over her head and tied it at the back. She would wear it for them. . .and see what happened.

Chapter 10

Allison watched the older couple walk toward the front door of Sweet Something. The man slowed and took his wife's hand as she stepped down into the gift shop. She stopped to admire the collection of teapots, and he waited patiently by her side, listening to her comments with an affectionate look in his eyes.

It was well past six, but Allison didn't want to hurry her final customers out the door. They appeared to be at least seventy-five and obviously enjoying their time together.

As they walked by, Alison smiled and waved good-bye. "Come back and see us again!" she called.

"Oh, we will. Thank you." The old gentleman held the door open for his wife. She passed through and took his arm. They exchanged contented smiles and headed down Nassau Street into the early evening twilight.

Allison's smile faded. Would she and Tyler share a love like that, one that lasted through the years? Closing her eyes, a prayer rose from her heart. *Please, Lord, take care of him wherever he is and bring him back to me.*

With a sigh, she turned off the outside lights, locked the front door, and flipped the sign to CLOSED. She glanced down at her KISS THE COOK apron and brushed off a few crumbs. Several people had commented on it, joking with her about the phrase. She had pasted on a smile and asked Tessa to take her picture for Haley.

A loud knock startled her out of her reverie. She turned and looked toward the front door. The reflection of the interior lights made it impossible to see through the glass. "I'm sorry, we're closed." She glanced uneasily over her shoulder at the empty tea shop.

"Allie, it's me."

Recognition flashed through her. She hurried over and unlocked the door.

Tyler stood in the doorway, wearing jeans and a soft blue shirt and carrying a large black portfolio. He looked at her with a somber, almost haggard expression.

She greeted him with a tremulous smile. "Hi."

He walked in and shut the door.

She stepped forward and hugged him, but he remained stiff and unyielding in her arms.

Fear moved through her, tightening her stomach. She stepped back and looked up at him. "What's wrong?"

A storm brewed in his brown eyes. "What's going on, Allie?"

"What do you mean?"

"I've just been through one of the toughest times in my

life. I needed you." His voice sounded hushed and strained. "Where've you been?"

Shock waves jolted through her. "What do you mean, where have *I* been? You're the one who disappeared without a word."

"I called you Friday night before I left."

"I waited here until after seven. The phone never rang. I went to Tessa and Matt's for my birthday, but the whole time I was worried about you."

A painful, confused look filled his face. "I'm sorry about your birthday. I called your house from the airport. I explained everything."

"What were you doing at the airport?"

"Didn't you listen to your answering machine?"

She lifted her hand in exasperation. "There was no message from you, only one that started with a long pause, and I knew—" Too late, realization flashed through her.

"That was me. I had a hard time getting started. I wanted to talk to you, not leave a message."

Allie sank onto the wooden bench. "I thought it was a sales call. I deleted it." She looked up and noticed the tired lines around his eyes. "Where did you go?"

"I had to fly to Florida. My dad had a heart attack."

She pulled in a sharp breath, regret tightening her throat. "Oh, Tyler, I'm sorry. Is he all right?"

"He had to have surgery, but it looks like he's going to be okay." He raked his hand through his hair and sat down on the bench next to her. "My stepmom's sister, Barbara, came down yesterday. She can stay as long as they need her. So I decided it was time to come home." He looked at her with a renewed tenderness. "I missed you."

"Oh, Tyler, I'm so sorry. I didn't know. I called your cell phone and your apartment. I left you a message each time. I was so worried about you."

"I dropped my phone in the rain on the way to the airport, and I spent almost all weekend at the hospital. I stopped by the office, but I haven't been home yet." He leaned back against the wall and closed his eyes. "Man, I can't believe this. We both tried to get hold of each other." He turned to her. "Did you think I'd taken off again?" His intense gaze focused on her, pain in his eyes.

She reached for his hand. "I was worried about you—and about us. I went over to your apartment on Saturday. When you didn't answer the door, I let myself in. I felt like a snoop, but I had to be sure you weren't lying on the floor with a broken leg or something like that."

Tyler nodded. "Of course I wasn't there."

"No." Allison smiled. "But I saw the photo of us on your laptop and the Bible open on your desk. I read the verses you underlined in 1 Corinthians 13. My name was written in the margin." She smiled. "Do you remember when you wrote that?"

He glanced away, looking embarrassed. "I don't know. Awhile ago, I guess."

"You dated it more than a year ago in February. That was before I even opened Sweet Something."

His face reddened, and he rose from the bench. "It doesn't matter."

"It matters to me. We weren't even talking back then. Why'd you write that?"

He looked down and fiddled with the bottom button of his shirt for a few seconds, then looked up at her. "When I read those verses, I realized love isn't just a great feeling, it's a decision you make every day. When you love someone, you take action. You believe the best about them, and you put their needs ahead of your own."

She smiled, warmed by his words. "So you decided to love me back then?"

His gaze met hers. "I never stopped loving you, Allie. I just decided it was time to do something about it."

Her thoughts spun back to that time in her life, the long hours she'd put into preparing to open Sweet Something, the money she and Tessa had scraped together to make it happen. A sudden thought struck her. She focused on Tyler. "Were you the one who sent me those anonymous checks?"

He glanced off toward the windows, frowning slightly.

She stood and faced him, certain she was right. "Tyler, please, tell me."

"I didn't want you to know."

She reached for his hand. "Why not? That was the sweetest, most generous thing anyone's ever done for me. How did you know I needed it?"

"My mom saw the article in the *Princeton Packet* about you opening your tea shop. She cut it out and sent it to me. It arrived the same day I read those verses in 1 Corinthians. I started praying for you, asking the Lord what I should do. And it was one of those times when He put a very clear impression in my mind. He wanted me to send you the money." He gently tucked a strand of hair behind her ear. "I wanted to help you, Allie, but I didn't want you to think I was trying to buy my way back into your life."

"So you sent them anonymously." A sense of wonder filled her.

He nodded. "When I first moved back to Princeton, I used to drive by here and try and see you through the windows. I wanted to come in, but I wasn't sure how you'd feel about that. I sent my assistant from work in a couple times. She told me the shop was beautiful, but business looked slow."

Allison lifted her brows. "You sent a spy?"

He smiled. "Yes, but I had good motives." He wrapped his arms around her. "I love you, Allie. I couldn't stay away. I had to see you again."

She slipped her arms around his waist and rested her head against his chest. "I'm so glad you came back. Thanks for believing in me and helping me."

He held her for a few more seconds; then he looked down into her face. "So, are you ready for your birthday present?"

She laughed softly. "You brought me a present?"

He nodded. Then he picked up the portfolio, took her hand, and led her up into the tearoom. "Let's sit in here." He chose a cozy corner table with a soft light shining overhead. "Why don't you have a seat right here?"

She smiled up at him. "What is it?"

"Close your eyes, and give me a minute."

She shut her eyes, heard him move a chair, and felt him turn the table just a little.

"Okay. You can open your eyes."

She did and gasped. Tyler had propped the open portfolio on a chair to display a large print of one of her paintings. The scene included a round, lace-covered tea table set with blue and white dishes and a large bouquet of pink, yellow, and white roses in a clear glass vase. "How did you. . .when did you?" She laughed. "I didn't even know you took it out of the closet."

The pleasure on his face erased all the earlier strain. "You like it? It's only the artist's proof. You need to okay it before they do the final run. And we have to make a decision about how many prints you want."

"I love it!" She rose from her chair and stepped into his arms. "It's the best birthday gift ever. Thank you." She kissed his cheek and focused on the print once more, her heart overflowing with gratefulness and love.

"You better sit down for the next one."

She turned to him in surprise. "You got me another present?"

He nodded and looked at her with a serious yet tender look. "I planned to give this to you last Friday after your special birthday dinner." He reached in his pocket and pulled out a small, navy blue velvet box.

Her breath caught in her throat, and she was glad he'd made her sit down because her legs suddenly felt shaky.

"We've been through a lot over the last eight years. Looking back, I can see how everything that's happened has made me love and appreciate you more. Our faith is stronger now, and I believe with God's help we can make it through whatever the future holds." He knelt in front of her and took her hand. "I love you, Allie. Will you marry me?"

Joy flooded her heart, and happy tears filled her eyes. "Yes! Oh, yes!" She reached for him, and they stood and held each other close for several seconds.

Finally, he stepped back and opened the box, showing her the sparkling, heart-shaped diamond nestled in a vintage platinum setting.

She blinked to clear her vision. "Oh, it's beautiful!"

"Not as beautiful as you." With love shining in his eyes, he slipped the ring on her finger. Then he gave her a kiss, achingly sweet and full of promise.

When he leaned back, he sent her a gentle smile and glanced down at her apron. "Where did you get this?" Amusement twinkled in his eyes.

She told him the story, and they laughed about the effect it seemed to have on each of the women who'd worn it. "We have to add our names, too," she said, untying the apron strings at the back.

"I have just what we need." Tyler reached in the zippered pocket on the side of the portfolio and pulled out a black permanent marker.

Allison slipped off the apron and spread it on the table. He handed her the pen, and she signed her name.

He added his signature with a flourish. "There's one more thing we need to do."

"What's that?"

Chuckling, he drew a *line* through the word COOK and wrote BRIDE. "There, now it's ready for you to wear."

Laughing, they embraced again, but soon lost themselves in another delicious kiss.

"Are you hungry?" she asked when she'd caught her breath.

He growled in her ear, making her laugh.

"I mean for dinner or dessert," she said.

He loosened his embrace so he could look toward the glass bakery cabinet at the back of the tearoom. "Do you have any lemon lush?"

She smiled and nodded. "I just made some this afternoon."

"That sounds great. And tea for two."

"Sounds good to me." Then she kissed his cheek, tied on the apron, and headed for the kitchen.

SWEET SOMETHING'S LEMON LUSH

CRUST:
   1 cup flour
   1/2 cup butter, softened
   1/2 cup walnuts, finely chopped

Mix flour, butter, and walnuts together, and press into the bottom of a 9 x 9-inch square pan. Bake 20 minutes at 350° until golden brown. Cool on a wire rack.

FIRST LAYER:
   1 (8 ounce) package cream cheese (regular or light), softened
   1 cup powdered sugar

Combine cream cheese and powdered sugar in a medium sized mixing bowl. Beat until smooth. Spread over cooled crust.

SECOND LAYER:
   2 instant lemon pudding mixes
   3 cups cold milk

Beat pudding mix and cold milk together with a wire whisk for two minutes and pour over first layer.

TOP LAYER:
   1 cup frozen whipped topping, thawed

Spread topping over pudding mixture and form soft peaks. Chill for 30 minutes. Serves 12.

CARRIE TURANSKY

Carrie Turansky and her husband, Scott, have been married for twenty-eight years and live in central New Jersey. They are blessed with five great kids, a lovely daughter-in-law, and an adorable grandson. Carrie homeschooled her children for many years, but she has recently "graduated" and now has more time for writing and being involved in ministry with her husband. She teaches women's Bible studies, speaks for women's events, and enjoys reading, gardening, and walking around the lake near their home. Carrie and her family spent one year in Kenya as missionaries, giving them a passion for what God is doing around the world. Carrie is also the co-author of *Wedded Bliss* and the author of *Along Came Love*. You may contact her through her website: www.carrieturansky.com.

Epilogue

by Kristy Dykes

Epilogue

HAM and I Together Again

Remember HAM? Haley, Allison, and Monica? The three women I met at the National Restaurateurs' Convention in Dallas two years ago? Well, I'm back, and so are they. We're supposed to meet here, at the convention reception. I scan the hotel ballroom searching for them.

A waiter rushes past holding a tray laden with yellow and white cheese cubes and crackers, then puts it down on a white-skirted table. A swan ice sculpture is nearby, surrounded by one of the largest and most exotic fruit displays I've ever seen. I make cerebral notes for my own restaurant, Angel Food. Fruit kabobs on short sticks jabbed in a pyramid of pineapples. Strawberries cascading out of a silver compote turned on its side. A creamy pink fruit dip in hollowed-out cantaloupes with zigzag edges.

I wait for HAM beside a bank of silk palm trees, enjoying

the ambience of the posh hotel. The crystal chandeliers give off a brilliant glow as people mill around in groups, chatting and laughing.

"Angel!"

I turn and see Monica walking toward me.

A big smile lights up her beautiful, caramel-colored face. "Hello, girlfriend!"

I hug her, as glad as all get out to see her again. "How's married life?"

"Couldn't be better." She shows me her wedding and engagement rings.

"What a unique setting. Congrats!"

"Thanks." She takes my hand and looks down at my rings. "And congrats to you too."

I smile, thinking about my *husband* Cyril. The word husband still sounds funny to me. "I can't believe I've been married a year."

"And I can't believe I've been married ten months. I hope you brought your wedding pictures because I did. I can't wait to see—"

"Monica!"

"Angel!"

I look to my left and see Haley and Allison coming toward us. They're waving furiously as they weave through the crowd.

Haley has a nice tan, and her eyes are sparkling. She's still floating on a cloud of newlywed bliss. I'm surprised she's even here since her wedding was only a month ago.

"Hey, there!" I lean in and give Haley a hug. "You look

wonderful. Honeymoons have a way of doing that, you know."

We all giggle as we exchange hugs.

"Especially honeymoons in the sun," Monica adds.

"Cancun was a dream." Haley sighs. "And so is Scott."

"You know what *honeymoon* means, don't you?" I wiggle my eyebrows at her. "Honey for a month."

"A month? You're right about that. Scott's with me. He's upstairs in our hotel room."

"Well, shut my mouth, as Sister Wilkins would say. She's my Sunday school teacher." I dip my chin and fake a guilty look, kindergarten-style. "Okay, HAM. I have something to confess. Cyril came too."

Monica bursts out laughing. "Gil couldn't stay away either."

Suddenly, a stab of guilt hits me, and it isn't fake this time. Allison—the only one in our foursome who's still single—might feel like the odd one out, and I can't let that happen. I decide to change the subject of husbands. I pat her forearm in a sisterly gesture. "How's Sweet Something doing, Allison? Everything going okay for you and your sister at the tea shop?"

"It's been a long winter, but business is definitely picking up." Allison grins mischievously then waves her left hand through the air, a diamond shooting glints in the chandelier lighting.

Monica squeals.

Haley gives her another hug. "I can't believe this. Why didn't you say something on the elevator?"

Allison laughs. "I thought I'd wait and surprise all of you at the same time."

KISS THE <del>COOK</del> *Bride*

"Well, you definitely surprised us," Haley says. "When did this happen?"

Allison's cheeks take on a rosy glow. "Two weeks ago."

"Who's the groom?" Monica asks.

"His name's Tyler Lawrence."

"Your engagement sure was quick, girlfriend." Monica playfully wags her finger at her. "The last time we emailed, you said a guy was helping you with promotional ideas for Sweet Something. Was that Tyler?"

Allison nods. "I've known him for a long time. We dated in college. When he moved back to Princeton this year, we both realized how much we still loved each other."

"I'll say." Monica grabs Allison's hand and stares down at the dazzling diamond.

Allison grins sheepishly. "We plan to get married in December, between Christmas and New Year's. Can you believe it? I still have to remind myself it's true."

"Remember how we were moaning about the sorry state of our love lives two years ago?" I ask.

"Yes," Haley says. "And then you bought that cute apron. . ."

"And here it is." Allison reaches into a colorful gift bag, pulls out the apron, and holds it up. "I was the last one to get it."

I chuckle. "You crossed out Cook and wrote Bride. You're too funny."

"It wasn't me. Tyler did it. I was wearing it the night he proposed, and, well. . .he. . .got creative." She giggles. She's probably remembering the moment.

"That sounds like something Scott would do," Haley says.

"Um-hm." Monica's chin goes up then down, a knowing look in her eyes. "Gil too."

I pick up a corner of the apron and examine the signatures we wrote across it as it traveled among us.

Angel and Cyril.

Monica and Gil.

Haley and Scott.

Allison and Tyler.

Haley looks serious. "Who would've believed we'd all fall in love about the same time?"

A funny feeling comes over me. I'm the one who started this whole thing by buying the apron and then sending it on to Monica. I'm not superstitious, and I don't believe in luck. But I'm glad we passed the apron around. It was a good way to stay connected.

Allison looks down at her ring. "It's pretty amazing, isn't it, what happened to all of us?"

I smile as wide as a dinner plate at HAM. "Every time I wore the apron, I thought about each of you, and how we were waiting on the Lord to send Mr. Rights into our lives."

They all nod.

Allison hands the apron to me, then glances around at each of us, a wise, thoughtful look in her eyes. "We all know the apron didn't bring us love. We have the Lord to thank for that."

"The Lord truly blessed us," Haley says. "He gave us the desires of our hearts."

Desires of our hearts? A mental picture of Cyril flashes

before my eyes, and my heart beats faster—even after a whole year of marriage. "Now that I have the apron back," I announce to HAM, "I can't wait to wear it again. It'll give Cyril another incentive to kiss the cook. . ." I look down at the words on the apron. "I mean, bride."

A Letter to Our Readers

Dear Readers:

In order that we might better contribute to your reading enjoyment, we would appreciate your taking a few minutes to respond to the following questions. When completed, please return to the following: Fiction Editor, Barbour Publishing, Inc., P.O. Box 719, Uhrichsville, OH 44683.

1. Did you enjoy reading *Kiss the ~~Cook~~ Bride*?
   ❏ Very much—I would like to see more books like this.
   ❏ Moderately—I would have enjoyed it more if _____
   _____
   _____

2. What influenced your decision to purchase this book?
   (Check those that apply.)
   ❏ Cover   ❏ Back cover copy   ❏ Title   ❏ Price
   ❏ Friends   ❏ Publicity   ❏ Other

3. Which story was your favorite?
   ❏ *Angel Food*   ❏ *A Recipe for Romance*
   ❏ *Just Desserts*   ❏ *Tea for Two*

4. Please check your age range:
   ❏ Under 18   ❏ 18–24   ❏ 25–34
   ❏ 35–45   ❏ 46–55   ❏ Over 55

5. How many hours per week do you read? _____

Name _____

Occupation _____

Address _____

City _____ State _____ Zip _____

E-mail_____

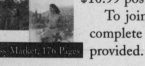